THE KILLERS

THE KILLERS

THE TALE OF A FIGHTING COCK AND A WILD HAWK

DANIEL P. MANNIX

ISBN: 979-8-3372-0036-1

This edition published in 2025 by Open Road Integrated Media, Inc.
180 Maiden Lane
New York, NY 10038
www.openroadmedia.com

THIS BOOK IS GRATEFULLY DEDICATED TO
EDMOND ROSTAND

I read his marvelous *Chantecler* when I was ten years old and it
made a profound impression on me.
There are those who may think I have been much influenced
by Rostand. They are quite right.

THE KILLERS

1.

THE GAMECOCK

Whitehackle was struggling in the tiny world of the eggshell. He was getting too big for its narrow confines and he felt cramped, yet he had no idea what to do. He peeped desperately and from somewhere came a soft, reassuring cluck that gave the tiny morsel fresh courage. He turned and stretched, tried to kick and struck against the shell with his soft beak. By accident, a tiny horny protuberance on the top of his beak—the "egg tooth"—hit the shell and cracked it slightly. Encouraged, Whitehackle struck again and again. More bits of shell flaked off until finally by a mighty heave he split the shell. The two halves fell apart and Whitehackle found himself lying on his back, wildly waving his legs. He was soaking wet and exhausted by his struggles, but he was free.

He was conscious of a warm, fluffy shape above him from whence came comforting sounds but he was too weak to move for a long time. Gradually his soft down dried and he was able to struggle to his feet. Other shells were breaking and there were other struggling bits of life around him. Whitehackle fought himself clear and found he was out from the protective feathers of the hen. He tottered about uncertainly on his thin legs and soon began to feel cold. The hen ignored him, brooding the other chicks and unhatched eggs, until Whitehackle started an indignant peeping. Instantly the hen turned to him, called and spread her wings so he could creep back under their warm protection. Whitehackle reeled back to safety, cuddled down with a contented peep and soon was asleep. His first day of life was completed.

The next day, all the chicks hatched out with the exception of three infertile eggs which the hen abandoned. Being both hungry and thirsty, she started out with her brood toddling behind her, the weakest constantly falling down and struggling helplessly, for they had not as yet grown used to their legs. Step by step the hen led them from the nesting box to the water fountain where she drank repeatedly. Water was new to Whitehackle but he was attracted by its brilliant reflecting surface and its motion. Duplicating the actions of the hen, he also plunged his beak into the trough: He got a mouthful but did not know enough to tip his head back to swallow it. He looked up at his mother and tried to peep, whereupon the water ran down his throat. It was cool and pleasant so Whitehackle tried again, and this time voluntarily lifted his head, opening his beak slightly at the same time. He was rewarded by another squirt of cool water and soon he and the other chicks were drinking eagerly and expertly.

Eating was more complicated. The mother hen scratched and gave her food call which the chicks instinctively recognized and came running. They watched her peck and then Whitehackle tried it. He had no idea what he was looking for, but he was attracted by round or oblong objects rather than square or angular. He soon found these oblong objects were seeds and good to eat. Still, even after this discovery he had trouble picking up an individual grain, as he had not learned how to coordinate his eyes. Since they were on both sides of his head, he received two different images and these images had to be brought together when the object was directly in front of him. Still, with a little practice he learned to use only one eye at a time by cocking his head to one side. Later, he found that by bobbing his head up and down he could bring the two images together when looking straight ahead.

At first, the chicks had made comparatively little noise, but they soon found that it was their peeping, not their appearance, that stimulated their mother to take an interest in them. After that, all the chicks peeped almost continuously except when they were being brooded. Cold especially caused them to peep, and the colder they were the louder and more frequently they peeped. Although the hen was a good mother, it was impossible for her to keep track of all her brood and some were constantly getting lost. Usually she could locate them by their peeping but as she could not count, as long as some of the chicks were with her she would go on looking for food quite happily even though some wretched little straggler had taken a wrong turning.

The morning of his second day of life, Whitehackle had his first alarming experience although at the time it affected him far less than one might think. There were voices in the chicken house and Whitehackle became aware of two monsters towering over him. Like all the chicks, he fled screaming to the hen, who first gave a *consoling* cackle to bring them under her and then a warning cry directed at the monsters. Even so, they came on. The hen's angry threats rose in pitch and frequency, and when she saw one of the monsters leaning over to seize her, she went up in the air at his face, striking with her beak and feet. Even though she had no spurs, she was able to do enough damage to make the man curse before he overpowered her. The other monster wore an apron and she expertly picked up the frantic chicks, one after another, and put them in the apron. Then they were borne off to what fate they did not know, although they all peeped madly for their mother and she answered them while still in the grip of the other monster.

This fearful experience lasted only a minute or so. Then Whitehackle found himself, together with the other chicks, reunited with their mother in a chicken coop set up on a stretch of green lawn. After batting around the inside of the coop until she found that she could not escape, the mother hen settled down, called the chicks under her and brooded them. When one of the monsters returned to install a water fountain and fill the feeding dish, the mother made threatening noises at him but continued brooding the chicks until he went away.

The coop was to be Whitehackle's home for the next two months. There was a small sliding door in the front, large enough for the chicks but too small for the mother. Every morning when the dew was off the grass, a monster went by and lifted the sliding door. At first the chicks ventured only a foot or so out on the green grass, but soon they grew more venturesome and went several yards, looking for seeds and picking at the grass blades. They were also fed several times a day by the monster, who also constantly cleaned and refilled the water fountain, as the mother hen insisted on scratching dirt into it. Although the chicks always ran from him, they gradually grew used to the monster and connected him with food. Water was especially important to them, as they ate only dry food and so had to drink every few minutes.

There were a number of these coops, shaped like inverted V's, on the lawn, each containing a hen and her brood of chicks. After two days, each hen could recognize her own chicks by their peeps, but the chicks were willing to go to any hen. One evening after a tremendous expedition of at least two rods, Whitehackle and another chick went to the wrong coop. As they were quite independent now and seldom peeped except when they wanted something, the chicks made no noise and the strange hen accepted them without question. Then Whitehackle's brother peeped to be taken under the hen's wing and brooded. Instantly she attacked him, seizing him by the head and beating him against the ground. Whitehackle fled in terror, the dying screams of his brother goading him on. He ran up and down among the coops, peeping hysterically until he heard his mother's anxious clucks and ran to her.

The next morning, a larger door was opened in the front of the coops so the hens could go out with their broods. Now that his mother was out in the sunlight, Whitehackle got his first good look at her. She had a light red head, whitish breast, brown wings and a green tail, but in general she gave the impression of being a wheaten color. Although all the hens were sisters to keep the bloodlines pure, there were several fights among them when they considered that their offspring were imperiled, and here Whitehackle's mother easily came out victor. One hen left these combats minus an eye, and several fled with bloody, skinned heads. Whitehackle's mother was prepared not only to defend her brood against other chickens, but also against dogs, cats or even the great monster himself. She was a "man-fighter" and would long ago have gotten her neck wrung had she not been so good a mother and always produced a line of dead-game cocks.

As Whitehackle grew, he learned to make full use of his excellent hearing and sight. Nearly all of his mother's calls he knew instinctively: food, warning, anger or the call to brood, but by experience he learned to know just where the food probably was, where the danger was likely to be and how imminent it was. He learned too, that not only his mother, but also all the chickens gave these cries, so by listening for them he greatly increased his chances of finding food or being warned of danger. This was the advantage of living in a flock. His sight did not improve after the first few days but he learned what to look for. At first any object moving overhead made him cringe instinctively, even a falling leaf. Later, he took alarm only at a fairly large flying bird with a short neck. Long-necked birds like ducks or geese did not bother him. Whitehackle was not conscious of the fact that hawks, which were dangerous, had short necks, while the harmless aquatic birds had long ones; simply, he was terrified by the silhouette of a short-necked bird. He was also upset by a swooping or darting flight, whereas the steady flight of ducks and geese was not alarming. In such matters Whitehackle was guided by overall patterns, not details; he relied on "field marks" that could be seen at a distance and instantly recognized. When the farm boy flew his kite, Whitehackle paid no attention to it, for the kite was not a sinister shape, but when a sudden current of wind made the kite swoop and dip, he panicked. The chicken's fright at such a harmless object as a kite amused the boy, but, of course, if chickens waited to identify every flying object by particulars, they would have become extinct centuries ago.

In only one faculty was Whitehackle deficient: he had almost no sense of smell. His ancestors had lost that with their ability to fly and so trusted to their wings to save them rather than being able to scent danger. Naturally with a winged predator, a sense of smell would have done him no good anyhow.

By the second month, the chick's pinfeathers began to force their way through the soft down. Before, the chicks had been darling little bits of fluff. Now they were awkward, homely objects, for the quills made them seem prickly. Only when the feathers broke through the sheathing of the quills would they look respectable again. But never would they regain the cute baby look which appealed to adult chickens and to a large extent protected them from being pecked—unless by mistake they tried to usurp the rightful place of other chicks under a protective mother hen. With this change, their own mothers gradually lost interest in them, so the adolescent chicks would soon be on their own and have to establish their individual positions in the flock.

Unaware of the struggles that lay ahead, the youngsters were delighted at escaping from the authority of the hen—although they still rushed to her in time of trouble—and gloried in their new freedom. They lost interest in the insipid chick starter feed and developed a taste for meat. They chased bugs eagerly, and gladly accepted the hamburger the man put out for them. They needed protein to make them grow and were especially fond of any mash with milk in it. They got plenty of that and it became the major part of their diet. The mash was made of oats, barley and the best grades of corn, all obtained from a mill where the grain was still "water-ground" between millstones to preserve the germ. The owner spared no expense in rearing them, for he knew that someday the cocks would enter the pit with several thousand dollars riding on their feathers, so the chicks were more scientifically fed than his own children.

Now that they were growing more independent, quarrels broke out among the chicks that were half play and half serious. Especially the young cockerels ("stags" their owner would have called them, as they were young fighting cocks) would square off at each other, striking with their still soft beaks or rocketing up with beating wings, their spurless feet hitting harmlessly. The pullets seldom took part in these playful duels, because they were no match for the aggressive stags, but they had their own disputes as they sought to establish dominance over each other. The mother hen would have fought to the death to protect her offspring from an outsider, but she never interfered in these squabbles, letting the children fight it out among themselves.

Of all the young stags, Whitehackle was the most independent, He usually won his mock duels and wandered farther afield than any of his brothers. His mother was a great ranger, taking her brood not only around the safe confines of the lawn and barnyard, but also into the fields and even up to the woods that grew beyond. Some of the weaker chicks were unable to keep up with her on these long expeditions and these were lost, but Whitehackle loved the trips. He liked exploring and sampling new bugs and berries. While the other chicks were only too glad to return to the coop when called, Whitehackle lingered. Several times he found himself left behind, but by giving a series of shrill peeps, three a second and very shrill, he was always able to attract his mother's attention. She would answer him with a reassuring series of repetitious, short, low-frequency clucks until Whitehackle, straining upward on tiptoe, could see her in the distance and run to her. Once beside her, he would give a happy twittering call, four peeps per second and much softer, to which his mother would answer with a purring note as she offered him her wing.

One afternoon, Whitehackle strayed from the hen even farther than usual. He had found a piece of deadwood crawling with termites and was happily picking them off when he heard his mother's alarm call that meant an aerial predator. The cry was a long scream, held until the hen ran out of breath, so it ended in a gasp and was then immediately repeated. Whitehackle knew it was a danger signal, but the termites were too tempting and he waited to grab a few more before running to her.

Because his eyes were on either side of his head, Whitehackle had a field of vision of nearly three hundred degrees. Rushing down on him through the trees he saw a shortnecked, swooping bird—all his unknown terrors suddenly brought to life. Whitehackle forgot all about the termites and ran for his life, squawking in terror. His mother was busy gathering the other chicks around her, but at sight of Whitehackle's danger, she left them to run to him. She was too late. Whitehackle heard a swish as the hawk dropped her banks of secondaries to brake herself for the bind. He gave a shrill, trilling cry all in one note, and as he did so, he felt scimitarlike talons plunge into his sides. The hawk lifted him with only a minor effort, and using the momentum of her rush, shot up toward the branches of the nearest tree. The hawk was a sharp-shinned, the smallest of all the accipiters or "bird hawks," and as soon as the impetus of her initial rush was lost, she had to put forth all her efforts to carry the struggling chick. She made it only to the lowest branch and sat there panting, holding Whitehackle with one foot and clinging precariously to the branch with the other.

If Whitehackle's mother had been an ordinary hen, he would have been doomed, but she was of fighting-pit strain. Bred back until she closely resembled the ancestor of all domestic chickens, the Indian red jungle fowl, she was not only fearless, but she also could fly far better than other breeds. Now she crouched down on bent legs, calculated the distance to the branch and went up in a whirlwind of beating wings.

The attack so astonished the sharpshin that the predator sat motionless, staring in disbelief until the raging mass of thrashing wings, stabbing beak and lashing feet struck. All three birds came whirling to the ground together, the hawk letting go of Whitehackle as she struggled to steady herself in the air. She hit the ground on her side, and before she could recover, Whitehackle's mother was on her, beating with her wings while her beak sought for the eyes. The hen was considerably heavier than the small hawk and the sharpshin did not like fighting on the ground. As soon as she could break away, she leaped into the air with a bound of her long legs and fled. The hen stood looking after her belligerently until the frantic peeping of the brood recalled her to domestic duties. But first she marched over to Whitehackle and stamped around him, giving a deep "cluk, cluk, cluk!" evenly spaced in reproof. After that, he was always the first to run to the mother when she gave the alarm cry.

As Whitehackle and the other chicks continued to grow, they became increasingly conscious of a Lordly Presence, an Imposing Being, who seemed to the awestruck stags nearly as big as the humans and far more impressive. This godlike creature paced about the lawn with slow, majestic strides, seldom bothering to look around him, and all got out of his way. He had only one eye but that detracted nothing from his imperious bearing, and his brilliant colors danced in the light of the sun. Not even Whitehackle's indomitable mother dared oppose this proud ruler, and when by an act of incredible condescension he deigned to tread her, she crouched humbly down with bent neck until he had had his pleasure. The young stags did well to be impressed, for this was their father, the brood cock, whose portrait, done in oils by a famous artist, hung in their owner's home. This cock was named the Mortgage-Lifter, a title he had won by his terrible steel gaffs and even more terrible courage.

The Mortgage-Lifter came of a long and illustrious lineage, going back to ancient Babylon. Themistocles, on the way to the Battle of Plataea, had seen one of the Mortgage-Lifter's ancestors fighting with another cock and stopped his troops so they could watch the contest. "See!" Themistocles had exclaimed. "These birds fight for nothing but honor. What shall we do then who fight for our homes, our families and our gods?" Later, St. Augustine, watching another of the Mortgage-Lifter's forebears in combat, had claimed they must be inspired by God, as mere animals could not show such skill and courage. Still later, Cocklane and Cockspur in London were named after others of his progenitors. When this great and distinguished line was brought to America, Washington and Jefferson had fought them in the committee room of Congress instead of attending to affairs of state. During the Battle of Lake Champlain, when the British squadron was overcoming the Americans, a round shot had shattered the coop of the Mortgage-Lifter's remote grandfather on board Commodore Macdonough's flagship. Instead of being frightened, the cock had flown to the bulwarks and crowed defiance, thus inspiring the Americans to go on and win as the Greeks had been inspired twenty-five hundred years before.

The Mortgage-Lifter himself was a worthy descendant of this noble race. During a main in Tampa, he had killed a black-gray by a brain blow in nine minutes, although the black-gray was two ounces heavier and the betting was five to three on him. In Dallas, he had killed a red Pyle in fourteen minutes even though the Pyle had blinded him. His owner proudly claimed he did better as a "blinker" than he had formerly, for the Mortgage-Lifter used to present his empty socket to an opponent, and when his antagonist struck at the tempting target, the Mortgage-Lifter grabbed him and then went to work with his deadly steel spurs at close quarters. No cocker will ever forget how he fought the famous duck-winged gray in Mexico City for a $10,000 stake and cut his enemy to pieces in eighteen minutes. But the climax of his life came when he triumphed in the Orlando Tournament in Florida and, by winning the $20,000 stakes, was christened the Mortgage-Lifter by his enthusiastic owner. So big, so impressive and so imposing was this great cock that it never occurred to the awestruck young stags that they could ever hope to attain to his size and power.

Yet when the stags were four and five months old, the brood cock did not seem quite so awesome. By then the stags' spurs were beginning to grow and their playful contests were taking on a more serious tone. Also, several of them were beginning to show an interest in the hens. As their genital organs developed, this interest increased, as did their combative natures, for the two traits were linked together. The hens also began to take a furtive interest in them, and being more experienced in such matters than the ingenuous young stags, often made the first advances.

One morning while Whitehackle was passing a hen, she not only lowered her head as a sign of submission, but also crouched down in a seductive way, even moving her tail to one side to expose her cloaca. Her actions triggered some deep instinct in Whitehackle even though he had no idea what to do. Automatically he began to waltz around her, dropping one wing and making little clucking noises in his throat. The hen crouched even more and the excited young stag sprang on her back, putting one foot on each of her outstretched wings and treading down, first with one foot and then with the other. The hen offered no resistance, but before he could progress further, Whitehackle was suddenly knocked sprawling by the furious impact of the Mortgage-Lifter, who stood towering over him with hackles extended, glaring down.

Automatically, Whitehackle struck with both his spurs. The spurs did not grow straight back but were slightly inclined toward the inside of his legs. The Mortgage-Lifter received the full force of the stag's short spurs on both sides of his body. He gave a gasp at the impact and staggered back. Instantly Whitehackle was on his feet, full of sudden confidence. The brood cock no longer seemed eight feet tall but simply another cock who could be hurt.

For a moment the two birds faced each other beak to beak, necks extended, hackles raised, legs bent for a spring, each watching the other for some sign of weakness. Then the Mortgage-Lifter rocketed into the air, trying to get above the stag so he could lock his spurs into the presumptuous youngster's head. Whitehackle went up at the same instant, but his legs did not have the powerful upward thrust of the old bird's, and the Mortgage-Lifter went higher. Bang-bang, so fast the eye could not follow the blows, he struck the stag twice, ripping open his comb and lacerating his wattles. Another fraction of an inch higher and even without steel gaffs on his legs, the Mortgage-Lifter might have ended Whitehackle's life then and there. Even as it was, Whitehackle reeled back bleeding and dazed. Knowing himself outmatched, he retreated, yet did not run. Head up, neck slightly retracted and wings in position, he withdrew. Though his tail was lowered, it was not dragging enough to show the white undercovers, so he could not be said to have shown the white feather. Significantly enough, the old cock did not follow him, so although defeated, Whitehackle was able to withdraw with honor. Whitehackle had not been cowed—"hacked" his owner would have called it—by the more powerful bird. He was still too small to take on his indomitable father, yet someday—someday!

That day was never to come, for the owner had seen the exchange and that afternoon the brood cock was penned up, to his intense indignation. The owner could not afford to have him kill, mutilate or even hack any of the young stags, for once thoroughly intimidated by him, it was unlikely they would put forth their best efforts in the pit if ever confronted by another cock of the same conformation and coloring as their conqueror.

Free to fight among themselves, the stags slowly developed a hierarchy, the "pecking order." At the top of the hierarchy was

Whitehackle. He had so clearly demonstrated his superiority that none of the other stags dared challenge him; he could peck any one of them and none dared to peck back. Directly below him was the number two stag, who would peck all the others with impunity and deferred only to Whitehackle. So it went down the line to one wretched bird who could be pecked by all but dared to peck none back. Meanwhile, the pullets were busy establishing their own pecking order, although they all deferred even to the weakest stag. This pecking order was not entirely rigid; some of the stags had won their positions mainly through bluff which would one day be called, others had had an off day and would later assert themselves, still others had not developed as rapidly as their brood mates. However, it remained more or less the same and was not unduly brutal, as no cock would pursue another who ran or attack one who refused to fight. They were fighters, not bullies.

The owner had been watching the stags closely, and when they were eight months old, he rounded them up and ruthlessly eliminated all that seemed unfit or had poor conformation. The rest were dubbed. While another man held a stag, the owner cut off the bird's dangling earlobes with a pair of razor-sharp, curved shears and trimmed the wattles. Then with a pair of straight shears he cut the comb. It was a bloody business but necessary from the owner's point of view, for it meant that in the pit a rival cock would not be able to grab the bird by the comb, wattles or earlobe and hold him down while using the gaffs.

Except for the sharp pang of the actual cutting, the operation was not as painful as it seemed, for the owner was an expert at the job. In fact, as soon as he was released Whitehackle began picking at his own former comb and ended by eating it, as he liked meat. What the birds minded most of all was being deprived of water for two days, as the owner believed this would make the bleeding stop more readily.

When the stags had recovered, the pecking order had to be reestablished all over again, for none of them recognized each other. As an uplifted head is a sign of defiance, two chickens when meeting first look at each other's heads, and so the stags identified other members of the flock primarily by their heads. Because of the dubbing, all heads were now different. These new fights caused some changes in the original pecking order but Whitehackle still stayed on top.

When the stags had recovered from the effects of the dubbing, Whitehackle's life on the home farm came to an end, for the time had come to separate the young cocks. They could not be left together indefinitely, for as they grew and their spurs became well developed, the fights between them would grow increasingly more deadly and the cocks lower in the pecking order would become hopelessly hacked. So one day Whitehackle and some of the other stags were decoyed into the chicken house with grain, captured and thrust into sacks.

Although indignant, Whitehackle was not frightened. Indeed, he crowed defiantly, and as he stood up and curved his neck, the sack took on the perfect silhouette of a crowing cock. Afterward, he was put in a car and, after a long journey, gently turned out of the sack.

Glad to be free again, Whitehackle shook himself and then strained up his neck to look around. His owner, together with a strange couple, were watching him but these humans Whitehackle ignored. He was interested only in his new surroundings. He was on a farm with a huge barn, a spacious barnyard and broad, well-kept fields through which a tiny creek flowed. In the distance Whitehackle could see woods, which he liked because of the interesting, eatable things he found in them. Pleased, Whitehackle began to cluck busily, taking short steps and bobbing his head up and down. Then he saw something far more interesting yet—other chickens.

Whitehackle had no idea whether these strangers were hens or cocks, so he crowed loudly. There was no answer, thus he suspected they were hens; a cock would surely have answered his challenge. Still, he was unsure. He moved forward deliberately until he was among the strange fowl. Some lowered their heads submissively but others did not. Whitehackle was unsure how to proceed.

In this situation, he resorted to tidbitting; that is, he scratched on the ground aimlessly. The gesture was much like that of a nervous boy's trying to dig a hole in the ground with his big toe. As scratching means the presence of food, several of the chickens ran over. Whitehackle gave the food call and even picked at imaginary grains. Naturally the chickens could find nothing and looked at Whitehackle in bewilderment. Whitehackle shook his head several times as a further sign of nervousness and, not knowing what else to do, crowed again.

Some of the younger chickens whom he was now reasonably sure were hens seemed properly impressed, but a grizzled old veteran in the background turned away. She had heard cocks crow before, and to invoke her interest, a cock had to do something more constructive, such as finding food. This old hen strode off in a determined manner, ignoring the handsome young stag who was so impressing the pullets.

Whitehackle watched her from the corner of his eye. She clearly knew what she was about and he saw her stop by the edge of a corncrib and start scratching. Whitehackle gave an authoritative crow and started after her with his best, stifflegged musketeer swagger, eagerly followed by the pullets. There was a crack in the crib at this point and corn had leaked down from the bin. Whitehackle gave the food call and started scratching in earnest.

As the pullets rushed over, the old hen who stood high in the pecking order furiously grabbed one by the back of the neck and prepared to punish her. Instantly Whitehackle was there and gave a deep-throated chuckle, suggestive of a growl. The old hen released her victim and eyed him. He was young and inexperienced, but he was a male and no female dared question the authority of a male—especially when the male had spurs which he was quite obviously prepared to use. Reluctantly she resumed her feeding, and Whitehackle felt that all these creatures were merely hens and he was their master.

What Whitehackle did not know was that his owner had spent many long weeks and a considerable sum of money inducing farmers with suitable farms to kill their brood cocks and allow him to "walk" one of his stags on the farm. It would be a year, perhaps two, before the stags would be ready for the pit and during that time they would have to be allowed to range at liberty with a suitable harem of hens to hold them to the farm and to allow their sexual prowess to develop. Not every farm could be used; there had to be open fields, woods, a stream of pure running water and above all no other cocks, not even within earshot. The crowing of a distant cock might serve to hack a young stag when he found his own vocal powers inferior to those of a more mature bird. Although Whitehackle's owner would have died rather than admit that a lowly "dunghill" rooster could ever compete with one of his lordly purebred game fowl, as a practical matter he knew well that the stags were nervous, unsure adolescents and that it was essential they build up confidence in themselves before entering a pit. Finding a farm suitable for a walk was therefore a difficult problem and Whitehackle's owner had given his prize stag one of the best.

These were happy months for Whitehackle. He not only learned to know the barnyard and the adjacent fields, but also took his harem to the woods where he introduced them to formerly unknown delicacies until even the old hen was impressed. When July came, Whitehackle began to molt and by November he was in full, mature plumage. Now he was no longer a stag but a cock, and what a cock. Weighing slightly over five pounds, his body was short and compact, with a broad chest and strongly curved back. His head was narrow with large, clear eyes and his neck long and thick. The butts of his wings were wide and strong, while his spurs were "medium-stationed," pointing neither too high nor too low. On both feet, the Tear toes pointed straight behind and served as braces so he could not be thrown backward in a fight.

His plumage was magnificent. His feathers were hard and elastic without being brittle. His head was red and his mahogany hackles were edged with gold. His breast was black and his tail, with its long, dangling sickle feathers, a dark jade green. His body was shaded ebony and a bluish-green. His wings were banded with green, red and blue. The saffron-colored scales on his legs gleamed in the sun.

Like his ancestor, the jungle fowl, Whitehackle was almost completely self-supporting. He was quite able to forage for himself winter and summer, and although the farmer, following detailed instructions, put out ground charcoal and oyster shell for him as well as a warm mash made with milk in winter, these luxuries were only to increase his bone and muscle. Whitehackle could have done quite well without them. Except for the single brief encounter with his father during which he had acquitted himself nobly, Whitehackle had never met anything that dared to challenge him and he was supremely confident, in fact, "cocky." And why not? He was undisputed cock o' the walk and cocksure of himself. He treaded his hens several times a day, and anyone watching him would have realized why a cock has come to symbolize the masculine generative organ.

That winter when his owner came to see how he was getting on, the man was delighted. Whitehackle was the reincarnation of the great Mortgage-Lifter, and when he curved himself into the semblance of a French horn to crow, he gave forth the same clarion call as the older bird. "As crows the old cock, so crows the young," the man reflected and resolved to leave Whitehackle on his walk for another year to allow him to grow to full maturity.

Late the following winter the owner returned, this time with a crate, for Whitehackle was now to pay him back for all his time and effort. Following orders, the farmer had left the cock severely alone, even putting out his food before daylight so Whitehackle would not associate the food with humans and become too dependent on them, for his owner wanted the bird to be as wild and free as possible. The man had no doubt of being able to catch Whitehackle, for he brought another cock with him. He knew well he would have only to show the bird to Whitehackle to have the young cock attack, and then he could easily be seized.

As matters turned out, the catch-cock was unnecessary, for Whitehackle attacked the man as soon as he entered the barnyard with a ferocity that forced him to retreat, protecting his face with his elbows. "A man-fighter!" said the owner, by no means pleased. Whitehackle's natural belligerency toward other cocks was a sexual trait greatly developed by selective breeding, but from his mother he had also inherited a general combativeness, so he stood prepared to attack any trespasser on his territory. This fierce protectiveness had nothing to do with his game-fowl blood, and most gamecocks do not possess it; murderous as they are toward another cock, they would never think of attacking a child, a dog or any other creature. These two forms of belligerency existed in completely different parts of Whitehackle's brain, and his aggressiveness toward interlopers by no means implied that he would for that reason be equally terrible in the pit; nor did it mean that he would not be. It did mean, however, that he would be a difficult cock to condition for the coming tournaments, as handling him would be a problem. Like all cockers, Whitehackle's owner disliked man-fighters, and if the cock had not been so outstanding in appearance and conformation, he would probably have wrung his neck right there.

Instead, he caught Whitehackle when the bird attacked him a second time and checked him for lice, sores or injuries. Finding the furious bird sound, he began to massage his neck in the direction of the feathers, rub under his beak and over his dubbed wattles and comb. The stroking of the man's hand quieted the bird, and after a few minutes Whitehackle relaxed and allowed himself to be placed in a shipping box, covered on all sides except for a few narrow slats near the top to admit air. In this box Whitehackle returned to the farm where he was born.

Not for him now was the freedom of open fields and attentive hens. He was entering his conditioning period or "keep" of twenty-one days to prepare him for the pit. He was taken to the cock house, a long, barnlike building with dozens of square pens called "stalls" on the sides. In many of these stalls cocks were already penned, as Whitehackle could tell by their crowing. He was placed in a stall and left to grow accustomed to his new quarters.

The next morning, Whitehackle was removed from the stall and weighed. He was in reasonably hard condition, yet still a few ounces overweight, so he spent some time in an outside wire coop some eight feet long, with deep straw in the bottom. A few grains of wheat were sprinkled among the straw, and in scratching for them Whitehackle not only developed his legs but also got enough exercise, so that, together with a purge and a strict diet, he was brought down to five pounds—his fighting weight.

He was then taken out, and soft leather balls called "muffs" were tied over his spurs. The owner's helper was present with another cock also wearing muffs. While the men held them, the birds were allowed to pick at each other and then when their fighting spirit was sufficiently aroused, put down on the ground a few feet apart. Instantly the cocks rushed together, bursting upward in a mass of beating wings and flailing legs, the muffs preventing any real damage. Two or three flies and a couple of hard blows with the muffs were enough to give Whitehackle's owner a general idea of the cock's willingness to fight, and of his style.

The cocks were now kept on an elaborately prepared schedule which varied from day to day during the period of the keep. Every morning each cock was put on a workbench four feet long and two feet wide, cushioned with straw and covered with burlap. The trainer ran the bird by pushing him along with one hand under the tail. At the end of the bench he turned the bird with his other hand and ran him back. This exercise was to strengthen the legs. Then each bird was "flirted," tossed up to fall with beating wings. They were also "flown." The trainer would turn loose the cock in training and then hold out another cock toward him. When the free cock leaped up to strike his opponent, the trainer would raise the captive cock slightly. By this method, a cock who would normally jump only a few inches could be taught to rocket up several feet in the air, thus giving him altitude over his adversary in a fight.

There were many other techniques the cocks had to learn, such as "sidestepping" and "whirling," but equally important was their diet. They were fed corn—not any corn, but a special hard grade, each kernel cracked by hand into three pieces—clipped oats and corn bread made with plenty of eggs and milk and then soaked in beef tea. But the trainer considered the most important item of diet to be his special cock bread, prepared by a secret recipe, handed down from father to son for many generations. The recipe called for fine wheat flour, oatmeal, two eggs and the whites of four more eggs, butter, candied sugar, cream, yeast and dry sherry. Each cock had his food measured out, and even his drinking water had to be distilled and given him drop by drop. Strenuous as the conditioning was, the birds prospered under it and during the period of the keep lived "like fighting cocks."

Although diet and exercise varied with each day and even with each cock, as their needs were by no means identical, Whitehackle's routine on the sixteenth day of the keep may be considered fairly typical. In the early morning he was flirted seventy times and after a twenty-minute rest fed the whites of hard-boiled eggs, oats and cracked corn. Then after fifteen minutes he was given a tablespoonful of distilled water. He received an hour's rest before being run for seven minutes. He was then bathed, dried and his feet rubbed with alcohol. In the afternoon he was put in an outside coop to sun himself and later given two flies at a held cock. After two hours' rest, he was flirted seventy-five times. In the evening he was fed cock bread and allowed two tablespoonfuls of water.

Whitehackle had been a problem to the trainer from the start. Because he was a "man-fighter," it took not only the trainer, but also an assistant and often the owner himself to put the cock through his paces. Only the owner could really handle the aggressive bird, and he did that by constant massage and rubbing. The soft stroking of the expert hands calmed the furious young cock as nothing else could, and often after an outburst of such fury that even the expert handler was cowed, Whitehackle would relax in his owner's hand, giving soft little chuckles of contentment, much like the soft purring of the hen when she comforted the chicks. The handler dourly prophesied that in the pit Whitehackle would more probably attack the other handler or the referee than the opposing cock, but the owner had fanatic confidence in the bird who so closely resembled the fabulous Mortgage-Lifter. As a result, Whitehackle received double the amount of attention given any of the other young cocks, and profited by it.

The last day of the keep, called "the point," was considered to be the most crucial. Each cock had a chart tacked to his stall, giving his daily weight, his individual diet and how he had responded to the conditioning. After consulting this chart, the trainer put each bird through his paces and then selected three birds for the contest coming the next day. Whitehackle was one of the three. All of the cocks already had had their spurs cut off with surgical saws, leaving only a three-eighths-inch stub to receive the steel heels or gaffs. Now they were trimmed for the fight. While one man held Whitehackle, the long drooping sickle feathers of his tail were cut, although the tail itself was left alone, as the cock needed it both as a rudder in a fly and as a brace when he threw himself back on the ground to strike with his spurs. The tips of his long primaries were trimmed, as well as his saddle hackles, so he would not be burdened with any unnecessary weight. Lastly, the feathers around his vent were cut away to allow for circulation of air in the heat of the struggle.

The fight was to be in two parts: first a "main," a private duel between two cockers who had agreed to fight a specific number of cocks of varying weights against each other. The main would be followed by a "hack," in which any individual might bring any number of cocks of any weights, the contests to be arranged at the pitside. Whitehackle's master intended entering the hack.

The fight was to take place in Pennsylvania, where cockfighting is illegal; it would therefore be held in secret and at night. The afternoon of the contest, the three cocks were put in their shipping crates and their owner, together with the handler, set out, timing their trip so they would arrive at the pit shortly after nightfall.

They drove to the barn of an old estate now converted into a country club. Already dozens of cars were parked around the barn, showing the license numbers of four states. In the loft of the barn, a portable pit had been assembled, its padded sides bolted together. The pit was some eighteen feet square and around it were wooden tiers of seats. A photoflood bulb in a reflector was suspended over the center of the pit, giving a brilliant, dead-flat lighting. The barn windows were covered with black cloth and the guests entered below through the former cattle stalls, where they paid five dollars' admission and then ascended to the loft by a flight of rickety stairs.

The guests were a mixed lot. Some were farmers, their woolen underwear protruding from their shirt sleeves; some were ladies and gentlemen in evening clothes; some were old men with deeply lined faces; some were excited boys who had never yet shaved; some were professional gamblers who communicated with each other by quick signals and code terms; some were drunk, some cold and calculating; some were men who spent their entire lives with the cocks, going from pit to pit in state after state, and these experts listened with barely twitching lips while gentlemen in dinner jackets explained to their eager dates the fine points of the sport.

Proscribed, condemned, archaic, cockfighting was still a sport followed by thousands, that could support four magazines in the United States and caused millions to change hands in bets. It took a good deal to beat cockfighting.

The cocks were taken to the scales for the official weighing. Although the main was already in progress, a crowd had collected around the scales, and here Whitehackle's owner arranged to pit his three birds against opponents in the hack, the weights of the fighters to be within two ounces of each other. Whitehackle was surprisingly indifferent to the noise and confusion around him. Far from being hacked by the hubbub, he cocked a malignant eye at the men who bent over to examine him, and would have attacked them if his owner had not kept a firm grip on his body and legs. He had no idea what lay ahead and was rather bored by the whole proceedings.

The main was concluded and the hack began. Whitehackle and the two other cocks, brothers of his, were heeled for the first time in their lives. Whitehackle's owner heeled the cocks himself. He opened a wide flat box to reveal a dozen partitions, each containing a pair of murderous, curved, steel spurs 1¼ inches long. Every spur was fitted into a leather band. The spurs curved upward, so when the cock struck, the steel points would plunge up into the enemy's vitals. Each pair of spurs was a right or left so the points could be curved at precisely the right angle to the cock's legs.

Whitehackle was held by the handler while his owner wrapped narrow wet strips of chamois packing around the stubs of his natural spurs and then fitted on the steel heels, making sure the needle-sharp tips pointed straight to the center of the leg and the socket of the gaff fitted on the "leader," the tendon running down the back of the cock's legs. The leathers were then tied on with waxed string, the string being crossed so it formed a series of *x's*. Whitehackle's owner knew his art, and when he was finished, the cocks were well-heeled.

Whitehackle's brothers went to the pit first. They were good cocks and fought gamely, but there were better cocks there that night, and one came back dead and the other coupled; that is, paralyzed by a blow in the back that left him helpless so he had to be killed. Whitehackle regarded the dead bodies of his brothers with indifference; the highly developed flock loyalty of crows or starlings does not exist among chickens. Then it was his turn.

On the handler's arm, he was carried into the pit under the glaring white light. Across from him at the other side of the pit stood another handler with something in his arms that Whitehackle could not see clearly. Only vaguely was he conscious of the shadowy crowd on the tiers of benches nor did he heed the roar of voices around him. "A hundred on the law-gray." "Okay, it's a bet," "Fifty on the Whitehackle," "Make it twenty-five." "All right, twenty-five." The two handlers moved around the ring so the crowd could see the birds, until the referee, a fat man with a sweat-stained shirt, stepped forward and ordered, "Bill your birds!"

Then the handlers moved together in the middle of the pit and with a sweeping motion turned the birds' heads toward each other. Now Whitehackle could see that the other handler was holding a gray cock. At the same moment the other cock saw him. At once the long necks shot out, the beaks clicked together and the eyes gleamed. The cocks struck furiously at each other, the handlers holding them back so neither cock could reach his opponent's eyes. Three times they were brought together until the birds were mad with rage and their beaks spotted with tiny feathers they had picked from the other's head.

"Places!" ordered the referee. The handlers stepped back on either side of the score marks, two parallel lines six feet apart. Whitehackle's handler set him on the line, making sure he had his feet well under him. "Pit!" shouted the referee and the handlers released their birds.

Both cocks rushed toward each other, hackles spread, heads strained forward, wings partly open. The instinct to attack any male opponent that showed fight, which originally had enabled the wild jungle cock to establish a territory for his hens and chicks, had been intensified to produce birds born for no other purpose but to attack and to kill regardless of punishment. Neither bird was even conscious of the noise around him, of the bright light or the unfamiliarity of the pit. Neither were they trying to establish a territory or defend their families. Each thought only of killing the other bird and, once released, nothing could have kept them apart.

They went shooting up together, each trying to get above the other so that as they came down the one on top could drive his pointing spurs up under the extended wings of his adversary. They met in midair evenly matched. Guided by their rudder-like tails, both birds arched backward and, twisting their legs forward, struck for the breast, hooking inward and upward with their spurs. Both missed and hit the ground together. Before the gray could recover, Whitehackle had seized him by the throat with his beak. Instantly the odds began to change and cries of "five to three on the red" went up. Before any bets could be taken, Whitehackle had thrown himself back and, using his grip on his opponent's neck for leverage, had struck once with his spurs. His right spur plunged into the gray's brain, killing him almost instantly.

The fight had been over in a matter of seconds and Whitehackle was not even winded as he stood over his dead foe and, arching himself into a curve, gave a triumphant crow of victory. His backers shouted with delight and bets were paid off while Whitehackle's proud handler picked him up and carried him from the pit.

His head was sponged off, his spurs removed and he was put down to rest while his owner and handler enthusiastically described the fight to one another and to everyone who would listen. "He's another Mortgage-Lifter!" shouted the owner, visions of the great Orlando Tournament already in his mind. He had lost heavily on the other two cocks, more heavily than he could afford, and now he regretted that he had not backed Whitehackle more lavishly. Perhaps after a rest the cock could go once more that evening. The owner returned to the pitside.

Two hours later a tall, thin man with a pronounced Southern drawl called, "I have a five-pounder," exhibiting a Louisiana blue-gray cock. Whitehackle's owner studied the cock a moment before calling, "What do you want to fight him for?"

"Five hundred." Whitehackle's owner hesitated. Five hundred dollars would more than recompense him for what he had lost and Whitehackle would be fully rested by now. "Short heels, of course?" he asked. Now it was the Southerner's turn to hesitate. His cock was one of the high-flying Southern birds usually fought with three-inch heels, as the longer gaffs best suited their dramatic if somewhat wild style of combat. To fight in short heels would give the Northern cock a decided advantage, yet the Southern cock was a "shuffler." Once he managed to hook his heels into an opponent, the cock would work his legs with machine-gun rapidity, as though doing a dance, each flicker of the legs driving the spurs deeper into his victim. The Southern cocker had an infinite contempt for any cock that did not shuffle, and he knew well the Northern birds were "single stroke" fighters who relied on one blow to do the work.

He nodded and the bet was made. Nothing was written down; there was not even a handshake. Welshing on a bet was almost unknown at the pit.

Both cocks were weighed and then heeled. When the next

bout was over, they went to the pit, the Southerner acting as his own handler. Again came the command, "Bill your birds!" and each man, holding his cock over his arm, crossed the parallel score lines and the cocks were swung together. Then the handlers stepped back, each to his own score. At the command, "Pit!" the birds were released.

The birds rushed toward each other and went up in the air. It was immediately apparent that the blue-gray was faster. The betting had favored Whitehackle, but now it instantly changed. "Watch that gray murder him." "Seven to five on the gray." "I'll take that last bet." "Double it?" "Hell no!" "Come on, you red!" "Jeez, did you see that gray bastard buckle?"

As the cocks hit the ground, Whitehackle tried for his beak hold but the blue-gray was too quick. As Whitehackle plunged forward, the blue-gray leaped over his extended head and came down astraddle of him. Instantly the blue-gray struck inward with his gaffs and began to shuffle. One of his spurs had caught in Whitehackle's wing but the other went home. Whitehackle gave an audible squawk as the spur knocked the breath out of his lungs.

"That hit his guts!" "Oh, look at that Southern bastard shuffle!" "Three to one on the gray!" "Make it four." "You've got a bet." "Shuffle, gray, shuffle!"

The blue-gray's spur hung up in Whitehackle's side and he toppled off, his spur still locked in the flesh. "Handle?" Whitehackle's handler pleaded. The referee nodded and both handlers sprang forward to make sure the other did not crush one of the cocks or drive in the spur deeper. The blue-gray's handler put an open hand on each cock to hold them while Whitehackle's handler pulled the blue-gray's heel out of his bird, taking care not to twist it and enlarge the wound. Every handler was entitled to take the spur out of his own bird; that was too ticklish an operation to trust to the enemy handler. As soon as the birds were separated, the referee started counting slowly as the men withdrew behind their score lines, carrying their cocks.

Whitehackle's handler swiftly examined him. He was breathing heavily but there was no rattle in his gasps and no blood on his beak. In spite of his shuffling, the blue-gray had not reached Whitehackle's lungs. Although uninjured, the blue-gray looked tired and the Northern cocks were reputed to have more stamina. If the Southern birds did not win quickly, they often did not win at all. Again the odds changed. "Even money on the gray." "I'll take that for a hundred; a cock that won't shuffle isn't any damned good." "Fifty on that gray; he's a bloody heel." "You're covered; he won't buckle no more." "Twenty says he will." "Right, it's a bet."

The referee counted slowly to ten and called, "Pit!" Both cocks left their score lines together but with notably reduced speed. The blue-gray tried to jump over Whitehackle's back again but this time Whitehackle managed to get his beak hold. With thrashing wings, the blue-gray strove to break the grip, but Whitehackle threw himself back on his spread tail and, swinging up both legs, drove his gaffs in under the extended wings as deep as he could before falling over on his side.

"Handle!" ordered the referee. This time it was Whitehackle's handler who held the cocks while the blue-gray's handler gingerly drew out the spurs. The referee started his rhythmical counting but there was a deep rattle every time the blue-gray gasped for breath. He threw up his head, sending a spray of dark-red blood across the handler's shirt. The handler put his mouth over the cock's beak and sucked out the blood that was strangling him, but it was no use. The cock's head and neck dropped straight down, blood pouring from his beak. He gave a few spasmodic flutters and hung limp, dying in the handler's hands.

An authoritative voice cut through the cursing and triumphant yells. "All right, nobody move. You're all under arrest."

There was instant silence and then women screamed, men leaped from the benches and the gamblers began throwing away their betting cards. Men in uniform started to force their way through the crowd while outside someone with a bullhorn was shouting orders. The lights went out.

Whitehackle felt himself snatched up but he was too tired to resist. His owner and the handler knew the place well and forced their way through the crowd to the old hay chute. The handler tore loose a hatch covering it and both men dropped through to the unused stalls, Whitehackle's owner still clutching his cock. The handler ripped out a window frame and they crawled out into the fresh air.

The car had been parked away from the others in case of just such an emergency, and the men raced for it, bending low in the shelter of the long lines of cars. The handler slid behind the wheel and switched on the ignition while Whitehackle's owner leaped in beside him. The motor thundered and the car lurched away without lights over the ruts. Another minute and they would be on the hardtop and free.

A searchlight hit them and there came the warning wail of a siren. The handler slowed down slightly, the pitch of the motor rose and then the car leaped away. The rear tires spun and screamed at the sudden thrust of power and there was a stench of burning rubber. The siren was louder now and a police car with a whirling red light on top sprang after them. They were on the paved road and the handler popped the clutch; mashing the throttle against the floorboards, he synchronized the clutch and gearshift with a swift movement so as to lose a minimum of speed. Whitehackle could feel the vacuum suck as the car reached out for high gear.

They were tearing down the road, and as now concealment was no longer possible, the handler switched on the lights. He popped the clutch again and they were in high. For a few seconds it seemed as though they had left their pursuer far behind, but then the police car reached the hardtop and began to gain. The speedometer reached sixty—seventy—eighty—and the police car was still right behind.

Whitehackle slowly recovered his breath. His side hurt him where the blue-gray's spur had gone in and he tried to struggle, but his owner pressed his wings to his sides. Without taking his eyes from the road, the handler snapped, "Get rid of that damned cock."

"You keep driving, I'll handle the cock," retorted the owner.

"You want to be picked up with a heeled cock?" shouted the handler. "Throw him out!"

The owner said nothing. They had hit a straight stretch of road and the handler jammed his foot down on the pedal. As the speedometer crept upward, the rear window cracked and at the same time there came the stunning report of a revolver.

"Get rid of the Goddamned cock!" screamed the handler. Another report and the car rocked wildly. "They'll hit the gas tank or a tire, you fool!"

A curve appeared just ahead. The handler fought the wheel and the tires screamed as the car keeled, nearly turning over. They went into a skid, only barely managing to stay on the road. The police car was coming up fast.

The owner turned down his window and, lifting Whitehackle, flung him into the bushes alongside the road. As the rush of air hit him, Whitehackle beat wildly with his wings and managed to break his impact. He lay on the bushes with extended wings as the car roared away, to be followed almost instantly by the police car.

Whitehackle lay there a long time, spread-eagled and gasping. When he finally recovered, he managed to get his wings under him and he fell heavily to the ground. Painfully he struggled to his feet and looked about him, but the night was overcast and he could barely see. He crawled through the roadside growth and found himself in a stand of evergreens. He ran his head against a low branch and by a great effort managed to half jump, half flutter onto it, for all his instinct was against roosting on the ground. It was too dark and he was too tired to go higher, so he roosted there, dozing off with his head under one wing. The throbbing in his side kept him awake for a long time, until he fell into a sleep so deep it was almost as though he had been anesthetized.

"Who-hoo! Who-hoo! Who-hoo! Who-hooooah!"

The grisly, ghostly cry rang out completely unexpectedly and Whitehackle came awake with a shudder that made his feathers rattle, the noise carrying a long way in the still night. His head popped out from under his wing and he sat trembling. The cry had been indescribably uncanny and menacing, sending shivers up his back, although he had no idea what creature made it. It was not repeated and after listening awhile, Whitehackle dropped off to sleep again.

"WHO-HOO! WHO-HOO! HOOOAH!" The banshee wail sounded right beside him. Whitehackle gave such a start he nearly fell from the branch, and had he done so that would have been the last of him, for not even a heeled cock is any match for that tiger of the woods, the great horned owl. A young crow roosting high above squawked with terror at the sound, and even though blinded by the darkness, tried to fly. Whitehackle vaguely saw a shadow that, as silent as a black cloud, swept through the evergreens after the noisy crow. Then came a scream of mortal agony that was quickly stilled. Quaking, Whitehackle huddled against the trunk of the tree. There was no more sleep for him that night, and never was cock so glad to see the black sky turning gray and hear the twitterings of the early-rising birds.

Whitehackle jumped down and limped through the woods. His wound had stiffened, he felt sore all over, and the tightly bound spurs made his legs ache, yet he was mainly conscious of a burning thirst. Somehow he must find water. He went on and on until ahead of him the trees thinned and he saw light through them. Forcing his way through a tangle of honeysuckle, he found himself on a hill overlooking a beautiful valley.

Even his beloved run could not match this delightful place. The air was fresher here without the stale odor of gasoline that had pervaded his, former home, and the winter wheat glowed with a special, living green he had never seen before, for it was well manured and the soil was richer than inorganic fertilizers could possibly make it. Below him was a huge barn with great round hex signs on the sides and beyond that a much smaller, though comfortable, white farmhouse. Along a dirt road a buggy drawn by a smartly trotting chestnut spun along, with a bearded man holding the reins. Beside him sat his sunbonneted wife. As the buggy vanished into the red cave of a covered bridge, Whitehackle could hear the echoing clip-clop, clip-clop of the horse's hooves on the board flooring.

Then the cock's eye caught the glisten of water. The stream that flowed under the bridge crossed the pasture, running clear and unpolluted between high banks on its way to Brandywine Creek. It was a long way to the stream for the weary bird, but Whitehackle set out at once. Being basically a ground bird, he preferred to walk, although he could have flown the distance in a few seconds. He struggled on, his spurs catching in the tall grass, until he reached the pasture. Here Whitehackle could run, and he ran to the water and drank and drank. The water was sweet, different from any water he had ever tasted before. After drinking, he stopped to gasp from its coldness and then drank again until he could hold no more.

Now he felt hungry. Whitehackle headed for the barnyard. In his experience, there was always food in barnyards.

On the way he passed a number of gray geese who hissed at him and some Muscovy ducks walking flat-footedly down to the stream. A drake stopped and examined him suspiciously, but Whitehackle hurried on, for once not being in a combative mood. He rounded a sheepfold and entered the barnyard by the open gate. Guinea fowl perching on the post-and-rail barnyard fence gibbered at him, and then he saw other chickens.

The chickens were scratching for grain in the manure pile and stopped to look at him with bright, questioning eyes. From their behavior they seemed to be hens. Several of them gave a nervous "cut-cut-cut!" call and moved away. Whitehackle headed for the manure pile, his head already bobbing as he sought to focus his eyes on any loose grains.

The call of the hens attracted the resident rooster, who came strutting out from the edge of a privet hedge where he had been dust-bathing. The rooster, predominantly Rhode Island Red, was far bigger than Whitehackle and he stalked impressively toward the smaller bird, giving the deep, growling chuckle that is a chicken's warning.

Whitehackle moved away, keeping his head up, yet with the neck slightly curved downward and his tail drooping as a token that he recognized the other cock's territorial rights. Had he met the cock on neutral territory, he would have fought at once, tired and wounded though he was. However, this was plainly the other cock's range and Whitehackle accepted the fact that he was an interloper and had no business here.

The big red took the strange cock's retreat as a sign of cowardice. Had Whitehackle stood his ground, the red would probably not have pushed the issue, for he was a fat, stupid bird who relied on bluster. He was too lazy and too absorbed with food to discipline the hens properly, and several of them exhibited the bloody heads and injured eyes that showed the pecking order had gotten out of hand. By chance the rooster had cut off Whitehackle from the barnyard gate, and the fighting cock found himself cornered under the overhang of the barn. He tried to turn to the right but the end of the overhang had been enclosed to serve as a windbreak. When he turned left, there was the red with extended neck and raised hackles.

Even now, Whitehackle tried to escape, but as he turned, the red charged him. The red was too heavy to go up in a fly and he rushed at Whitehackle like an angry bull, intending to pin him against the enclosed end of the overhang.

As the red reached him, Whitehackle sprang up and struck once with his right spur. The dagger-like tip went through the rooster's eye and he dropped with hardly a flutter, his entire nervous system paralyzed. Whitehackle stood looking at the twitching body for a moment and then, going over to the dung-heap, started to scratch.

The farm dog, a half-collie, half-Airedale cross, had been dozing by the back steps when the anxious cry of the hens awakened him. It was not a real alarm signal so he continued to doze, only opening one eye. Through the green, five-barred gate that led from the barnyard to the turnaround behind the house, he saw that the rooster was after something. Instantly alerted, he jumped up, ducked through the hedge by a hole he knew and loped into the barnyard. So quick had the duel been that, when he arrived, the red was already dead and the strange cock was looking for grains of corn as though he belonged there.

The dog was sure that nothing had the right to kill the poultry under his protection, yet this interloper was also a chicken and therefore safe from molestation. Uncertain, he went over to sniff at Whitehackle, who promptly put down his head and spread his golden hackles. The dog recognized the danger signals, but not wishing to provoke an attack, could not get close enough to get the bird's scent. As he relied on his nose more than his eyes, he was not perfectly sure just what this creature was. Standing still, he started to bark.

Almost instantly a man and woman came out of the farmhouse kitchen and hurried toward the barn. They were the same couple Whitehackle had seen in the buggy, strict Pennsylvania Mennonites who continued to live as their forefathers had who first settled this region two hundred years before. The woman saw the dead rooster and gave an exclamation of surprise and regret. Her husband, going to the barking dog, saw Whitehackle who, deciding that the dog meant no harm, had resumed his feeding.

While his wife was mourning over the dead rooster, her husband approached Whitehackle. Whitehackle looked at him suspiciously. He considered attacking the man but he was in strange territory, weak and tired. Also, this man seemed to know chickens, so he allowed himself to be lifted gently while the man examined his steel spurs wonderingly. The man took out a knife, cut the waxed strings, and to his intense relief, Whitehackle was free of the constricting things.

The couple conferred while feeling Whitehackle's broad breast and powerful thighs. They had to have a cock, and as this bird had killed their rooster, it was only fair he should take the dead bird's place. If he could, there was no need to buy a new bird. They decided to give him a chance.

Whitehackle soon showed that he knew his duties. He kept the hens bred and any that resisted were run down. He also quickly put a stop to any quarrels that flared out among them. The sight of fighting instantly triggered Whitehackle's combative instinct, and if a hen high in the pecking order began abusing one of her weaker sisters, Whitehackle instantly raced across the barnyard and flung himself into the fray. The hens were promptly knocked apart while Whitehackle stood between them, glowering, an eye on each bird. The weaker hen automatically made the submission signal of drooping neck and lowered tail, but the more aggressive hen, whose blood was up in the delight of bullying, would remain for a second with uplifted head and tail. That was enough for Whitehackle, who would wheel on her and give the arrogant hen a beating she long remembered. Thus, although the pecking order still existed and the weaker hens deferred to the stronger, fights were practically eliminated, nor were the hens low in the order kept from the dust-bath pockets and food. Skinned heads healed, eyes were no longer pecked and the entire flock took on a healthy, happier look.

The farmer loved to watch Whitehackle in action. "Dot rooster, he's a regular policeman," he often delightedly told his wife. The woman agreed, but without enthusiasm. She knew as well as her husband that the hens had to be kept in order, but just as he instinctively rejoiced in this exhibition of masculine supremacy, she just as instinctively resented it.

Whitehackle soon learned to know every part of the barn, the barnyard, the pasture and the lawn, and even took his harem up to the woods after new delicacies, to the alarm of the farmwife, who was sure something would happen to them. Whitehackle had no such fears. His spurs were growing back now, although his comb and wattles would never return, and he felt entirely confident of his own powers. He was lord over this pleasant, peaceful valley where nothing could harm him or his flock.

One morning while Whitehackle was luxuriating in a dust

bowl under the privet hedge, he heard the fearful alarm cry go up from half a dozen throats—the repeated, long scream that meant an air attack. Instantly the guinea fowl chimed in, the turkeys fled for shelter, while from the pond came the honking of the geese as they hurried to the water.

In the moment of peril, Whitehackle thought only of himself. His atavistic fear of a winged figure, reinforced by his awful experience as a baby chick, drove him insane with fear. He raced for the chicken house, knowing that there he was safe from an aerial raider. Here was no dignified retreat; he ran with his neck stretched out flush with his back, his tail down and his wings flapping to add to his speed. As he raced past the line of stalls, he saw that the double doors of one stall were open, and inside two birds were fighting.

Being now under the overhang, Whitehackle was less afraid of an attack from the air, and no gamecock could be indifferent to the wild struggle in the stall. One bird was screaming the alarm call at the top of her lungs. Now the other seized her and the hapless hen screamed "Awk! Awk!"—a cry that sounded almost exactly like "Help! Help!" They came down in the straw together.

Whitehackle did not realize that the screaming bird was one of his hens and the other a hawk. Whitehackle could not recognize a hawk on the ground, nor if he had would it have made any difference to him. He had no fear of hawks per se; he was afraid of a flying outline of long wings and short neck, especially if the silhouette dove or swooped. He would have been as much afraid of a big Silver King pigeon as of a hawk. But he would not have been afraid of the Silver King on the ground, for then the pigeon would have been just another bird, and now he was not afraid of the hawk that had bound to the screaming hen and was staring at him over her open, panting beak with murderous yellow eyes. He saw only two birds in a fight, and true to his game-fowl blood, whenever there was a fight, he was determined to get in it. His golden ruff rose, and with long, snaky neck extended, Whitehackle charged the ancestral enemy of his race.

2.

THE HAWK

She was struggling in the eggshell, one foot twisted around her neck, forcing her little egg tooth against the hard covering that had been a warm, sheltering world around her but was now a suffocating prison. The shell flaked off and a minute hole appeared, letting in sweet, fresh air and a hint of light. She forced her egg tooth against the shell again and again until she was too exhausted to make another effort, and started a plaintive chirrp-chirrp, appealing to some power to help her, she knew not what. Instantly she heard a reassuring voice and from without came deft blows. The shell split away and she rolled out, pieces of the shell still clinging to her wet white down. Above her towered a great, white bulk with flaming scarlet eyes, but the bulk was warm and fluffy and made soft sounds. A terrible hooked beak, capable of tearing the life from a screaming rabbit, swooped down upon her and delicately peeled away the remains of the shell until she was free.

Her down dried quickly in the warm May breeze and almost at once she realized that she was ravenously hungry. She began to cry again, a "chip-chip-chip" call this time, and struggled to turn over on her stomach. She could not quite make it and her mother had to turn her over with that wonderful beak. On her stomach, she opened her mouth as wide as possible and cried again.

Somewhere from far away came a distant "kik-kik-kik!" call and even the newly hatched baby recognized its insistent nature. After a quick check to make sure she was all right, the mother gave an answering "ca-ca-ca" and dropped from the nest head-first. The baby cuddled down beside the other three eggs from one of which was already coming a series of anxious chirps, and waited. She did not know for what she was waiting, but she was contentedly confident that the great white-breasted bird with the marvelous, gentle beak would know what to do.

From afar she heard the sounds of an angry dispute, the shrill tones of the "kik-kik-kik" call mingled with the deeper sounds of her mother's irritated answers. Then there was silence for a few seconds. The nest suddenly jarred and automatically she opened her mouth and cried again. There was the mother bending over her and in her foot the adult hawk had a dead starling, already plucked. Neatly, the hawk bit off a tiny bit of the breast with her sharp beak and offered it, holding the morsel skillfully at the extreme tip between the hook on her upper mandible and the straight lower beak. The baby eagerly snatched for it, but once she had it did not know what to do next and dropped it. Patiently, her mother cut off another sliver and offered it. The sight of the red blood excited the baby and, grabbing for it, she found the meat in her mouth. Her mother was ready with another piece, and in her efforts to get that one, too, the baby swallowed the first bit. It tasted delicious and now she knew what to do. She ate and ate, her crop bulging out until the mother was forced to turn her attention to the second pipped egg and free the little captive.

In the next twenty-four hours, all four of the eggs hatched out, and now the mother ran an almost continuous shuttle service from the mysterious place where the shrill "kik-kik-kik-kik" voice called to the nest, each time bearing some new quarry. The greedy youngsters jostled each other for the food, for the mother simply offered the tidbits, and the first baby to grab the food got it. The baby female soon discovered that she had a longer neck than two of the other babies, who were males, and had to fear only the competition of the other young female. The two females ate first and only after they were satiated and resting their necks, tired from constant stretching, on the edge of the nest, did the smaller males have a chance. Luckily for the males, there was plenty of food that year. Had there been a shortage of prey, they would not have survived, and in case of an extreme shortage only one of the females would have pulled through, for the mother made no attempt to distribute the food evenly. Ruthless as this system seemed, it was necessary, for if there were a shortage of game, it meant that there must be a corresponding shortage of predators to keep the controllers in balance with the controlled.

Although the babies were soft and downy, they could hardly be called cuddly. They had huge hooked beaks that made them look like miniature Punches, and naked, sprawling feet. Their eyes were pale blue with a brown tinge and they seemed to have a perpetual startled expression, for they had not as yet learned to coordinate the double images they received from both eyes simultaneously. The little female found herself in a world of strange, unrelated dual pictures that floated around her and occasionally came together when she tried to focus her eyes on something directly in front. It took the young hawk some time to learn that by bobbing her head she could coordinate these two forward images because she was usually not looking in front but to the left and right; as her eyes were on either side of her head, she could do this without turning. Once she mastered the bobbing trick, and learned to distinguish between the two pictures on each side, the world gradually came into focus around her.

The nest made a perfect observation tower, for it was sixty feet up in a tall beech growing near the edge of a grove that overlooked miles of rolling farmlands. Even though with four of them the nest was crowded—it was only two feet in diameter and crudely made of dead twigs—she was quite content to lie quietly in the bark-lined central cup and study this strange new world. She was too weak to be energetic and had no desire to walk, which was lucky for her, for if she had been as active as a young chicken she would have gone crashing down to the ground far below. Her mother guarded her constantly night and day, while the devoted "kik-kik-kik" creature worked constantly to bring in food, so all was well. To the baby, the mother hawk seemed huge and all-powerful. In spite of her great three-foot wingspread, she swept through the interlaced tangle of branches without seeming trouble, always carrying some succulent quarry in her mailed fist. With her wings folded, she was less awe-inspiring, for she weighed less than two pounds and was not nearly as big as one of the gigantic turkey vultures the baby often watched soaring in vast circles over the grove. Still, the mother had a dash and determination that not even the powerful red-tailed hawks who also nested in the grove possessed, for she was a Cooper's hawk, a species found only in North America and hated by sportsmen, farmers and conservationists alike as the most ruthless of all predators. The popular names given the Cooper's hawk—blue darter, swift hawk, quail hawk, privateer, striker and bullet hawk—show they have not a friend in the world. Even so, the mother was a strikingly beautiful bird with a white breast heavily cross-barred with cinnamon-brown stripes. Her long legs were butter yellow and her back was slate-blue. Her eyes were blood-red, for she was an old bird, possibly approaching her twentieth year. That she should have remained alive so long in a hostile world was a tremendous tribute to her intelligence and skill.

Even when the babies could not see her, she was never far from the nest, for the male did all the hunting, allowing her to give her undivided attention to the young. One hot day when the scorching sun shone too fiercely through the leaves and the babies began to suffer, the little female anxiously raised her voice in the "chip-chip-chip" call that meant something was wrong. She had only to give it a few times before the mother dropped out of the foliage and stood on the edge of the nest with extended wings to provide shade. When it rained she was there again to shelter them, and during the cool nights she brooded them with partly open wings to make sure none caught a chill before their feathers were in.

By the end of three weeks, the little female was able to stand. Now she was able to look over the edge of the nest and see all the wonderful things about her. From the concealment of her tree-house nest, hidden by the broad leaves of the beech, she could look down on the forest floor and the open fields. She was intensely curious and watched the flight of birds, the motions of insects and even the erratic, jerking fall of leaves with solemn interest.

These were golden days when dozens of flowering plants competed for the newly awakened honey bees so they could be fertilized and grow pregnant by midsummer. The young hawk watched fascinated as the bees, dragging their pollen basket sacks, buzzed among the tiny blue blossoms of alehoof that formed a mat under the waxen flowers of the dogwood.

The hawk could see colors well, perhaps better than a human, but she was primarily attracted by motion, so the flowers meant little to her. In a distant orchard, the apple trees were covered with perfumed snow and the fields were golden with wild mustard. With her telescopic vision, the young hawk saw them clearly, but mainly she watched, instead, small birds in the orchard and among the mustard. She could see details of the birds' plumage and study their manner of flight better than a man could have done with field glasses, for the glasses limited his range of vision while the hawk, with three times as many visual cells as a human, could see not only the distant birds in detail but also the rest of the countryside. She watched the azure flash of bluebirds among the saffron forsythia that was already turning green, and the flicker of redwinged blackbirds over the pastures studded with yellow dandelions and buttercups. Around the dooryards the purple lilacs were in flower, brilliant against the pinkish-purple of wisteria, and the hawk saw an orange-and-black Baltimore oriole pause for a moment on the vines on his way to the orchard to look for a good spot to swing his hanging nest.

More than anything, she watched the distant red barn with its great circular hex signs, for here a score of different kinds of birds congregated. The overhang of the barn was alive with barn swallows as they flicked in and out, building their mud cup nests that clung like wasps' nests under the eaves, while the chimney swifts darted in their batlike flight over the roof. On top of a high pole was a multicompartmented martin house, and even though starlings and sparrows had taken possession of some of the compartments, the martins were there by the dozens, bringing in nesting material or sweeping low over the farm pond to snatch a mouthful of water as they flickered past. A scarlet tanager flamed for an instant on the white candles of a huge horse chestnut that provided shade for the black-and-white Holstein cows, and from the fields came the screams of mating killdeer as they chased each other in insanely erratic mating flights. The young female watched this strange, new world entranced, taking in every detail.

The young hawk was interested in the small birds only because they were moving objects and brightly colored. She did not regard them hungrily, simply because she did not know they were good to eat. She had been fed nothing but small pieces of meat held out by her mother, and she no more connected this food with the live birds than a small boy would have recognized a steer as the result of having eaten a hamburger. She was equally interested in the farmer plowing with a six-horse hitch and watching the plow turn over the dirty yellow stubble of last year's harvesting and leaving behind the new rich brown soil. As the team turned and began to ascend the rise that led to the grove, the big Belgian workhorses threw their weight into the collars and the farmer slipped off his seat to lighten their load. A dozen small birds that had been following the plow in hopes of worms flew up and the young hawk watched the man, the team and the birds with equal attention.

At the end of two weeks, her feathers in quill sheaths began to push their way through the cottony down. As they grew, the down shredded away and soon the nest and adjacent twigs were covered with it. The small birds in the grove used the down to line their own nests, taking it with impunity, as only the male hawk hunted during this period, and he did not hunt in the nesting area, which he regarded as sacred to the female and her brood. As the babies' feathers grew, the mother stopped sleeping with the young birds at night, knowing that the feathers would keep them warm. Instead, she roosted a few yards away to give them more room, as they were growing bigger now.

Now that the babies were growing stronger, the mother started to bring whole birds to the nest as well as an occasional red squirrel or chipmunk which the father hawk had brought in. The young hawks were perfectly capable of carving up the prey themselves but they much preferred to let their mother do the job for them. One day when the mother left a starling, most of the brood sat on the edge of the nest, regarding the newly killed quarry as though they had never seen such a looking thing before in all their lives and crying to be fed, but the big young female cautiously approached the dead bird and picked at it. Finding it did not hurt her, she pulled out a few feathers. The others stopped their crying to watch. She managed to tear through the skin and reach the dark meat. Now all the young birds were really interested and ran toward her. Giving an angry cry, she covered the starling with cupped wings, turning her back on the others while she ate. When the mother came in a few minutes later with a robin, the rest of the brood decided that, if they wanted to eat, they would have to learn to carve. The other female grabbed the robin and from then on the young birds fed themselves, the two females eating first and the little males getting what was left. Dimly, the young female began to realize that this food was somehow related to the live birds she could see from the nest, but how it was obtained she still had no idea.

As she grew older, the young female began to take an ever-increasing interest in her father, whom she recognized as the meat getter of the family. She learned to recognize him not only by the "kik-kik-kik" call he used to alert his mate when he arrived with prey, but also by sight. He was marked much like her mother, but he was about one-third smaller. As each of the four nestlings devoured an average of 250 items of prey during the six-week period of growth, the male was almost constantly on the wing providing food for them. When they were downy babies, he had been in the habit of taking the quarry to a fallen maple caught between two other trees which he used as a butcher block, or rather as a plucking place to deplume the quarry, and so save the harassed female trouble. Now that the young were almost full-grown and their constantly expanding feathers drained nourishment from their systems, they were continually and insatiably hungry, so he had no time for plucking. He would call to his mate, and if she did not instantly respond, he would scold her and bring the prey to the nest himself.

Although as with all raptors, the male was considerably smaller than his mate and could not make large kills, he was quick and tireless. Much of his booty was young starlings who had not learned to look out for themselves, but he also killed dozens of songbirds. Meadowlarks were a favorite quarry, as their erratic flight seemed to attract him. The plucking tree was littered with their yellow feathers as well as with the red of cardinals and the purple of grackles. When the cherry trees were in fruit, they attracted hundreds of birds, and the male Cooper's haunted the orchard to the vast delight of the Amish farmer, who hated the songbirds that were ruining his crop. He had even put wagon wheels in the trees, hoping the hawks would use them as a foundation for a nest, not knowing that the Cooper's hawks were far too shy to nest in such an exposed place.

Only by the tireless devotion of the male could the four young have been raised, for the mother had to stand constant guard over them. The woods were full of deadly predators who would have been glad of a meal of young hawks. Now that the babies were older, she did dare to leave them occasionally to take a bath in the stream that ran under the covered bridge or just to exercise her wings. At these times, the male would baby-sit for her. He was not strong enough to be of much protection, but in case of danger his shrill alarm cry would bring the female to his aid. He would also do little housekeeping chores while his mate was away. He cleared the nest of garbage, such as bones, feathers and castings. These castings quickly accumulated and if left too long became noisome. When the hawks ate, they swallowed the feathers or fur of the quarry and later regurgitated this indigestible matter in the form of small, firmly packed pellets. These castings removed the slime that tended to form on the lining of their stomachs and were as necessary to their health as the grit swallowed by chickens. The adult birds followed the same pattern and usually would not fly in the mornings until they had cast. When the male cleared the nest, the young birds moved over to one side while he rearranged the bark lining and removed the debris. The young female, who had hitherto considered her mother the only important creature in the world, vaguely came to realize what role the male was expected to play in family life.

Yet there were some dangers against which even the devoted parents, working as a team, were helpless. Late one cloudy day, a raccoon wandered through the grove on his way to the creek. The young female, crouching in the nest, heard him coming—not with her ears but through special sensitive organs in her legs that could pick up ground vibrations. As she crouched lower in the nest among her brothers and sister, she heard, or felt, the coon pass under the tree. Then he stopped and began sniffing. The young birds were "nest-broken" by now and when defecating would back to the edge of the nest and squirt their feces over the side, so the ground was striped with the white streaks. The coon had found the "slices" and knew what they meant. The trembling fledglings heard his deep breathing as he circled, making sure that the nest was in the beech. Then he began to climb the tree.

The fledglings' mother was watching from a nearby perch, hoping the coon would go away if she gave no sign. Now that concealment was useless she took to the air, screaming her shrill "ca-ca-ca" alarm cry. The male was coming in to the plucking tree with a freshly killed kingbird, but he dropped the quarry and sped to her help, flying low among the trunks of the trees to avoid the branches and make better time. As long as the coon was close to the ground, the hawks could not get a good run at him for their strafing type of attack, but as he shinnied up the trunk, the female turned over and, shooting in at an angle, raked him across the head. The coon hissed, and hanging onto the rough bark with one paw, raised the other to fend her off. While he was watching her, the male struck him. As the coon turned to face this new attack, the female did a wingover and dove in again. Fur flew as her long hind talons ripped home, and the coon snarled in pain.

To the hawks, the coon was as formidable an enemy as a grizzly bear would have been to humans, but in defense of their young, neither bird hesitated, the male pushing home his attacks as recklessly as did the big female. While one bird was striking, the other was turning over for a fresh dive, and so perfectly did the hawks coordinate their attacks that the coon was constantly being buffeted, first from one direction and then from another. Even so, the determined couple was fighting a futile battle, and the coon would have triumphed if there had not been a noise in the underbrush and a man appeared, staring with astonishment at the curious duel.

The man was a Dunker, another of the many Pennsylvania Dutch sects, who had come to the woods to gather ginseng. Earlier that year he had marked a good stand of the plants, whose roots would bring him twenty-five dollars a pound when properly dried and prepared. At the sight of the man, the coon promptly dropped to the ground and ran, while the hawks, who had not seen the intruder, chased him screaming.

The Dunker watched the little episode with amusement. Not being either a chicken farmer or a fruit grower, he was indifferent to hawks one way or the other. He did, however, admire the hawks' courage, as he knew from personal experience that an enraged raccoon can be a dangerous adversary. The young birds were doomed in any case, for after nightfall the coon would return and in the darkness the hawks would be blinded and helpless to defend their babies.

As the Dunker continued on his way to the ginseng stand, he passed the plucking tree and saw the dead kingbird. Instantly he stopped. He knew that kingbird, or "bee hawk" as he called it. For weeks now it had taken up a position over his beehives and caught bee after bee. He had tried vainly to shoot it. He not only depended on the bees for honey, but also he needed them to fertilize his crops of clover, alfalfa, lima beans and cabbages. The Dunker picked up the dead bird, examined it and looked thoughtfully at the nest before continuing on his way.

Late that afternoon the young female was aware of another trespasser in the grove, even before she heard her father's warning "gek-gek-gek" cry that meant the presence of danger but not an actual attack. Her mother was on the nest and the older bird slipped quietly away, for she saw it was a man and hoped to escape notice. The man was the Dunker and he went straight to the tree, carrying several large sheets of tin. When the parent birds, watching from a distance, saw he was definitely headed for the nesting tree, not even their fear of humans could stop them. Shrilling their "ca-ca-ca" alarm cry, they swept in for the attack. The Dunker had his dog with him and not daring to attack the human, they turned on the dog. The dog was not nearly as tough an adversary as the coon and after a few cuffs on his tender ears, he fled yelping. The hawks followed him to the edge of the grove and then hurried back. By the time they had returned, the man was gone, leaving the tin nailed around the trunk. The mother ignored it and settled down to brood her precious young.

When night fell, the young female heard the coon return and felt him trying to climb the tree, but the slick tin defeated him and he departed, grumbling to himself. Although during the day the little bird had been terrified of the great, hairy monster, at night she was scarcely conscious of her narrow escape. It was an especially black night, and in total darkness the hawk became strangely calm. Unable to scent her enemies, she depended almost entirely on eyesight, and if she could see nothing, she feared nothing. The coon tried one more night to reach the nest and then gave up the attempt.

When the young female was a month old, all her feathers had come in and her baby down had disappeared except on her thighs, which gave her the appearance of wearing pantalettes. The irises of her eyes had turned a bluish-gray, and although she could not fly as yet, for the blood was still circulating through the quills of her feathers, which made them soft and flexible, she was growing more active and adventuresome. The nest had seemed a broad, ample platform. Now it was cramped and confining.

For once, the little males took the lead. Being lighter and more nimble than their big sisters, they jumped from the nest to nearby branches and sidled along them until they could spring to yet farther branches. The young female watched this venturesome proceeding with grave doubt, but the temptation to get away from home was too strong and she tried it. At first she was clumsy and nervous, but within a few days she learned to balance herself and even reached the topmost branches of the beech. The other female followed her, and soon the young birds became so agile at this sport that a man trying to catch one would have found that the long-legged youngsters could go through the branches faster than he could.

When the mother came in with food, she had trouble finding the young hawks, even though they all set up their eager food call of "eeeee-eeeee-eeek" at the sight of her, so she solved the problem by dropping the food on the nest and leaving it there. At first the young "branchers" regarded this as an outrage and sulkily decided to wait until she brought the quarry to them. The young female, however, had tried before to outwait her mother over learning how to carve. Now she hurried back, jumping down from limb to limb until she landed on the nest. She found a squirrel there and had it all to herself while the rest watched this strikebreaker resentfully. When the mother came in with a flycatcher and the young female grabbed that, too, the rest decided this had gone far enough and they scrambled down, screaming with indignation. The female screamed back, protecting her meal with spread wings and tail. She was able to retain possession of the flycatcher but after that, whenever the mother appeared with food, it was a race to get back to the nest. In their eagerness, the young birds began to use their wings to help them, for the feathers were full-grown now and the blood had withdrawn from the quills. The quills were becoming stiffer and could support the weight of their bodies in flight.

The young birds seemed fascinated with their plumage and devoted great care to the morning ritual of preening. They behaved as though they knew that their lives depended on these feathers—as indeed they did. The big young female was especially meticulous in performing this rite. First, with the hook on the tip of her upper mandible she carefully lifted each individual feather on her neck and breast, making sure that the delicate plumes had not become matted or disarranged. These were the feathers that kept her warm at night. Next she separated the tiny alulae feathers on the shoulders of her wings. These little "thumb" feathers seemed to have no functional purpose, but when the birds were flying with outstretched wings, the minute protuberances stood out stiffly and were highly sensitive to air currents. Somewhat as a cat's whiskers signal the cat in the dark when an obstacle is in the way, so the alulae told the bird of every fluctuation of the wind.

Then she turned to the primary coverts, the layers of feathers that lay like plate mail at the base of the long primary feathers on each wing. The hawk could separate or bring together these primaries like fingers and it was the primaries that would give her speed in flight. Then she cleaned the primaries themselves, separating each one and stroking the webbing of the feathers into place. Next she attended to the secondaries. The secondaries were all the same length, whereas the primaries differed in size. They could not be moved individually but were raised or lowered as a bank, like an airplane's wing flaps. Although the primaries were also used in flight, their main purpose was to allow the bird to brake her forward passage suddenly or go up and down. The young hawk then oiled her feathers from a special oil gland near the vent. This oil served to protect the plumes and partially waterproofed the fine webbing. Lastly, she used her hind talons to comb the feathers on her head where her beak could not reach.

These were exciting days, for spring was giving way to summer and the first fledglings were out of the nests, making awkward flights among the yellow-centered, white-leaved mock orange bushes or coming plunging down on the multiflora rose hedgerows powdered with white blossoms. The clumsy efforts of these birds made the young hawk shiver with excitement as the sure, expert behavior of the adult birds had never done. She watched a brood of young pheasants trickle through the pasture studded with blue-eyed grass, and she longed to chase them. A young catbird sat in a mass of green honeysuckle spangled with white, tan and gold blossoms, screaming for his mother to come and feed him. The young bird's obvious helplessness inflamed the hawk so that she half opened her wings as if to fly, only to close them again. Tiny brown rabbits crept through the purple helmeted skullcaps, taking care never to get too far from the shelter of the pink wild roses, and the young hawk followed their every motion with longing eyes.

After watching this enticing quarry, she would return to the nest, which was now used only as a dining room and sun porch by the branchers, and jump up and down on it in a passion of frustration, grabbing at loose twigs and bounding around with them, gripping first with one foot and then with the other as though killing them. The other nestlings kept out of her way at such times, regarding her with somber eyes from a distance, and even her father when he came in with food, hurriedly dropped it on the nest and departed without stopping.

After one of these rages had passed, the young female was relaxed again. The others ventured back to the nest and took their turn at the food, even the little males being condescendingly ignored by the big young hawk. She had made short flights already, volplaning from branch to branch, but only for a few feet. She began to try in earnest to keep herself aloft.

Going down turned out to be easy. She had only to stand near the end of a branch, spread her wings and dive off headfirst. With wings stretched to their uttermost, she could coast across an open space to the next tree. Landing was considerably more difficult. As she swept toward the tree, the young hawk had no idea how to stop herself. On the first few tries, she crash-landed into the foliage, making frantic clutches for any twig she saw, and then lay with spread wings, gasping for breath. It took some time for her to get her wings under her again and crawl through the leaves until she could get a safe footing on a limb. Then she tried wildly flailing the air with her wings just before she hit. This tended to break the force of her impact, but it was only after several near-disastrous attempts that she learned to hack with her wings and throw her legs out in front of her. Trying every possible combination she could think of, she finally learned to drop her twin banks of secondaries, which stopped her almost dead in the air, and then, before going into a spin and falling, to shoot out her long legs, grab a branch, come up on it with spread tail, which served both to balance her and also to check her forward progress, and close her wings.

Flying upward was something else again. At first the effort was too much for her, and after a landing she would hop up from limb to limb until she was high enough to make another trial flight. When she tried to fly upward, she beat madly with her wings but still could not seem to gain any altitude. She did become fairly adept at flying in a straight line, especially when she kept low to avoid the tangle of branches through which her parents threaded their way with deft weavings of their bodies and quick turns of their rudder-like tails. Her usual style was to take two or three hard flaps, glide for a while, take another few flaps and so on.

One afternoon while flying along only a few yards above the forest floor, she saw her mother come into the nest with food. Fearful that the other young birds would get there before her, she put on her best burst of speed and then, when she came close below the nest, dropped and spread her tail, at the same time twisting the tips of her long primaries at an angle. She had learned this trick, which made her rise, but she was quite unprepared for the result when going forty miles an hour. Without any further effort on her part, she suddenly shot almost straight up without needing to beat with her wings at all. She went so fast she nearly overshot the nest and had to brake with her secondaries and twist her tail at a forty-five-degree angle to her body to stop herself. After that, she seldom attempted to beat her way higher; instead, she put on a burst of speed and then by altering the positions of her wings and tail allowed her momentum to rush her upward.

The young female now felt that she could really fly and there was nowhere in the grove she did not dare to go. One day when her mother was not around and she heard her father's "kik-kik-kik" cry at the plucking tree, she set out to meet him herself, screaming "eee-eeeek!" as she flew. Her father was on the maple with a young pewee in his talons, but at the sight of his giant daughter rushing down upon him he dropped the pewee and fled. In her efforts to catch the falling bird, the young female went into wild convulsions, lost her air speed and stalled out, crashing down near the dead pewee. She lay panting on the ground for several minutes before recovering enough to walk over and grab the bird. After eating it, she was too tired to fly, and had to walk to the nearest tree, jump onto one of the lower branches and then work her way up limb by limb until she was high enough to cruise back to the nesting tree.

For a day or so she had all the kills to herself, as she was able to meet the father at the plucking tree and none of the other youngsters dared to make so long a flight. Still, indignation at seeing their sister gorge herself while they went hungry finally overcame the others' reluctance, and they followed her to the plucking tree. After a few days they were sure enough on the wing to fly for fun rather than food.

Delighted with their newfound dexterity, the young birds

played games through the woods, chasing each other, diving on an unsuspecting playmate or trying to catch a falling leaf. Sometimes they would fly down to the forest floor, pick up a stick, hop around with it clutched in one foot, then take to the air, drop the toy and, turning over, plunge down on it before it could reach the undergrowth.

The venturesome young female was the first to leave the safety of the grove with its convenient trees and trust herself to open country. She picked a day when the hot sun made a nice thermal draft rise from the hillside. Sitting on the projecting limb of a walnut, the young hawk could feel this thermal. Simply by spreading her wings and leaning forward, she could catch the draft, which lifted and carried her over the green meadows. By turning the tips of her primaries and twisting her tail slightly, she could ride the air currents without flapping. This was really fun and she soared in great circles, turning whenever she felt she was being carried out of the draft. Coming down turned out to be harder than she had expected, and she had to make a considerable effort to force her way down through the draft and pitched, alighted, on the limb of an all-but-dead willow growing by the bank of the stream. The sight of the water charmed her and she cocked her head first on one side and then on the other to make sure the dual images she received were not playing her tricks. At last she dropped down on a mud spit to examine this strange substance more closely.

She had never seen water before, receiving all the moisture she needed from the fresh blood in her food. Now she walked with easy strides into the shallow water and touched it with her beak. It felt cool and pleasant. She bit it and found her beak full of water which she swallowed. Delighted, she drank long and deep—"booze" as the old falconers would have called it, meaning to take an abnormal pleasure in drinking. Then she noticed her long toes distorted by the ripples and tried to bite one of them. To her astonishment, she missed her grab owing to the refraction of the water. The young hawk tried again and again, unable to understand why she could easily locate her toes on land but not in this substance. In her exasperation, she struck with a fury that would have hurt the knitting-needle thin pounces if she had ever connected. Unable to solve the mystery, she squatted down in the cool substance, swaying her body back and forth to squirt water along her sides, and at last scooping it up in the shoulder cup of each wing and pouring it over her back. When she was soaking wet, she left the stream and was concerned to find she had trouble flying. She made it to a lower branch of the willow and sat there with extended wings until she dried off.

The next day the other youngsters followed her to the stream and they all bathed. They, too, discovered the fun of riding the wind without the restriction of trees, and swooped and swirled over the pasture, taking care, however, not to get so far from the grove that they would have trouble returning to it when they were tired. Flying into a really strong wind or getting down from a powerful thermal were techniques they had not yet mastered.

The young hawks made no attempt to pursue the small birds they saw. They were well fed and regarded their natural prey with curiosity rather than aggression. The young female did make a few halfhearted dives at the starlings and cowbirds that followed the cattle, but they easily avoided her. So far their mother had let the male do all the hunting, but seeing her young in full flight and noting the awkward attempts of her most forward daughter, the adult bird began to hunt. When the male saw her in action, he relaxed his perpetual quest for quarry, knowing that at long last his wife was prepared to help him. As usual, the parent birds worked as a team in training the young in the skills that would mean life or death to them.

The young birds were now in the habit of flying to the edge of the grove to look out for their parents returning with food, so their first lesson was here. The mother stationed herself high in a black walnut at the edge of the grove and waited until she saw some cowbirds following the Holsteins in the pasture below. She sat perfectly still and made no effort to attack until one of the cowbirds disappeared in a patch of bunch grass. If she could not see the cowbird, he could not see her, and at once the hawk dove in a long, slanting glide from the tree. The rest of the cowbirds saw her and took off in time, all except the one in the bunch grass. The hawk was almost over the patch when the cowbird heard the warning cries of his friends and popped his head out to see what was the trouble. As she passed over, the hawk casually dropped one long leg, grabbed her victim and then, making a long sweeping turn, carried her prey to the top of the walnut where the intrigued young were waiting. She allowed one to snatch the kill away from her, content to know that the young birds now clearly realized the connection between these live birds and the dead quarry they had been eating.

Thrilled, the big young female took her mother's place in the walnut and waited for more cowbirds. None came. Impatient, the young hawk remembered seeing starlings around the willow tree by the stream at that time of day and set off on her own. Like many animals, the hawk had a "mental clock" and could tell time in that she recalled certain events happening at certain hours. The starlings also had this "mental clock" and were creatures of habit; they nearly always went to the stream to drink at the same time and always under that particular willow. They were there when the young female arrived.

Without taking any precautions, the hawk rushed straight at the starlings who were popping in and out of the mint that grew close to the water's edge. She came down from the hill with the slope in her favor and went so fast that the starlings were hard put to escape. They reached a raspberry patch only a few feet ahead of her. The angry hawk tried to crash through the spiked vines after them and hit the tangle so hard she became caught in the cat's cradle of thorny stems. In her efforts to free herself, she tore out one of her primaries, a serious disaster, for the missing feather left a gap in her wing through which the air rushed when she tried to fly and threw her off balance. Not until the feather grew in again did she have complete control of her movements.

This misfortune discouraged the young bird and she refused to do any more hunting for several days. The other youngsters were no better. They were all a little afraid of live quarry, and by the time they had made up their minds to chase a bird, the quarry would have escaped. Even though the Cooper's hawk is notorious for its reckless courage, these hawks were nervous adolescents, unsure of themselves, and it was important that at this stage of their training they should not be daunted. The parents seemed to realize this danger.

Now the father hawk took over. Waiting until he knew by her actions and shrill cries that his most promising daughter was hungry, he started skimming over the hedgerows, diving occasionally to put up a small bird, while the hungry young female followed him, pitching on the nearest tree and watching his progress anxiously. Her father led her to the dead willow and there were the starlings. Instead of making an outright attack, he dropped low, flying only a few inches above the ground, taking advantage of every rise, clump of grass and finally the tree itself as cover. Only at the last possible moment did he unleash his rush.

The starlings exploded in all directions, screaming so loudly their noise itself bewildered the watching young female as she jerked her head back and forth trying to follow each member of the flock. In seconds she was hopelessly confused, but not so her father. As he came in for his final rush, he focused on one bird and now followed that bird regardless of the noise and confusion. As the fugitive twisted and turned through the flock, trying to shelter himself behind the wings of the others, the hawk's wings knocked the other starlings out of the way as he followed his chosen victim. In a last desperate effort to escape, the starling turned on one wing and tried to fly over his pursuer's head. As he did so, the male Cooper's turned over on his back and grabbed the bird from below. Both came plunging to the ground, the starling screaming in terror. Holding the struggling bird was difficult for the little male, yet strangely enough he did not dispatch him at once by sinking his talons into the brain. Instead, he sat holding him in the close-cropped grass and waited.

The young female could contain herself no longer. She leaped from the willow and flew toward her father, screaming her food call. When she was only a few yards away, the male released the starling. The bird instantly took off, but he had been mauled so badly he flew erratically and slowly. The young female swerved and followed him. When she saw that he was headed for the raspberry tangle, she put on all her speed and managed to get below him. Still leading her, the starling closed his wings and dropped like a stone for the bushes, but the hawk had learned from watching her father. Putting on a last burst of speed, she turned over on her back and the starling fell right into her pounces. It was her first kill and she felt inordinately proud.

Gradually, the young female learned her trade. When she saw a flock of birds feeding in the open, she did not make a direct attack but flew from tree to tree until she was as close as possible before turning loose her charge. She learned to wait until one bird had his head turned away and then went after that one. She never chased a bird more than a hundred yards; if she couldn't get him in that distance, there was no use trying. She developed an almost psychic ability to detect the weak, the crippled and sickly, as these were far easier to catch than healthy game. Luckily for her, the young of her quarry were growing up at the same time as she was learning to hunt, and these fledglings were comparatively easy to catch. Many of them were undernourished, for the songbirds, like her own parents, fed indiscriminately and only the strongest young got an adequate diet. The rest were condemned to death, either from predators or when winter came.

She learned to dive at woodpeckers on the trunk of a tree to make them fly. The older birds refused to fly and dodged around the trunk until she got discouraged, but the youngsters would become panicky and take off. As all woodpeckers are clumsy fliers, she could then pick them off easily. In spite of her experience with the raspberry bushes, she wasted a lot of time striking aimlessly at tangles, trying to make sparrows fly out of them; "beating around the bush" as the old falconers called it. By watching her parents she learned the knack of sweeping up and down the side of a hedge, raking it with her claws, and then suddenly shooting over it. Often inexperienced young sparrows would try to make a break on the far side of the hedge, thinking the hawk would not see them. She also learned that a squirrel "out on a limb" was easy pickings, but if he was close to the trunk, he could dodge around it like the woodpeckers and outwit her.

Her first attempt at big game was a half-grown cock pheasant. She was sitting in a tree, keeping an eye out for squirrels, when the cock ran below her. He had been flushed by something, possibly a fox, and was scuttling away, concentrating on the danger behind rather than above. The young hawk had never seen a pheasant before and was not sure if the creature was good to eat, but she took a chance and dove after him. She grabbed him by the base of the tail but the cock twisted around and, with his dagger-like beak, hit her a blow that knocked her over. For a long time after that, she left pheasants severely alone, until one afternoon while she was sitting on the roof of a springhouse looking for cowbirds, the farm dog sent up a young hen who came gliding across the pasture toward her. The pheasant did not see the motionless hawk on the roof and was headed for a patch of pokeweed near the springhouse door. She passed almost directly under the hawk and the temptation was too much. The young hawk came straight down on her, knocking the bird to the ground. The pheasant struck at her and in self-defense the hawk grabbed the game bird by the head. Her talons went into the brain, but the dying bird thrashed about so madly that the hawk could barely hold her until she got a grip with her other set of talons at the base of the pheasant's wing. This gave her a good hold and she hung on until the convulsions stopped. She killed several pheasants after that, although always young birds, taking care to grab them by the head and the base of one wing.

Large quarry could be dangerous for the young hawk; she was, after all, very flimsily built, being nothing but two sets of talons and a beak transported from one place to another by her great sails. Once while she was chasing a sparrow across a meadow, a rabbit got up under her and started to run. She checked off after the rabbit, easily overtook the bounding brown animal and grabbed him by the rump. The rabbit was a tough old buck, and he gave her a kick with his powerful hind legs, tipped with sharp claws, that ripped open her breast and left her lying semiconscious on the grass. It was over an hour before she recovered enough to fly to the nearest tree, and so crippled was she that, had not her father found her and fed her, she would have died.

By autumn, she had completely recovered although she left rabbits alone. She was abnormally big for a Cooper's hawk, almost as large as a male goshawk, and correspondingly powerful. Her eyes were beginning to turn a lemon-yellow and the new feather that had grown in was blue and white—her adult coloring. Not until the molt that spring would the rest of her plumage match it. She and one of the young males were the only two of the brood left. Her sister had been killed when she crashed into a barbed-wire fence, chasing a meadowlark, and her other brother had been caught by a redtailed hawk while he was struggling with a mourning dove. She had not seen her parents for several weeks now, but hardly missed them, as she was quite self-sufficient.

As the days grew shorter, she began to grow increasingly more restless. Even a few minutes' lack of daylight bothered her and she went on long soaring flights that took her higher than she had ever been before. Quarry was growing increasingly scarce and more difficult to catch. The awkward fledglings of summer were gone and those who survived had learned to avoid predators almost as well as their parents. Great flocks of starlings polka-dotted the fields in the evenings on their way south, but these she could not catch. They had too efficient an alarm system organized, and when she attacked they formed such a dense, compact mass that wheeled and wove around her that she could not cut out a single bird from the great flock. The songbirds were beginning to go, too, all heading south.

Then in October, a low which had centered over the Great Lakes began moving down the St. Lawrence Valley, followed by a broad cold front coming down from Canada and reaching over Pennsylvania. In her soaring, the young female had encountered a long ridge running north and south. The wind hitting the side of this ridge was deflected upward, forming an ascending stream of air on which she was able to ride south as though floating on an invisible river. Hardly bothering to flap, the young Cooper's was carried south until near dark a storm broke. Unable to see in the growing darkness, she came down in a city, attracted by the lights, and roosted under the over-hanging eaves of a building.

When dawn came, she found the building was infested with hundreds of pigeons. Their white droppings lay in great caked masses of stinking stalactites on its sides, and the air was filled with their cooings as the cocks strutted up and down the windowsills after the hens. The hawk had chased barn pigeons a few times, only to find that they were much too fast for her, so hungry as she was, she ignored these birds. Then she made a great discovery.

The pigeons had increased so in numbers that not only were their droppings defacing the buildings, but the enormous flocks had become a definite health hazard. An exterminator had been hired who had first tried trapping the birds, only to find they soon grew trap-wise. He had then used poisoned grain, but the sight of dying birds struggling in their death throes on the streets and pavements had aroused so much public resentment he had been forced to abandon this practice. He had then hit on the ingenious device of empaling grains of corn on barbed fishhooks tied to strong lines. When a pigeon ate one of the grains, the hook caught in his mouth. By keeping his hooks on the roofs of the public buildings where they could not be seen, the exterminator was able to avoid public indignation and also make some dent in the pigeon population. He visited his hooks every two or three days to collect the dead and dying pigeons.

The young hawk soon discovered these helpless birds. Here was a bonanza indeed. With so much good food about, she ate only part of the breasts, first dispatching the tortured prisoner with a quick grip of her powerful talons. Sheltered by the tall buildings and with a plentiful food supply, she gave up all idea of migrating and settled down to spend the rest of her life in the city. She was not alone, for other hawks passing over the city in their southward flight also saw the thrashing pigeons and came down to feed. The predators soon found that although barn pigeons were fast fliers well able to protect themselves, these city pigeons were fat, stupid creatures who could be easily caught even when they were free. This was a situation made to order for the hawks and they moved into the city in considerable numbers. By their combined efforts, the pigeon population began to drop. No one bothered them and the janitor of the building where the young Cooper's had taken up her abode used to lean out a window and cheer her on when she was hunting.

One sunny afternoon the young Cooper's was sitting on her favorite perch, a cornice of the building where she was protected from the wind but had a good range of vision. Below her was a park where an old lady was feeding the pigeons. One black-and-white bird was obviously the lady's favorite, for he flew to her hand and allowed her to stroke him. The striking black-and-white markings attracted the hawk's attention. When the bird fluttered away, the hawk went into a long dive, seized the pigeon before he could land and carried him off to her perch, disregarding the woman's hysterical screams.

She was not to enjoy her meal in peace. The old lady returned with a policeman and angrily pointed out the hawk to him. The officer drew his service revolver, took careful aim and fired.

The bullet barely chipped the shoulder of the hawk's right

wing but the concussion and shock partly stunned her. She came plunging down, turning over and over, while a group of little boys who had gathered to see the fun rushed to catch her, shouting with excitement. The hawk had managed to break her fall with outstretched wings and, when she saw the children coming, limped under the shelter of some ornamental holly bushes planted around the building. The boys had a dog with them and they started to beat the bushes, yelling with delight while the wounded and dazzled bird threw herself back on her spread tail so as to have both sets of talons ready for the inevitable battle.

Then came on interruption. The janitor burst out of the building, bellowing with rage. Crouching under the holly, the hawk heard his shouting, the furious answers of the woman and the bewildered voice of the policeman. It ended with the boys being ordered away and the policeman and the old lady leaving. Then the janitor came looking for her. He could not find the hawk, so well had she hidden herself, and he returned to the building muttering to himself.

The wounded hawk remained hidden the rest of the day and all that night. At dawn, half mad with hunger and thirst, she left the shelter of the hollies and scuttled along the side of the building, looking not unlike a large rat. There was no one about to see her at that hour and she was lucky enough to find a pool of rainwater, from which she drank feverishly. She picked up some scraps from overflowing garbage cans and then hid in a used-car lot. That evening she was able to catch a rat by running him down as he skulked along the side of a tenement building. The rat saved her life, for he provided both food and moisture.

Against incredible odds, the hawk was able to survive until her wing had healed sufficiently for her to fly. The damage was permanent. The delicate, hollow bones would never entirely knit, but she still could fly. As soon as possible she left the dangerous city and returned to the farming areas where there were trees and the possibility of game.

That night, an early snowstorm buried the whole countryside in fourteen inches of snow. The hawk had roosted in a stand of pines before the storm struck and their thick, feathery branches protected her, but when the dawn broke, her situation was desperate indeed. The whole world had turned white, there was no chance of her finding even a field mouse, and the few birds she saw were far too fast on the wing for her to catch in her crippled condition.

Flying through the woods, she came on a covey of quail that had taken refuge among the pines from the storm. The quail were so surrounded by snow that they could not run and they dared not fly for fear of coming down in the soft snow and being engulfed. The hawk stayed with them for ten days, taking a quail a day, until the covey was wiped out. Then she went on, insane for food.

She spied a barn with pigeons on the eaves and hopefully took out after them, but these pigeons were knowing birds, fast on the wing, and even if she had been in perfect condition she could not possibly have caught one. Once she thought she had one trapped in a pocket under the eaves and hurled herself after him with the fury of desperation, but the pigeon knew where a hole was and slipped through it, leaving the hawk clinging to the stone side of the barn. From the corner of her eye, she saw a brown form running around the corner of the barn. It looked something like a female pheasant and the hawk dropped on it, killing it with one fierce clench so that it was able to utter only a feeble squawk. On investigation, she found the bird was not a pheasant. It was not like anything she had ever seen and for that reason she would ordinarily have left it alone, as she was suspicious of strange creatures, not knowing what their powers were or whether they were good to eat. However, she was now too maddened by hunger to be cautious, and she fed. The flesh was very good, better even than pheasant, and she gorged herself.

She returned early the next morning but the remains of the chicken were gone. However, that made little difference, as there were plenty of others in the barnyard. She went straight in and made her kill without trouble, although this time she was not quite so skillful and the chicken squawked wildly. Instantly the formerly peaceful barnyard exploded with sound: chickens screaming their alarm call, guinea fowl chattering, ducks quacking as they fled for the pond with frantically beating wings and a dog appeared from nowhere and attacked her. Bewildered by the noise and the sudden charge, the hawk took off. As she rose a woman rushed from the house with a shotgun in her hands. The gun meant nothing to the hawk but as she rounded the barn, she heard the stunning crash of the report and the patter of shot on the stone wall. Then indeed she flew, for she had heard the report of a gun before and knew what it meant.

Afraid to return to the farm, she spent two days hunting in vain in the woods and fields. Then by chance she alighted in an apple tree that was part of an orchard. It was coming on evening and she felt that unless she was able to eat before dark, she would be too weak to live through the cold night.

At last fortune favored her. From a hedgerow, a rabbit hopped out, sat up, tested the air with twitching nose and loped toward the trees. He and his friends had already girdled several of them as high up as they could reach, for their grazing was under snow and the bark of the young trees was their only food. Those trees would never bear apples, for stripped of their bark, they were doomed to die.

The hawk dove for him, taking care to keep between the rabbit and the hedgerow. Ever since her former experience with a rabbit, she had been afraid of them, but now hunger over-balanced her fear. She was fast, but the rabbit saw her out of the corner of his eye. He made no attempt to double back but raced for a root fence surrounding the orchard. He plunged into a familiar hole, with the hawk so close behind him she nearly hit the tangle of roots. At the last second she altered the angle of her wings, spread her tail and zoomed straight up, shooting over the hedge and dropping on the other side straight down.

The rabbit had stopped in the safety of the roots, but they were far apart and the hawk reached in and grabbed him. He tore free, leaving a patch of brown fur, and ran for the orchard. Here he dashed from tree to tree, the hawk banking around the trunks right behind him. With each turn she cut in closer and closer until her inner wing seemed to scrape the bark and the rabbit, seeing that eventually he was sure to be caught, spun around and tried to bolt back to the fence. The hawk hit him full and fair, knocking him flat. Unfortunately for her, she also knocked the wind out of herself.

For a few seconds the hawk and rabbit sat scarcely a foot apart, both unable to move. Then the rabbit got up and limped off. The hawk watched him go and painfully got to her own feet and started to run after him. The rabbit went faster. So did the hawk. Then the rabbit began to run in earnest. The hawk left the ground and began to fly, although her beak was still open and she was panting hard.

The rabbit reached the fence and tried to slip through, but he was not at the familiar hole and was held for a moment by the tangle. Only a moment, but then the hawk had come up. She dropped to the ground beside him, reached into the tangle with one foot and grabbed the rabbit. The rabbit kicked and plunged like a bronco but the hawk hung on until she could grab him by the head with the other foot. Spreading her wings on either side for leverage and bracing with her extended tail, she held him down and squeezed with her long, needle talons until his hind feet stopped kicking.

Too exhausted to eat, the hawk sat astraddle of her kill until a slight noise made her look up. There was the Amish farmer who owned the orchard watching her. She wanted to fly but she hated to leave the rabbit, so she remained where she was with spread wings and open beak. If the man had taken another step toward her, she would have torn free from her quarry and flown, but instead he slowly walked away, went through a gap in the fence and continued on his way, leaving the hawk to gorge on her kill in peace. She was saving his orchard.

From then on, the hawk haunted the orchard. Even though she could apparently fly perfectly now, she could not turn loose that last terrific burst of speed that enabled her to take winged prey in fair flight, and to a Coopers hawk this meant the difference between death and survival. Rabbits, however, which had to run along the ground, were comparatively slow, and killing them was mainly a matter of strength and cunning. The big female already had the strength and she developed the cunning. She learned what rabbits were likely to do and how to outwit them. Unfortunately, there was not an unlimited supply of rabbits, and after a few weeks she had killed all except the wise old-timers who did not expose themselves and always were on the alert. These she could not catch and she soon abandoned the attempt, leaving them to reproduce their kind when the spring came.

Occasionally she was able to catch a squirrel, or a grouse or a pheasant, but not often; her injured wing was too much of a handicap. There was nothing for it but to return to the chicken yard.

She was far more cautious in her approach now. She flew to a branch high in a huge buttonwood tree that stood near the house and sat there studying the situation. She saw the chickens far away on the other side of a stand of winter wheat. Not knowing anything of their flying ability, she did not dare make a direct attack. Instead, she decided on strategy.

Plunging head foremost from the branch, she shot down like a dropped knife with her wings flat to her sides and her long tail closed and sticking straight out behind her. Six feet above the ground, she opened her tail like a fan, giving it a quick twist and at the same instant spreading her wings and dropping her banks of secondaries. This maneuver turned her over on her side, and going at top speed she banked sharply around the house. Now the barn was between her and the chickens so she used it for cover. Keeping low, she swung around the barn and dropped into the wheat.

It was higher than her head and offered concealment. She walked through the field with long strides and stopped at the edge, still securely hidden, to watch the chickens. The flock was well spread out, with none as close to her as she would have liked, so she waited patiently for a good fifteen minutes until one of the hens wandered within range. Then she rushed out of the wheat, and with a bound took to the air. The chicken saw the motion and turned to look. Instantly she screamed with terror and began to run, but now the hawk turned in the air, her lower primaries almost scraping the ground, and hit the hen so hard she bowled the quarry over. As the hen went down, she grabbed her by the base of one wing with her taloned foot and seized the screaming victim by the head with her other set of talons. One squeeze of her long hooks and the hen lay flapping feebly.

Meanwhile the rest of the flock had scattered in all directions, looking like feather dusters without handles, squawking hysterically as they raced for shelter. The hawk paid no attention to them. As soon as the hen had stopped fluttering, she dragged her under the shelter of some greenbriers, hopping on one foot and pulling the hen along with the other. She began to tear out the feathers with her hooked beak, throwing them around with flirts of her head so they formed a circle. She was too hungry to finish the job and, tearing off mouthfuls of meat, skin and feathers, bolted them whole. When her crop was so full it protruded like a tennis ball from under her neck, she stopped, wiped her beak thoroughly on a piece of dead wood and cleaned her long, thin toes, then seeing the form of a human, with a bound sailed away across the pasture.

In the house, the Mennonite woman heard the hubbub and rushed out with the shotgun in her hand, accompanied by the barking farm dog. By the time she arrived, the chickens were back in the barnyard, cowering under the privet hedge or hiding in the chicken house. The woman wasted time searching the barnyard and only later went out to the wheat field. On the far side she saw the telltale ring of feathers at the edge of the greenbrier hedgerow and was just starting toward it when the hawk took wing.

The woman watched with helpless fury, for the bird was far out of shotgun range. When spring came and there were small chicks that the hawk could easily carry off, the robber would surely return day after day until they were wiped out. By farm custom, chickens were the property of the woman; she depended on them for "egg money," her only source of revenue for the few simple luxuries that meant the difference between merely existing in a life of ceaseless toil and having something to look forward to. Now even that pitiful little pleasure was to be taken from her. Nothing either she or her husband could do would prevent the raids, for neither had time to mount an all-day vigil over the barnyard, and keeping the flock penned up would entail more cost and trouble than they were worth. Deeply devout, the woman wondered why a merciful God had ever created a hawk.

Only the chickens enabled the partly crippled Cooper's to survive that long winter. She studied the flock and the farm with the same cool cunning she had used in learning how best to catch her natural prey. She soon learned that the big Rhode Island Red rooster whom she had at first regarded with apprehension was an abject coward and contemptuously eliminated him from her problems. Although she caught other game when possible, she had become a confirmed chicken hawk. There is no one species of hawk that can be called a "chicken hawk"—a chicken hawk is simply a hawk that has taken to killing chickens—but the Cooper's, because of its method of hunting and tendency to live near farming areas, is more likely to become a chicken thief than any other species. The buteos are big, soaring birds living mainly on rats and mice; the harriers live near swamps and feed on frogs and snakes; the falcons take their prey high in the air; and the great goshawk is a bird of the deep forests. Still, even Cooper's hawks seldom attack chickens, as poultry are not their natural prey and they have a certain reluctance to enter such an alien world as a barnyard. So although the Cooper's is the most friendless of all hawks, the wounded bird had become a degenerate even among her own kind. She was an outcast among outcasts, a pariah's pariah, a female Ishmael of the bird world.

Ishmael cared nothing for her outcast status; she sought only to survive and with her injured wing that meant running the risks of chicken stealing. She lived alone, never seeing another of her own kind and rejecting the world as completely as the world had rejected her.

March came and with it appeared the tiny white flowers of snowdrops on their fragile green stems. These delicate little flowers that signal spring is on the way meant nothing to Ishmael. She only knew the days were growing longer and each additional minute of the thin sunshine made strange emotions stir within her. The starlings had come back and were looking for nesting holes and there was an occasional robin.

Flying through the woods that topped a ridge overlooking the farming country, Ishmael for the first time felt lonely. For some reason she could not have explained, she gave a plaintive series of soft "ca-ca-cas" not unlike her alarm call but far more gentle and lower in pitch. For several days she flew through the woods uttering her sad protest against fate until one day, to her astonishment, she heard an answering "kik-kik-kik" in a voice much shriller than her own. Then she saw a male Cooper's flying through the woods toward her and Ishmael saw he was carrying a dead female downy wood-pecker.

The male beat furiously with his wings a few times to give himself added speed and shot up to land on the branch near her. Ishmael shrank away from him with obvious distrust even though she was much bigger than he was. She was not used to friendly advances. The male plucked a few feathers from the downy and then pranced up to her, bowing, ruffling his feathers, opening his wings and giving little, hopeful cries. Ishmael was hungry and she remembered how her father had brought her food. She arched her neck and opened her wings belligerently and, jumping sideways along the branch, seized the woodpecker. The male made no effort to defend his kill and seemed pleased that she had decided to accept his love token. Ishmael bolted the downy and then, fluffing out her feathers, she drew one foot up under the soft plumes of her panel and stared steadfastly out into space. The male continued to woo her, making short flights around the tree as though tempting her to follow, but Ishmael continued to ignore him, looking everywhere except at the anxious male.

After she had put over the food from her crop and partially digested it, she began to follow the male's pleading flights with her eyes, cocking her head first on one side and then on the other to watch. Several times she half spread her wings and bent her legs as though to join him, and then thought better of it. It was not until the male seemed to be growing tired and was preparing to leave that Ishmael made up her mind and, slipping from the branch, swept after him.

Delighted, the male altered his manner of flight and flew with long, leisurely strokes, bringing his wings up so high above his back that the tips of the primaries almost met, and then with a downstroke sweeping them below him until they touched. At the same time, he fluffed out his creamy undertail coverts so the plumes spread out on either side of his long tail. Ishmael duplicated his actions and the two birds rose above the trees and continued their courtship flight over the grove. So slow and soft were the wing strokes that the birds flew almost like moths. They were no longer the fearful assassins of the forest but creatures of fairy-like beauty, looking somewhat like snowy egrets, as they wheeled and glided above the trees in complete control of their environment.

When they had finished, Ishmael led the way back into the grove and pitched on a broad limb, leaning forward with wings and tail partly spread. The male took the hint and, swinging up behind and above her, came down lightly on her back with fast fluttering wings. Ishmael took a firm hold on the branch and spread her wings and tail even more. The actual mating took only a few seconds and both birds gave gasps of what seemed to be pure delight. Afterward, they preened. That night they roosted in the same tree, only a few yards apart from each other. As the night was cold, both birds fluffed out their feathers to make air pockets under the plumes to provide insulation against the chilly air. Instead of the sleek look they had during the day, they now seemed soft and fluffy, almost like downy youngsters.

At dawn the next morning, the male flew to the top of a hog hickory and began to sing in his high-pitched voice. The sounds he produced were surprisingly musical and soon Ishmael joined him and chimed in with her deeper contralto. Between them, the birds produced an astonishing variety of notes and seemed supremely content with the result. They did not sing to establish territory, as did most of the songbirds, or for any apparent reason except sheer joy in being together. They sang their strange duet for nearly an hour and then flew side by side down to the little creek that ran under the covered bridge to bathe.

The male kept them both supplied with food for several weeks, and Ishmael reveled in being petted and spoiled after the long months of semistarvation and loneliness. Then one morning the male was late in coming and she grew impatient. She gave her "ca-ca-ca" call several times, following it with a few irritated "waas." Then she decided to go hunting on her own. For a long time she had not been near the barnyard and she had a craving for the soft, white meat of chicken.

By now she had learned to follow a regular route to the farmhouse. Leaving the grove, she swept across an open space, alternately flapping and gliding. Here a high tension line had been run, so she lit on one of the insulators to look around. Satisfied there was no danger, she slipped off the insulator and flew swiftly along a line of trees, doubled around them where the line turned, and with the slope in her favor glided down a hill toward the farmhouse. In the middle of the pasture, a few trees had been left around a sinkhole in the limestone that lay only a few feet beneath the soil. Ishmael made for this clump, pitched in a cherry and looked around again. All safe. Again she took to the air but dropped sharply, and, keeping a hedgerow between her and the barnyard, slipped around the house to where the buttonwood stood. Gaining momentum with a few hard wing-beats, she shot up to one of the topmost limbs and froze into immobility.

There were no chickens on the turnaround so she shifted her attention to the barnyard. Through the high privet hedge which had been allowed to grow wild, she saw the chickens in the barnyard None was of convenient carrying size so Ishmael waited.

Watching the chickens, she saw there was a new cock. This seemed to her like a very different bird from the old barnyard rooster she had seen before. The new arrival had longer legs, a longer neck, broader chest and powerful thighs. He marched about with light confident steps and his every motion suggested alertness. Even though Ishmael had no fear of chickens, she regarded the newcomer with a slight tinge of doubt. Of course he would panic as chickens always did before her rush; still it might be as well to avoid him.

There came a flicker of small, moving shapes through the brown twigs. Ishmael leaned forward and bobbed her head to bring them into better focus. Ah, one of these chickens was small enough to be carried.

She dove head foremost from her limb, darted through the dangling branches of a circle of elms, never taking her eyes from the chicken, and banked sharply around the hedge. Here was nothing but open pastureland and a post-and-rail fence. Ishmael flashed over the fence and rocketed into the barnyard.

At the moment she started her plunge, the pullet had seen some grains of feed in the entrance of an open box stall and started to enter it. With a twist of her tail and a slight turn of her extended primaries, Ishmael was after her. The pullet managed to reach the stall a few wingbeats ahead of the hawk, but there she was trapped and Ishmael without hesitation followed her in.

By now all the alarm systems of the barnyard had gone off; the cries of the chickens, the calls of the guinea fowl and the quacking of the ducks mingled with the angry chittering of starlings who dove at the hawk, one or two of the bravest even following her into the stall. Ishmael ignored them. She saw the pullet running about and went for her. Before, the pullet had only been giving the alarm call. Now with the hawk upon her, her cackling went up to a shrill crescendo and she fluttered up, seeking a way over the top of the stall. Ishmael spread her long tail and, shooting up, seized her. Both hen and hawk came down together on the straw, the chicken's screams becoming deafening. Ishmael sank both sets of her long talons into her quarry's sides, spreading her wings and tail to hold the struggling bird. Once the pullet was limp and dead she could carry her more easily, so the hawk began clenching hist with one set of talons and then with the other to drive the points home.

Something came charging into the stall, its snaky neck extended, its hackles spread like a ruff showing their white underparts, its long legs going like pistons. This creature came rushing at her, and to her astonishment Ishmael realized it was the new cock and he was attacking. He obviously intended to save the hen or die trying, and Ishmael knew that she was going to have to fight for her life.

3.

COCK O' THE WALK

Whitehackle hurled himself at the hawk with all the berserk madness of his gamecock blood. He was not fighting to save the hen; he wanted only to get his spurs in the intruder who had dared to start a fight in his territory. True, he regarded the hen as his property and this added to his outrage, but the sight of the struggle was enough to inflame him. Duplicating the technique he had found so effective in the pit, he seized the hawk by the breast feathers and then, throwing himself back, he prepared to use his thorn-sharp daggers.

Ishmael found herself at a hopeless disadvantage. She was not equipped for beak-to-beak fighting on the ground and the cock was more than twice her own weight. She was designed for and accustomed to overtaking fleeing quarry and being able to pick her hold as she came in from above; if the pursued animal had ever turned to face her, she would hardly have known what to do. To make matters worse, Ishmael's talons were locked in the body of the squawking pullet and she had taken so fierce a grip she could not relax her hold any more than a bulldog can release his grip once he has locked his jaws in flesh. Her talons were her main weapons, so momentarily she was handcuffed and all but helpless.

She still had her beak. Whereas the cock's beak was a spear, the hawk's beak with its curved upper mandible was a hooked pair of shears. It was designed for gripping and tearing, and Ishmael had ripped many a rabbit to death with it while the bunny plunged and kicked in the grip of her ice-tongs talons. Though she could not strike straight out with it, now that the cock had seized her by the breast, she was able to grab him by the remnants of his comb.

The hooked mandible went right through the soft red flesh and the cock's blood spurted out over both birds. Whitehackle felt the chill shock of the hard, sharp beak cutting through him, and he stabbed for his life with his newly grown spurs. Ishmael had spread her wings to make herself look more impressive, and as she had thrown herself backward to meet the attack, her extended sails did not act as shields as do the open wings of a cock who is rushing head foremost at his opponent. Whitehackle's spurs hit her unprotected sides bang-bang and Ishmael gasped as the blows went home. Had Whitehackle been heeled, she would have been killed almost instantly, but although the bony spurs plunged through the soft body feathers, they did not kill. Whitehackle felt his spurs go home but, with the blood pouring over his eyes and beak, knew he would have to win fast if at all. For the first time in his life he shuffled, his legs going with sewing-machine rapidity as he strove to drive the spurs in deeper.

The birds were grappled together, Ishmael with her hooked mandible through the top of the cock's head and Whitehackle with his spurs locked in the hawk's body. Unable to use any other weapons, both fought with their wings, beating blindly and trying to throw the other off balance. Ishmael struggled to free her beak so she could strike again. Whitehackle forced himself against her in the hard, rolling rhythm of a ground shuffle. The hawk was weakening fast and he could feel it.

In her agony, Ishmael's leg muscles relaxed and she felt her talons come free. At the same instant she was able to rip her beak loose. She was barely in time, for the spurs were stabbing and pounding her to death. As the screaming, hysterical pullet fled from the stall, leaving a wake of feathers, Ishmael with a gasp of relief threw herself back on her spread tail and grabbed the cock by the chest with both feet. Thinner than spurs, the needle-like pounce talons slipped between Whitehackle's breast feathers, and as each one perforated his skin, he felt a spasm of the purest pain leap through him. Then Ishmael was able to bring her hooked, powerful hind talons into play and drove them in with all the power of her great leg muscles. In spite of the torture, Whitehackle still tried to shuffle, but even gamecock flesh and blood could not withstand the fearful punishment of the hawk's grip that began to paralyze him. Whitehackle tried to tear himself free, and for a few seconds the two birds bounced around the stall like a gigantic feathered rubber ball. Then they came apart and faced each other panting and bloody.

Whitehackle was almost blinded by the blood pouring from his mutilated scalp but he was still dead game and perfectly prepared to continue the battle. Ishmael, on the other hand, desired nothing except escape. She killed only for food, and the whole conception of fighting simply to achieve victory over an opponent was entirely alien to her nature. She could see the open door of the stall and beyond it light and freedom, but the cock stood in the way dand she was too battered and breathless to fly. Even so, she tried to reach the doorway, running forward on her long legs and attempting to dodge around the cock. Whitehackle thought she was attacking. Almost unable to see because of the flowing blood, he could hear her coming and sidestepped. As the hawk rushed by, he went up in a fly and managed to come down on top of her. Grabbing her by the back of the neck as though she were a hen he was treading, he began to shuffle. The cock's weight threw the hawk down, and she lay struggling in the straw while the spurs vibrated against her sides. She could use neither her talons nor her beak and all her efforts to turn under her oppressor were useless. She began to lose consciousness.

The farm dog had burst into the stall and was barking furiously. He would have been glad to come to Whitehackle's help but he was afraid to bite, for he could not tell one bird from the other in the struggle. He was still barking and snapping at the combatants when the farmer's wife ran in. She gasped when she saw the two birds and, bending over, grabbed the hawk away from Whitehackle and tried to wring Ishmael's neck.

Now Ishmael was no longer helpless. Once she was free of the cock, she twisted around to bring her legs into play and buried her right talons in the fat of the woman's hand. The woman screamed and tried to tear the hawk loose with her free hand while the dog grabbed the hawk's tail with his jaws and Whitehackle rocketed up in fly after fly, indiscriminately striking at the woman, the hawk and the dog. Ishmael's rear talon had gone right up to the socket in the woman's flesh and the pain was excruciating. She tore the bird free by main force and flung her on the straw, two of Ishmael's tail feathers coming out in the dog's mouth at the same time. The dog spit them away and plunged forward while Ishmael went over on her side with raised talons to meet his attack. Whitehackle, virtually blind and drunk with fighting fury, saw only the great shape bearing down on him and attacked the dog. Ducking his head to protect his eyes, the dog tried to get around Whitehackle but the few seconds' delay had saved Ishmael. She had fallen on the stone doorstep of the stall, and between her and open sky was nothing except the overhang of the barn. Ishmael rolled over, got her feet under her and with a bound leaped upward. The dog sprang after her as she flashed away, his snapping teeth missing her tail by inches as she shot out under the overhang, swung over the chicken house and was gone.

She left chaos behind her. The clean, yellow straw and white-washed planks of the stall were splotched with blood from Whitehackle and the woman's hand, there seemed to be enough feathers strewn about to stuff a pillowcase, the Mennonite woman was sobbing and half hysterical from the pain in her arm, Whitehackle was still attacking everything he could see, including the sides of the stall, the barnyard was in an uproar and the dog had rushed outside and was barking. In the excitement of the fight he had not been listening to the alarm cries of the poultry, and now, hearing them for the first time, he decided that the hawk was returning to the attack.

When the farmer returned from the fields that evening, walking well behind his great, feather-footed team and guiding them by the long reins, he listened amazed and incredulous to his wife's story. A cock that would attack a hawk in gallant defense of one of his hens was unheard of. He went out to see the hero and found the completely blinded Whitehackle staggering around the barnyard, his eyes sealed shut with clotted blood. The man caught the champion and, carrying him tenderly into the kitchen, washed his head with warm water and applied some cobwebs to his wound. As soon as he could see, Whitehackle drank water eagerly, but the farmer insisted on pouring some peach brandy down his throat which made him cough and choke. Even though the scalp wound had bled so copiously, it was not serious, and by next morning Whitehackle was back in his usual shape which was more than could be said of the woman, for her hand swelled like an inflated rubber glove from the crushing force of Ishmael's grip. Word of Whitehackle's exploit flashed through the district, and for days afterward there was a steady procession of buggies as the Plain People came to see the rooster that had engaged a chicken hawk in hand-to-hand battle and defeated the raider. While the men stood about in the barnyard admiring Whitehackle and commenting in astonishment on his conformation and glowing colors, the women collected in the great farm kitchen before the huge fireplace, commiserating with the farmer's wife, suggesting home cures and, more practically, doing the cleaning and preparing enough meals to tide her over for the next few days until her hand was usable again.

The farm wife had at first resented Whitehackle, holding him in some way responsible for her injury. Now the general awe in which the strange rooster was held began to affect her. Considerably more to the point, everyone wanted young cockerels who were the descendants of this heroic bird, and the woman felt she could count on a most profitable season. There still remained the problem of the hawk. The woman well knew that blue darters were death on young chicks which could be easily snatched up and carried. She gravely doubted Whitehackle's ability to protect the broods, even if he had the will to do so. She realized far better than her husband did that Whitehackle had attacked the predator only because of special circumstances. Whether the cock would or could fight off the same hawk in the open was extremely doubtful. That the hawk would return she had no doubt; once a chicken hawk, always a chicken hawk. She was as helpless as ever to protect the barnyard, everything depended on this strange, new rooster, and she feared that he would be of no more help than the great, glaring hex signs painted on the barn which, as the woman fully knew, had no magical properties; they were "just for nice."

Whitehackle had no such doubts. He only wished the woman had left him alone to finish off that hawk which he had been perfectly capable of doing. His victory had impressed all the other birds on the farm, from the swaggering turkey cock to the grim ganders. Whatever the reason, this arrogant little rooster had attacked the most terrible of all enemies and driven it away. Just as they relied on the dog to protect them from ground predators because they had seen him drive off foxes, stray cats and weasels, so they relied on Whitehackle. At least for the time being, Whitehackle was king of the barnyard.

Whitehackle accepted the tribute as being only his due. Although his primary concern was with the chickens, he also recognized a certain responsibility for the other fowl. He ruled not only a kingdom but an empire, and never was an empire so diversified as to territories and ethnic groups. On the farm were chickens, geese, ducks, turkeys, guinea fowl, and even peafowl, for the farmer had found he could get twenty-five dollars each for the magnificent peacocks, and they were no more difficult to raise than turkeys, as they belonged to the same genus. There were also wild birds on the farm that did not come directly under Whitehackle's supervision yet had to be taken into account, if only as competitors for food. These included pigeons, pheasants, starlings, sparrows and crows. Even the mammals such as the sheep, cows, horses and definitely the dog entered into the skein of government.

In general, each of these highly complicated societies kept to its own territory: the geese near the pond, the ducks to the stream, the pigeons to the barn roof, the guinea fowl to the fields and the peafowl to the lawn and trees, but the territories often overlapped and varied according to the time of year. Now that it was spring, the geese and ducks came to the barn and sheepfold to find nesting places, and this interfered with the nesting hens. As the turkeys and peafowl were both pheasants, terrible battles took place between the cocks, not only for territory but also because each suspected the other had designs on his hens. Two pairs of Canada geese were nesting by the pond and the ganders had established limited territories around the nests. Curiously, the Canadas did not fight with the domestic geese, who respected their territorial rights, but they did fight with the sheep. As both the sheep and the geese ate grass, the struggles were over grazing rights near the nests. One stubborn ewe nearly lost an eye when she insisted on grazing too near a nest, and the old ram butted a belligerent gander so hard that the bird limped about with a dragging wing for several days.

Apart from interracial conflicts, there were constant feuds going on in each group. Not only did each group have its own variation of the pecking order—which was constantly changing according to circumstances—but some like the chickens were polygamous; others like the geese were monogamous; and still others like the ducks were promiscuous. There was even homosexuality, for the stronger of the young cockerels would sometimes tread their weaker brothers when Whitehackle kept them away from the hens.

Generally Whitehackle did not interfere in the intertribal disputes unless they took place in the barnyard, which he regarded as his special domain; still, he was not entirely indifferent to them. He felt a sort of proprietary interest in the whole area and any kind of disturbance bothered him. Usually he demanded the sign of submission—a lowered neck—from every bird he passed, although this depended on circumstances and his own disposition at the time. A very nice balance had arisen between him and the other males that was partly an armed truce, partly a recognition of territorial rights, partly a feeling of mutual respect and partly habit.

Whitehackle's domain extended from the picket fence east of the house to the five-acre truck patch north of the house and barn, through the orchard to the south and west to the stream and pond. Around this well-known and safe area was a no-man's-land where he frequently ventured, depending on the time of year, but where he felt no proprietary authority. This fringe area included the dirt road that ran past the house and the weeds on the far side (the road was excellent for dust baths and there were often seeds on the weeds). North of the truck patch were wine berries, chokeberries and sheepberries where he would sometimes lead his hens. The orchard could nearly always be counted on for a supply of grasshoppers, crickets, caterpillars and beetles, especially after the grass had been mowed and it was easier walking. If not, he would take his harem to a line of evergreens planted beyond the orchard as a windbreak. The cross-cropped pasture around the stream and pond he generally left to the water birds, but especially in spring one could often pick up succulent shoots by the stream and occasionally catch small frogs and grass snakes. It was also a grand place to chase the white cabbage butterflies, as you could run across the turf with your head up and not bother about tripping. Beyond the pasture were the woods where grew all sorts of exotic delicacies, but this was a haunted land full of strange sounds and colors. When entering this enemy country, Whitehackle always went first, ahead of the flock, walking with slow strides, making many stops and constantly turning his head to get a distinct image with each eye while listening intently.

When off his home range, Whitehackle was easily hackled by any determined adversary. On his home range, he was far more aggressive, yet even here he did not go out of his way to pick a fight and avoided, while not seeming to do so, a passing gander, peacock or drake. In one place and one place only was Whitehackle determined to insist on his unquestioned authority: in the barnyard he was to be the undisputed ruler. Here he would fight to the finish against any challenge to his rights.

To a human the barnyard did not seem to be much larger than a tennis court, but to Whitehackle it was a very considerable territory indeed and he knew every square inch of it with a minute attention to detail impossible to a tall, lumbering human. He knew each stalk of the privet hedge that bordered the yard on the side nearest to the house, where all the holes were and which ones would admit the dog, which a chicken and which a rat. He knew all the stones, too, and it bothered him if one was moved or a new one added. Sometimes when the farmer was busy he threw the manure from the stalls into the barnyard instead of hauling it away to the manure pit, and it formed a pile some five feet high. This dungheap seemed like a hill to Whitehackle and he loved to climb on top of it several times a day, not only for the insects it attracted, but also because it gave him a magnificent view over the pasture. It made a good crowing point and Whitehackle crowed here several times a day.

The barn, Whitehackle also regarded as part of his fief, although he seldom entered it except on rainy days. He knew it almost as well as he did the barnyard. In summer the barn was always cool, for it was built into the south side of a hill to provide shelter for the stock in winter and make it possible by use of a low ramp to drive the heavily loaded hay wagons into the loft which was above the lower section where the cattle were housed. Whitehackle preferred to stay outside in good weather, as he liked the warmth, and the shade provided by the elms was enough for him, but several of the hens spent almost all their time in the cool darkness of the barn, especially when they were hot and broody. Whitehackle learned to walk surely along the dark, narrow passageways between the stalls and he knew the location of all the mangers where there were always a few oats or traces of sweetfeed. He knew how to jump from the mangers to the tops of the stalls and from there to the joists for roosting in inclement weather. Usually he preferred to find his food outside, but when the horses and sheep were being fed, he learned to slip into the stalls and sheepfold and snatch oats and corn away from the clumsy brutes. With a little practice, he grew adept at avoiding the great, hairy hooves of the Belgians and the stupid, wild rush of the sheep to the feeding troughs, and glided back and forth between the animals' feet with an almost weasel smoothness.

Whitehackle's day began just before sunrise when the first false light of dawn made it possible to distinguish between the shadows and the open. He roosted high in the privet hedge, right under the eaves of the barn where he was protected from owls and too high for prowling raccoons to find him without making so much noise that he would be warned. The guinea fowl who also roosted in the privet were always the first down, and Whitehackle let them scuttle around, crane their necks and check the terrain before he descended, for he had found from long experience no enemy could hide from the watchful guineas who, in spite of centuries of domestication, were still as alert as their African ancestors. If the guineas did not give their rattling alarm cry, he would fly down and after a quick check either pace slowly and majestically to the top of the dunghill or fly up to his favorite perch in the post-and-rail fence. There he would give his morning crow, arching his neck and beating with his wings as though pumping the clarion call out of his lungs. After each crow, he would listen carefully for an answer. If the wind were exactly right, he could barely hear the crowing of a cock on the next farm, also proclaiming his territory. The two birds would crow defiantly to each other for a minute or so and then, each satisfied with his own prowess and confident that he had definitely established his own property, go about the business of the day.

Whitehackle's crow was the reveille that brought the sleeping barnyard to life. One after another the hens would plunge out of the hedge on heavily beating wings to crash-land on the hard-packed earth of the barnyard and then run off into the dew-laden grass to look for crickets and other nocturnal insects that might still be abroad or to check the edges of the cesspool for tardy night crawlers. The ducks would appear from under the wagons in the carriage shed, standing on tiptoe to stretch their wings before heading for the stream. The geese who had slept beside the pond would start out to graze on the tender, damp grass, and the turkeys would fly down from their perches on top of the stalls.

As the barnyard awoke into life, Whitehackle always seemed nervous, as though suddenly conscious of his responsibilities at the start of a new day. He rushed around among the chickens as though counting them to make sure none had vanished during the night, chasing one hen as though about to tread her, turning away to pursue another and stopping frequently to crow nervously. Not until he had quieted down and gone to the stream to drink did the young cockerels dare to crow in their cracked, uncertain tones, like adolescent boys whose voices are beginning to change, and then fly down themselves. They knew better than to interfere with their father until the old fellow had had something to eat and drink. Cocks are always irritable upon first rising.

Whitehackle made a ceremony of drinking. After the long night he felt dehydrated and he savored each mouthful of the deliciously cool water like a gourmet savoring fine wine, tilting back his head and letting the sweet fluid trickle down his throat. This morning he drank thirty-five times before he was satisfied and returned to the barnyard.

Now it was full light although the sun had not as yet lifted above the ghostlike white wall of mist. Vapor was rising from the pond like steam from a boiling kettle. Individual pigeons were making trial flights in the steel-blue sky to test the wind, air temperature and thermal drafts. So far, everything had been silent except for Whitehackle's crowing, but now the barnyard noises began. Three of the guineas had found a pilot black snake returning to his hold under the corncrib, and they set up their hard alarm roll. The scolding of the sparrows in the ivy started and the quarreling of the starlings; without constant disputes these birds could not live—fighting gave their whole lives flavor. The barn swallows were slicing the air with their darting flight, looking for late mosquitoes. In the lilacs came the angry mew of a catbird, reinforced by the locust-like buzz of a red squirrel. They might see a skunk, opossum or a raccoon, but whatever it was the creature was headed for home and posed no menace to the farmyard. Far away in the distant woods came the rallying call of a crow, promptly answered by many other crows who came flapping in from all directions to join in the attack. Almost surely they were after a late owl who had not managed to find a roost deep enough in the woods before daylight caught him.

The geese were now spread far out over the pasture, grazing, leaving green trails behind them where their big webbed feet had knocked the glistening white dew off the grass. The farm dog came half out of his kennel, yawned, stretched, came out entirely and stood looking around and testing the morning breeze. At the sight of him, several wise old Muscovy ducks started for the pond. Until the dog was up and around, they had refused to leave the shelter of the barn. High on the eaves and chimneys of the house, the peafowl looked down but did not stir. They were always the last to move. The turkey gobbler led his nervous, high-stepping harem of slender hens toward the stream.

As Whitehackle headed back for the barnyard, pigeons slipped from their nests under the overhang of the barn and drifted down to the salt blocks in the pasture where they started to peck. There were a few night-feeding rabbits about who scarcely moved to get out of Whitehackle's way. In the distant woods, a cock pheasant called, looking for his hen. The oldest of the young cockerels waltzed around the hens, hoping to make time before the old cock returned.

The round red ball of the sun rose above the mist curtain. The sky turned a robin's-egg blue. The peafowl came coasting down from the roof, the cocks trailing their incredible long trains behind them. Whitehackle quickened his pace, for he knew the peafowl would make short work of any insects still too cold to fly. As he hurried on, some hens came out from squatting under a bed of Turk's-cap lilies and joined him. The rays of the sun struck this bed first and they were luxuriating in the warmth.

Whitehackle strode on with a quick high-stepping walk suggestive of a pacing horse and started picking among the grass, managing to get a few flies inoperative from the damp and cold. He and his hens worked in feverish competition with the peafowl but there was no quarreling. Some ducks joined them, eating the grass but occasionally finding a worm, too. When one got a worm he ran with it while the others pursued him. Small groups of starlings came scudding in to favorite trees and a jay started his strident call, to be instantly answered by another jay. Then a robin joined in with her "tut-tut-tut" call. Whitehackle raised his head and paused to listen. So did the oldest peacock. The starlings started scolding and several swooped low. Whitehackle and the peacock strained their necks upward to watch.

The hens, intent on the protein-rich insects their systems craved, paid no attention to the birds. They had spread out like a fan, picking feverishly. An eager pullet came close to the low-hanging branches of one of the two great Colorado spruces which had been planted a hundred years before as small, ornamental trees but now towered above the house. The untrimmed bottom branches spread like open hands touching the grass. The robin had her nest in the nearest spruce, and now her warning cry rose in intensity and the "tuts" came closer together.

A domestic cat gone feral exploded from under the concealing spruce branch and bounded for the pullet. At the last instant, the chicken skitted sideways and avoided the blow, screaming, "Awk! Awk!" Instantly Whitehackle and the peacock charged, both going up in the air to strike with their spurs in precisely the same motion. The cat swerved to avoid them while the chickens and peahens scattered like beads from a broken string, yelling, "Kaaaaah! Kaaaaah!"—the cry for a ground predator. Having missed her rush, the cat did not pause but kept going while the cry of the poultry changed to "Cut—cut—cut, cattah, cut—cut—cut!" meaning the predator was still in sight but not attacking. In seconds the dog was there, sprinting up the gravel drive as hard as he could go while the wild birds joined in the uproar. The dog saw the cat crossing the drive, but she made it to the honeysuckle-wild grape tangle around the old snake fence well ahead of him and escaped.

Whitehackle instantly withdrew to the greater safety of the area between the house and the barn, with the anxiously clucking hens following him, the peacock withdrawing more slowly, being a bigger bird and helped by the younger cocks who assisted him in covering the flights of the peahens. The whole barnyard had been alerted, and the ducks with quivering tails were giving their jerking quacks and the turkeys their worried calls that sounded like drops of water hitting a tin roof. Even far away on the hill, the ever-vigilant guineas gave their warning cries although they had no idea what the trouble was all about.

It took nearly half an hour for the excitement to die down and quiet to be restored to the barnyard. Even then Whitehackle avoided the front of the house. Instead, he led his hens to the great copper kettle near the blacksmith shed where apple butter was made in autumn. It was used for other purposes and there were occasional scraps to be found here. Next he went to the cucumber pump and allowed the hens to scratch for worms in the damp ground, keeping a sharp lookout to grab the first worms for himself. The next stop was by the Gegusse eise Kessel, the kettle-furnace built into the house to maintain a supply of hot water. There was a wood-pile here that was constantly replenished and often wood borers and beetles could be found under the sticks. Then came a long walk under the wild plums, lindens, sassafras and white ash, past the tobacco drying shed to the old limekiln where bugs often hid under the stone slabs.

Now the sun was high in the sky and it was growing unpleasantly hot, so Whitehackle led the way to a single huge white pine. Here the thick lower branches had killed the grass under them and the soil was dry and powdery. It was ideal for dust baths. All around the south and east sides of the pine were a series of cup-shaped depressions. Whitehackle selected the best, as was his right, and wriggled down in the delightfully soft dust that drifted up through his feathers, discouraging the lice and mites. For the better part of an hour he and his faithful hens lay there, luxuriating in the delicious sensation, shifting slightly from side to side. When they finally had had enough,

Whitehackle led them to the shade of a trumpet vine where they stood or lay about, waiting until the sun dropped.

At four o'clock, they started out again, this time going to the truck patch to look for eatables and then making a detour through the pasture to drink at the stream and ending in the orchard. The grass was getting a little high here for comfort, but Whitehackle followed the sheep paths and there were open spaces under the trees where the sheep collected during the heat of the day. The hunting was good here, especially tent caterpillars and Japanese beetles that fell from the trees, and the chickens returned to the barnyard with full crops and contented minds. It was evening now and the ducks were drifting up from their day at the stream to collect under the farm wagons for the night. On the bare spots around the salt blocks, the cock pigeons were strutting after the coy hens, spreading their throat feathers to make the late light dance on their iridescent hues. Their activities may have given Whitehackle ideas, for he treaded several of the hens before going to roost.

Courtship was not the slap-bang affair that anyone watching Whitehackle's pursuit of a reluctant hen might suppose. Whitehackle had two approaches, one to a familiar hen whom he knew would receive him and one to a reluctant or strange female. With a new hen, Whitehackle went through an elaborate procedure. He would first waltz around the hen, dropping the wing nearest to her and fluttering it spasmodically, while kicking with the other leg. If the hen did not respond, he would give the food call and pretend to feed. If she ran, giving loud squawks, Whitehackle would then indignantly run her down and, grabbing her by the top of the head, hold her down and mount her, his feet pressed against her outstretched wings, convulsively grasping and relaxing much like the motions Ishmael made when killing her quarry. In fact, the whole business of mating was curiously like fighting, for the waltz with dropped wing, the comb grip and the rapid shuffling motions of the legs were exactly those motions used in fighting. When the young cockerels challenged each other in the barnyard, they approached with the same waltzing step and if possible got the other cock down, straddled him and held him down by the comb. Fighting and mating were so closely identified in the cocks' brains that only by the behavior of another bird could they tell if he were male or female. If a cockerel succeeded in getting a weaker cock down and the victim attempted to save himself from further punishment by moving his tail to one side and erecting the cloaca, the dominant bird would breed him as he would a hen. This, however, rarely happened, as usually another cock would fight when approached and, if pursued after defeat, stop and prepare to fight again, so the dominant cockerel would seldom have entire control over the situation.

With a quiescent hen, Whitehackle did not employ the elaborate courtship dance. He would simply approach her from the rear and extend his head over her with hackle raised, and giving the soft chuckling sex call. The hen would promptly squat down to receive him, moving her tail to one side and lifting her body so his vent could join hers. The actual mating was only a matter of seconds, and when it was over, Whitehackle would step away, leaving the hen to rise and shake herself.

Whitehackle's daily routine varied somewhat according to the season. When there was plowing, he and his hens followed the plow to watch for worms; when different weeds were in seed or bushes bore fruit, he would be on the lookout for them. Otherwise, he followed the same schedule so strictly that at any time of day it was possible to foresee exactly where he would be almost to the minute, for Whitehackle seemed to have a clock built into his brain that told him the precise time, and he liked to do things in an orderly manner. All the other farm animals possessed this same faculty; the cows came to be milked at the same hour, the farm dog trotted down the lane to meet the children returning from school at the correct moment and the pigeons flew down to feed and sunbathe at the same time each day with scarcely a minute's variation.

Only on rainy days was Whitehackle's schedule upset. If it rained during the night, the eaves of the barn gave him some protection, but if it was a heavy rain and blowing, by morning he and his harem were miserable. They hated to get wet, never bathing except in dust, and once wet they were hopelessly waterlogged. There was nothing to do except crouch unhappily in the barn until they had partly dried off. At such times, Whitehackle would usually make his way to the loft—to him as huge an area as Carlsbad cavern. He always entered the loft slowly and cautiously, looking about as he high-stepped in, partly because he was slightly suspicious of the place (he had occasionally found stray cats and owls there) and also because sometimes he could surprise a mouse. If the barn doors were left open, the peacocks hunted the loft for mice as systematically as Whitehackle hunted the lawn for crickets, for they were practically carnivorous and by no means above killing the baby chicks and ducklings. However, if the doors were closed they could not get in. Whitehackle had his own secret means of entrance by jumping on a feed bin, then moving along a joist to the top of a closet where the harness used on Sundays was kept, then up through a broken board in the floor of the haymow and so into the main part of the loft. If there were any mice trusting to the closed doors to keep them safe, he was generally able to get one. On a few occasions, he had even been able to kill a rat, breaking the animal's back with a plunging blow of his dagger beak. Eating his kill was a complicated process, as he could not cut off pieces and had to pick at the dead animal over and over, although he often tried to make it come apart by shaking it as hard as possible. Still, the invigorating meat was worth any effort. If there were no mice, he took a bath in the dry chaff that covered the floor as a substitute for the dust holes under the white pine.

During the early weeks of spring, the barnyard community lived together fairly amicably, but as the days grew longer and the time for nesting came nearer, fights became first sporadic and then epidemic. Territorial lines grew more rigid and were more fiercely defended and to establish dominance became a matter of life and death for all males. The females seemed indifferent to this strife and yet by their ceaseless competition for the best nesting spots and the most spacious and preferred areas for their broods, they were really the instigators of the battles and by no means unconscious instigators, for every duck, hen and goose was determined to do the best possible for her own brood and damn every other consideration. The females were not nearly so passive as they seemed and were quite capable of using the ultimate weapon against the male of withholding their favors if he did not obey their wishes. That many male birds are forced to develop brilliant plumage in order to attract a mate, even though this gaudy coloring makes them extremely conspicuous to predators, is visual proof of the female's power; the most dramatic example being the great tails—or rather "trains," since the feathers grow from the back—of the peacocks.

Despite Whitehackle's arrogant aggressiveness in treading his hens, the hens could not actually be forced against their will; a hen had only to keep her tail down and avoid raising her cloaca to frustrate the cock. Helpless as they seemed, the hens were really in control of the situation, as Whitehackle soon discovered. Whitehackle was on quite good terms with the drakes and turkey gobbler and, of course, hopelessly outweighed by the gigantic ganders, and so, except for occasional skirmishes, the males were content to let well enough alone. So were the females until the fatal Ides of March which roughly announced the beginning of the nesting season. Then the males were supposed to provide adequate nesting areas, and as every female had highly inflated ideas as to what might be considered adequate, the males were goaded into battles for which they often had little enthusiasm.

Each hen had her own special nesting box, arranged according to her position in the pecking order, and as this order was not immutable there were constant disputes. During the winter Whitehackle had been able to break up these female fights without trouble, but now that the hens were fighting for the new life within them, it was a different matter, and to his surprise and annoyance, Whitehackle found himself largely helpless to control the situation. But if the hens fought among themselves, on one matter they stood together with unreasoning conviction—it was Whitehackle's duty to keep all other nesting females out of the barn and chicken house for the hens' benefit. If he seemed remiss in his duty, the hens did not actually band together to refuse him their favors but they did become sullen, reluctant to please and avoided him. In a dozen subtle feminine ways they let him know that he was being remiss in his responsibilities.

Confined as they were by the artificial restrictions of the farm, the various bird families were in more acute competition than they would have been in the wild. The geese were luckily no problem, for here even the indomitable Whitehackle was hopelessly outclassed, but the geese preferred to nest in the sheepfold or among the outbuildings and so did not offer direct competition. Neither did the peafowl and guineas, as both nested in the fields. It was the ducks and turkeys who presented the main threat.

Whitehackle was brave but he was not crazy, and he knew well that the heavy Muscovy drakes far outweighed him while the big turkey gobbler was an opponent only slightly less overwhelming than one of the ganders; hence although he was prepared to stand up for his rights, he had not gone out of his way to pick a fight with any of these formidable opponents. Also, both the drakes and the gobbler had regarded the cocky little rooster with a certain amount of awe. He was clearly very sure of himself, always ready for a fight, and anything that could defeat a hawk was worthy of respect. So even though there had been occasional raised hackles and angry hissings, combat had never actually been joined, both sides retiring with honor. Now goaded by the females, the truce was at an end.

However, it caused more than the females to precipitate the fight. The head drake was a bellicose, short-tempered old bird built like a cube except for his long neck. The morning after a heavy, all-night rain he had been reveling in one of the freshly formed pools in the pasture which all the ducks liked far better than either the stream or the pond. The shallow puddles were just right for their short feet, it saved them the trouble of swimming and there was no current. In addition, the distilled rainwater had a taste and quality they liked. This morning the old drake had felt so rejuvenated by his bath in the puddle he had set off after an attractive young duck, but to his fury the sleek female had easily avoided him. He had tried several others who also refused to squat down and yield to his approaches, and he was too big and heavy to catch them. To make matters worse, one of the younger drakes who had ambitions to take over the flock had challenged him, and even though the old drake had won, it had been closer than he liked. Being hungry after his exertions, the drake had come stamping back to the barnyard to look for any stray kernels of corn that might be around. He was in no pleasant mood as he waddled along, shaking his head and muttering deep in his throat. As he came through the open gate, he encountered Whitehackle. Whitehackle had been having a hard time himself with the hens that morning and the damp weather annoyed him. The water running off the roofs of both the barn and the chicken house combined at this point to make a sizable pool, and Whitehackle swerved to avoid it. He collided with the drake who was marching along, looking neither to the right nor left. The lighter cock was knocked back by the impact while the drake kept on giving an angry hiss. That did it.

Even in his rage, Whitehackle had too much sense to attack the drake directly as he would have done with another cock. He came in tacking from side to side, keeping one wing lowered and constantly interposing it between his body and the drake's stabbing bill. He wanted to get his favorite hold-grabbing his opponent by the breast feathers with his beak and then using his spurs—but almost at once he realized that the drake with his longer neck had the reach on him and could hold him off. Whitehackle retreated and came in on the fly, starting from a point four feet away from the drake, something he had never done before. He expected the drake to go up to meet him in a buckle, but the drake was too heavy to leave the ground except by a great effort and Whitehackle easily topped him. Left! Right! he struck with his spurs and at each blow the drake's head reeled with the impact. Before, the drake had only been annoyed; now he was hurt and furious. He charged forward with extended neck but Whitehackle easily avoided the rush. Again, the cock went up, and although this time the drake dropped his head to avoid the blows, Whitehackle got home on his chest and shoulders. Hissing like a boa constrictor, the drake charged again and again, but each time Whitehackle eluded him, leaping over the ponderous bird to get in his blows. Bloodstained spots appeared on the drake's white feathers and a deeper shade of red showed on his red comb.

The drake saw he was losing but he was too stubborn to admit defeat. The next time Whitehackle rose in a fly, clumsy as he was the drake flung himself up to meet the attack. This maneuver was so completely unexpected that Whitehackle was thrown backward, and before he could recover himself the drake had grabbed him by the breast with his broad, flat bill. There were toothlike projections on the drake's bill to permit him to strain water through it while looking for food, and these serrated edges clamped down on Whitehackle's feathers and held him prisoner. Realizing his advantage, the drake used his weight to throw the cock down and then stamped on his prisoner with his big, webbed feet. There were formidable claws on the drake's feet which, if not as long and as keen as those of Ishmael's, were thicker and more powerful. In addition, the drake used his wings to beat the cock into unconsciousness, and each blow was as strong as the slap of a powerful man.

For the first time in his life, Whitehackle knew panic in a fight. If he could not break the drake's death grip on his breast, he was finished. He hooked upward with his spurs under the drake's flapping wings and the two-inch daggers sank deep into his opponent's sides. The drake gave a whistling gasp as the breath was knocked out of him, but he was coated with layers of fat and he did not let go. Whitehackle shuffled, then seeing that was getting him nowhere tore his spurs loose and struck again. The punishment was frightful but the drake had not battled his way to top place in the flock without learning how to endure pain. Yet he knew he could not stand many more such blows. He dragged Whitehackle into the pool of rainwater and tried to drown him, deliberately holding him underwater while continuing to stamp him.

As both birds were beating with their wings, the water flew in showers, blinding the drake, and Whitehackle managed to fight free. It was only a temporary respite, for the drake seized him again and flung him back into the pool. Whitehackle would have certainly been killed had not two passing ganders seen the disturbance and rushed into the fray with extended, cup-shaped wings, heads arched back and honking loudly. This was not the ganders' usual fighting pose but was one they adopted when not sure of themselves. In this case, they may have thought that the drake, being also white, was another gander or they may have been simply excited by the sight of combat. They broke up the battle and allowed Whitehackle to escape, soaking wet, half-drowned and partly plucked.

When the ganders quieted down and departed, the old drake, no whit discouraged, went looking for Whitehackle to resume the battle, hissing loudly as he marched around the barnyard, his neck going back and forth continually as he peered around the cylindrical white pillars that supported the overhang or examined the hedge. Whitehackle was hiding in the hedge, and he remained there until the cross-grained old fellow had huffed and hissed his way back to the rain puddles. Whitehackle was sore and bruised for days afterward, while the drake victoriously took over the barnyard and proudly brought his ducks into the most exclusive nesting places. However, even though beaten, Whitehackle was not hackled. He took to hiding in the hedge, and when the drake plodded past, Whitehackle would dart out and spur him from the side or rear, instantly rushing back to the safety of the hedge. The drake was too big to follow him and too clumsy to avoid the lightning-like attacks. Finally, a compromise was reached. The ducks nested in the stalls and hayloft while the chickens used the chicken house and lower part of the barn. From then on whenever Whitehackle and the drake met, they studiously ignored each other.

It had been a sobering experience for Whitehackle. He was forced to admit that he was not omnipotent in the barnyard. Still, as the drake made no effort to take over control of the territory and kept pretty much to himself, Whitehackle could still feel that he was king. Even if he could not defeat the drake in open combat, he knew now how to handle the stupid bird, so there was none to challenge his authority—at least until the hawk returned.

4.

QUEEN OF THE WOODS

Ishmael barely made it across the pasture, and collapsed rather than lit on the familiar bough of the black walnut. She was in a bad case of shock. Being far more delicately constructed than the sturdy Whitehackle, she could not take rough handling. Nor did she have the cock's single-minded, phlegmatic nature. She was highly temperamental and easily upset when faced by unaccustomed situations.

Although not seriously hurt physically, she was so shaken by the experiences that even when her anxious mate brought her a female hairy woodpecker he had just killed she was unable to eat until late that evening. When it was almost dark, the prospect of going through the long night with nothing in her stomach alarmed her sufficiently to start feeding on the limp, cold ball of feathers. When she slept she did not doze off as usual but instead fell into an almost sporadic trance, hardly even shifting from one foot to the other during the night.

Ishmael was awakened by the sound of a scolding jay. She pulled her head out of its wing blanket to listen. The sun was not yet up but the clear, hard glitter of the stars had taken on a washed-out appearance and in the east they were starting to fade. The outlines of the trees stood out against the blue-black sky but under her the forest floor was still black as at midnight. Ishmael sat listening to the angry jay until she was able to make out the form of the cat stealing along the edge of the grove, returning to his lair after hunting. Ishmael watched him indifferently. She yawned and stretched, extending one leg and the corresponding wing in turn and shook herself. She was still sore but no longer in a state of shock. Her movements awakened the male who also stretched and roused.

After casting, the hawks preened themselves. Then the male slid off the branch and volplaned through the grove, hardly using his wings at all and steering with his long tail. Ishmael followed and the two hawks slalomed among the trees as though tied together by an invisible thread. In the open they flew side by side, constantly dropping until they reached their favorite pool in the creek. Being smaller and lighter, the little male alighted easily on a mud spit, but Ishmael had to drop her banks of secondaries, lower and spread her tail and reverse her wingbeat before pitching beside him. Then they walked into the water and bathed. The sun was well up when they had finished and both hawks flew heavily to a tree and sat with wings extended to dry.

Their feathers had fluffed out and they were doing a little preening when they heard the sounds of bird warfare—the staccato cries of an angry woodpecker and the nasal chittering of starlings. The hawks stopped their preening to listen. Then both took to the air, flying fast and silently toward the noise. They kept close to the ground so as not to betray their presence unnecessarily.

In a half-dead cherry tree, a frantic hairy woodpecker whose mate the male Cooper's had killed the day before was trying to ward off the attacks of a pair of starlings. The woodpecker had just completed a nesting hole which the aggressive starlings intended to take over for their own home. The hairy was clinging to the rough bark, striking wildly at his attackers, but the black robbers kept out of his way. They took turns diving at him, so while he was warding off one assailant, the other was stabbing him in the back. When the woodpecker took to the air to escape them, one of the starlings instantly dove into the hole. This was too much for the property owner to stand after all his hard work. He flew back, ducked into the hole and drove out the interloper. The starling burst out screaming with outraged indignation and joined his mate on a branch of the cherry where they waited for the hairy to emerge so they could continue the harassment. They would keep up this game until the woodpecker finally gave up in disgust and was driven from his nesting hole.

The cherry tree was on top of a rise well above the stream, so the hawks were flying upgrade. They altered their flight to take advantage of a sumac clump that would conceal them from the starlings although the robbers were too intent on diving at the woodpecker every time he stuck his head out of the hole to pay much attention to anything else. Ishmael, who was in the lead, deliberately slowed her flight as she approached the sumac tangle, waiting until one of the starlings left his perch to dive at the hairy's head as the harassed bird tried to escape from the hole that had now become a prison. As the starling struck at the hairy, Ishmael did a sudden bank around the sumac and, turning on all her speed, flashed across the intervening space. Her broad, flat wings enabled her to build up tremendous speed very quickly, and although with her injured wing she could not maintain it long, she could still make a short rush. The starling was returning to the limb after driving the woodpecker back into the hole when Ishmael hit him. She bound to him with both feet and kept on going.

The starling's mate was so astonished by this sudden attack that for an instant she sat motionless. Then she took to the air, screaming frantically, while starlings from all over the pasture answered the cries. As she flew, the starling turned her head to watch Ishmael. The male Cooper's had followed Ishmael around the tangle but had kept low. He was now flying only a few feet above the ground, paralleling a hedgerow of honeysuckle, wild rose and poison ivy that grew over an old stake-and-rider fence. As the starling flew over the hedgerow still intent on Ishmael, the male hawk shot up, turned over on his back and grabbed the starling from below. The struggles of the starling were so desperate that the small male had to come down to the ground with her. Once on the ground, the male hawk let go of his captive's body and with one foot grabbed the flapping bird by the head. His long talons went through the starling's skull into the brain, and after a few convulsive wingbeats, the quarry was dead. Immediately the male took to the air again and flew toward the grove with his prey, for the quarry's dying screams had brought starlings from all directions to help their friend. Flying just clear of the ground, the male made it to the woods before he could be seen by the dozens of yelling starlings who were rushing to the scene.

After furiously circling around the district, the starlings gave up and retired. However, they felt uneasy about the place and the death screams of their unfortunate friend were still ringing in their ears. They avoided the vicinity of the cherry tree in the future.

The bewildered woodpecker stuck his head out of the hole and looked around. The whole business had taken only a few seconds and being in the hole, he had no idea what had occurred. All he knew was that the belligerent starlings had somehow disappeared and he was left in peace. With a sense of intense relief, he flew off to find the female hairy for whom he had been building the hole. She was not to be found but he eventually located another lady who was only too delighted to find a male in command of such comfortable quarters. Later they raised a large family, cheerfully unaware that the hawks had made their nest building possible.

The male carried his kill to a fallen tulip poplar where he plucked and ate it. Ishmael preferred to eat hers high in a hickory. After they had finished and had meticulously cleaned their pounces and wiped their beaks free of blood, they set off on another of their ballet-like courtship flights.

The starling was the last kill that Ishmael made, for the male kept her well supplied. This was the period of their honeymoon that made up for the long months of loneliness and isolation. They soared on the thermal drafts that the increasingly warm sun sucked from the hillsides, mated, played tag through the trees, mated again, bathed and slept. The first flush of green appeared on the branches, sulfur-colored patches of daffodils colored the roadside banks where two hundred years of heavy wagons had worn the roadbeds five feet deep into the soft loam. Along the white picket fences of the farmyards, the yellow tendrils of forsythia were coming into flowers and, spotted here and there in the low ground, the red of swamp maples stood in brilliant contrast to the young green of the other budding trees. Now great dull green patches of the Mayapples' umbrellas with a few clumps of exquisite white bloodroot studded the forest floor. These spring flowers were more delicately made than the later blooms, for while there was still often a scum of ice on the horse troughs in the mornings, the early bloomers had no competition to fear as did the flowers that blossomed in full richness of summer.

Early each morning, the male made his distinctive soaring flight over the grove to establish territorial rights to the group of oaks, maples and hickories. There were other raptors nesting in the general area—a pair of redtails, two pairs of sparrow hawks, a pair of marsh hawks, a pair of screech owls and a pair of great horned owls. None of these birds offered any real competition to the Cooper's hawks. The redtails were buteos and lived mainly on rats and mice which they caught while soaring over the open fields; the sparrow hawks were largely insect eaters while the marsh hawks lived on frogs and small snakes. The owls hunted at night and so tended to feed on a different sort of quarry. However, when a sharp-shinned hawk entered the grove also looking for a nesting site, Ishmael's mate furiously drove him away, as the feeding habits of the sharpshin were so similar to those of the Cooper's there would have been short rations when both families had to obtain food for their young.

Ishmael made no effort to help her mate establish property rights to the grove despite the fact that she was bigger and fiercer than he and equally concerned over the fledglings to be. Once the eggs were laid, she would join him in protecting the nest but establishing territorial rights was a male's job. Meanwhile she was content to be petted and fed and made love to, although by the middle of April, she began to show signs of restlessness.

The male recognized the symptoms of a female who wanted a home for her children and promptly set to work. Flying at full speed toward a hickory, he grabbed a small dead branch with his yellow feet as he shot past. The weight of his body plus his speed snapped the branch off clean, and the male carried his prize fifty feet up to the crotch of a white oak near the trunk where three main branches came together. For some time the male had had his eye on this crotch as a possible nesting site, and after laying the foundation stick, he landed on a branch to see what his mate thought it.

Ishmael was a hundred yards away, yet she instantly became intensely interested and bobbed her head up and down to focus on the crotch. Then she slipped from her perch and glided over to the oak to inspect the job. The stick was not placed just to her liking so she adjusted it slightly with her beak. Now the male was sure of his choice and flashed around through the trees, each time returning with a fresh stick. Like establishing a territory, nest building was work for a male, so Ishmael retired to a comfortable branch a few yards away, but she continued to watch the male's activities with a critical eye. Occasionally she would give a shrill cry when the male was not doing things to please her as though giving him exasperated instructions. Industrious as the male was, he was also impatient with details and would only stay at the nest long enough to deposit his stick before flying off for a new twig. Disgusted at such slipshod masculine methods, Ishmael was forced to fly over to the nest several times and rearrange the sticks to suit herself. At each visit she would cuddle down in the growing nest to try it for size, wriggling her body around to make sure the cup forming in the center was comfortable.

Building the nest took two weeks even though the male could have done it in two days. He stopped often to mount his willing mate and there was always the hunting to be done. In the evenings they roosted together near the oak and in companionable silence listened to the shrill pipping of the spring peepers in the marsh where the skunk cabbages were unfolding their curved tongues. At sunset they could hear the splash of mallards alighting in the creek, their good-night quacks and the swish of a trout rising to an early May fly that had fallen on the water. Full and comfortable, they would at last put their heads under their wings and sleep.

In the early mornings, the forest came alive with birdsongs as the brightly colored males staked out their territories by flying from tree to tree and singing, stopping to listen after a few notes to see if a rival answered before flying on to the next tree. A male fox trotted through the woods and, stopping at a prominent white stone, lifted his leg to throw a spurt of strong-smelling urine to establish the boundaries of his range. Birds, having almost no sense of smell, had to rely on sound or color, while the fox was color-blind but had a keen sense of smell. Meanwhile the male Cooper's, being neither especially colorful nor a songbird, practiced his spectacular soaring flight over the treetops as a warning to others of his species, undisturbed by the sound of the farmer who was nailing up "No Trespassing" signs around his fields.

The nest was no longer a pile of sticks but was definitely taking on shape, a flat top with a shallow cup in the center. It was about two feet in diameter and a foot and a half high. It looked much like a crow's nest except no branches with leaves had been used, as the male broke off only dead twigs. As a result, even the central cup was hard and prickly, and when Ishmael lowered herself into it to try it for size, she got scratched. She was developing brood patches, two parallel strips of bare skin running down her breast where the feathers had dropped away. When the eggs were laid, these brood patches would enable Ishmael to bring the eggs directly against the heat of her bare skin without the insulation of her feathers and make incubation possible, but now the sharp edges of the twigs sticking into the naked brood patches made her most uncomfortable. She tried to stamp down the twigs with her feet but the broken edges still remained. Also, she was beginning to feel "broody" and irritable. Her metabolism was changing as the developing eggs drained nourishment from her body, and she was passing into the special psychological state that enables a female bird to sit for hours motionless on her clutch to allow the embryo life beneath her to germinate and grow. Ishmael became increasingly finicky over her diet, complaining with loud "ca-ca-cas" about everything the male brought her, fussed over the nest and took full advantage of her delicate condition to make life miserable for her mate.

This heavy, querulous, unreasonable bird was very different from the sexually exciting female, loving companion and swift hunting partner he had known, yet the male remained loyal and devoted. After all, on her would come the full burden of egg laying and brooding the young. When she went into temper tantrums, jumping up and down on a limb in a rage because the food was not to her liking or plunging down to the forest floor to seize a handful of dead leaves in her talons, he hurried off to catch some new kind of game she might prefer. He did his best to make the nest suitable, yet it was not until Ishmael, in obvious exasperation at masculine stupidity, had flown over to a hickory, edged along a limb to the trunk and peeled off a strip of bark with her beak that he got the idea. Feverishly he flew about among the trees until, spotting a good piece of loose bark, he plunged down on it as though striking prey, ripped it loose with his talons and after thoroughly "killing" it by clenching first with one foot and then with the other so he could shift his weight with each grip and put his full force into the clamp, he carried it triumphantly to the nest. Ishmael supervised its placing and then the male wore himself out bringing in fresh strips until the cup was well lined. Although the nest was now finished, as a climax he brought in several green pine sprigs and carefully stuck them around the edges. The sprigs had no functional purpose; they were just for nice.

Heavy with broodiness and indifferent to everything except

the crucial miracle of birth, Ishmael was content to stay in the nest while the male hunted for both of them. There were many small eatable birds nesting in the grove—flycatchers, pewees, nuthatches, red-eyed vireos, several varieties of warblers and even a succulent pheasant hen incubating her clutch under a tangle of greenbriers. The male made no attempt to catch any of these local residents because they knew all about the hawks and constantly had an eye out for the predators. This made them too hard to catch. There were many songbirds nesting now, and these were so absorbed in their domestic arrangements they could easily be caught. Also, there came a period of heavy rains that flooded out the meadow mouse passages in the nearby orchard, forcing the mice to the surface. As it was still too early in the year for the grass to be high enough to hide them, the little mammals were virtually helpless, and the male Cooper's made the best of the bonanza, often being able to catch a mouse in either foot. Several times he saw the orchard owner, a lean young Amish-man whose beard was just beginning to sprout, watching him, but as the man never interfered, the Cooper's soon lost all fear of him. The man had no intention of interfering, for all that winter the mice had been stripping the bark from the roots of his fruit trees and had killed several. And he had no objection to the hawk killing songbirds, as they picked at his fruit and made it unmarketable.

The eggs were laid toward the end of April. It had been a good season for game and the hawks were fat and healthy, so there were five eggs, more than the usual number. Ishmael laid one every other day, always in the early morning. At first the eggs had a pale sky-blue tint, but this gradually faded until there was only a faint bluish tinge.

Both birds were inordinately proud of the eggs and Ishmael brooded them constantly except when eating whatever game the male had brought in to the plucking tree, for the hawks never plucked their quarry at the nest, as this would leave telltale feathers about and betray the nesting site. Ishmael allowed only one interruption in her maternal duties. Each morning the pair resumed their duets. When the male began his morning song of pride and pleasure, Ishmael would leave her precious clutch to fly up and sit on the branch with him so they could sing together. She never dared leave the clutch for more than twenty minutes or so for fear the eggs would cool, so long before the male had finished his song, she would fly back to the nest and start brooding again.

Formerly the hawks would quietly slip away from the nest when any danger threatened, but now with the precious eggs laid, they became fiercely protective. When a red-shouldered hawk happened to light near the nest, both Cooper's hawks lit on nearby branches, giving their harsh "ca-ca-ca" call and threatening him until he left. A great horned owl who decided to visit the nesting area one cloudy morning got even a more violent treatment, for he was potentially a far greater menace. Both hawks dove at him repeatedly, raking him with their hind talons and screaming until he flapped away with his deceptively clumsy flight. If the owl with his tremendous strength, silent wings and acute hearing ever located one of those hawks at night, he would have his revenge.

For over a month Ishmael brooded her eggs with her long tail protruding over the edge of the nest, and the time passed slowly for her. Bored, she watched every passing bird and insect, leaving the nest only to sing with the male in the early morning, feed and defecate. When she returned after an absence, she would turn the eggs with her beak to make sure they were being evenly warmed on all sides and then carefully worm her way over them before settling down to brood. The eggs had to be constantly guarded not only to keep them warm but also to prevent robbers from stealing her precious clutch, and the woods were full of robbers: red squirrels, jays and, above all, crows.

Crows were the greatest danger, for these big, black fearless birds loved eggs and seemed to take a fiendish joy in outwitting brooding mothers. Egg stealing was a game with them as much as a search for food. If a crow found an unguarded nest, his method was to fly silently to it, plunge his V-shaped beak through the shell and then tilt his head back with the egg impaled on his beak and allow the contents to run down his throat. The process took only a few seconds and he could destroy the entire clutch before the mother returned.

There were three crows who spent much of their time in the grove keeping an eye on the hawks' nest. The male tried to chase them away, but the crows, working as a gang, attacked him from all sides and drove him off. After several such experiences, the male swallowed his pride and went to Ishmael for help. Ishmael could hear the triumphant cawing of the crows and could tell by the male's nervous fluttering what had happened. Leaving the nest in his care, she slipped through the branches and flew fast and silently, taking advantage of every bit of cover the trees afforded her. The crows were so busy congratulating each other over their victory they did not see the big female until she was on them. Then they fled, cawing in shrill terror. Singling out one, Ishmael chased him while he yelled futilely for his friends to help. Big as she was, Ishmael did not care to bind to a crow; she had too much respect for their pile-driver beaks, powerful wings and clawing feet. Instead, every ten feet or so she would shoot out one of her long legs and pull a handful of feathers from the black robber. When the crow finally closed his wings and dropped into a sumac tangle, she left him alone and returned to the nest. The crows never came back to the grove.

At long last came the thrilling day when in response to Ishmael's soft murmurs there were little peeping noises from within the eggs. Now Ishmael positively refused to leave the nest for any purpose whatsoever, even defecating while sitting, and the male fed her on the nest. It was only for a day or so and then the eggs began to crack. The babies had none of the charm of newly hatched chickens nor did they need it, for they were not living in a flock where their "cuteness" was necessary to protect them from being pecked by adult birds. But to Ishmael and to the excited male, they were exquisitely beautiful and well worth all the long hours of nest building and brooding.

After the hatching, Ishmael cleared the nest of all broken eggshells and carried the pieces well away from the white oak. The babies had recovered sufficiently to sit up by the time she returned, their pale bluish-brown eyes regarding the strange world doubtfully and entirely unaware of what their role in it was to be. Ishmael brooded them contentedly while the male rushed off to get food for his growing family.

Even though Ishmael did no hunting, she worked as hard as her mate. She had to brood the youngsters, protect them from predators, shield them from rain and sun, feed them and keep the nest clean. When she cleaned the nest, she made the babies move over to one side and then rearranged the bark lining before letting them come back.

By the beginning of July, the young hawks were on the wing and beginning to hunt for themselves. Spring had given way to summer. The dandelions had gone to seed, and instead of their enticing golden glory, they were feathery, contented balls of pregnancy. The white flowers of the dogwood had faded, for they were now fertilized, and bunches of red seeds appeared on the maples. There were untold hordes of insects, from the tent caterpillars in their white web nests surrounded by bare branches stripped of leaves, to the clouds of blowflies that whirled around even the smallest piece of carrion. This was lucky for the hundreds of young songbirds just leaving the nests, as they were still too clumsy on the wing to have survived except in a world loaded with food. The young hawks were able to catch these fledglings, especially as the songbirds had such large broods that they were not able to feed all the young equally well and so many of the birds were weak and unable to shift for themselves.

Heretofore, the hawks had taken few game birds but now haying had started and also the cutting of grain crops. This left the fields bare and the hen pheasants with their broods could no longer hide. The hawks harried the young pheasants to such an extent that the farmers, who were usually also keen sportsmen, cursed the raptors and took to carrying their shotguns with them in the fields. Two of the young Cooper's hawks were shot before the rest learned to avoid the men, the adult hawks being much too wary to show themselves when men were around.

The game birds were not nearly as hopelessly outmatched by the hawks as the men supposed. One of the young Cooper's hawks, a bumptious female, set out after a pheasant hen who, with a brood of half-grown young, was nearly a quarter of a mile away across an open field. The mother pheasant saw the hawk coming, for the inexperienced young female made no attempt at concealment. Instead of panicking, the pheasant gave a few sharp clucks that caused her brood to drop where they stood and freeze, their brown feathers mingling perfectly with the fresh-cut stubble. Then the mother crouched down but, instead of freezing, shuffled swiftly away toward a barbed-wire fence. Not until the Cooper's was almost directly overhead did the hen herself freeze, and then she was almost a hundred feet away from where the hawk had first sighted her.

Puzzled, the young female circled and then landed to look around. As soon as the predator was on the ground, the pheasant sprang to her feet and raced toward the fence. The hawk saw her and took to the air, but the Cooper's needed time to build up speed and the pheasant had a long lead. She kept running until it was obvious that the hawk was rapidly overhauling her, and then she too began to fly. Keeping low, she headed for the fence. The Cooper's turned on her final burst of speed and ate up the space between them, but the pheasant's timing had been perfect. Just as the hawk threw out her long legs for the bind and backed with her wings to lessen the shock of collision, the pheasant slipped between the lower strands of wire. The hawk struck the barbs in the worst possible position, still going all out and with wings extended. Her body hit the wire, her neck whipcracked and that was the end of her.

Later, Ishmael made a try for this same pheasant. The hen had had an early nesting, the young had grown up and left and she was ready to lay again. A strange cock from another district came in to court her and Ishmael from her watchtower on top of the black walnut saw the two birds busy with their mating rites. Ordinarily Ishmael would have been reluctant to attack a full-grown pheasant, but when two birds were fighting or mating they were especially vulnerable, and the antics of the pheasants attracted her and aroused her hunting instinct. Far more experienced than her unhappy daughter, Ishmael dropped straight down from the tree until she nearly hit the ground, straightened off and, after a few quick, powerful wingbeats to give herself momentum, glided across the field with extended, motionless wings toward the two birds, going so low that she seemed sure to strike one of the high stalks missed by the reaper. Never taking her yellow eyes from her quarry and steering by almost imperceptible motions of her long, thin tail, Ishmael skimmed over the stubble like a skipped stone over water. She was almost on top of the pheasants before the hen saw her.

The hen made no attempt to crouch and freeze; the hawk was far too close for that. She took off at once for the barbed-wire fence with the cock after her. Banking slightly Ishmael was after them, turning loose her closing rush.

The hen slipped through the wire strands, but to the cock, the fence was as unexpected an obstacle as it was to the hawk. He hit the wire full on and was hung up on it. Ishmael close on his tail hit him, but she hit the wire too and was also hung up. For several seconds both birds thrashed and struggled on the wire before the cock was able to tear loose. He fell heavily to the ground with the hawk still clinging to him. The two birds rolled over and over, only the tips of their wings appearing above the high stubble, until at last Ishmael was able to get her grip on the base of the wing and head. That finished the struggle.

By infinitesimal degrees the days were beginning to grow shorter, but the animals sensed it. The days were as warm as ever, for Indian summer was setting in, yet the loss of those few minutes of sunshine was enough to alert nature that winter was coming. Some of the weaker, more sickly trees shed their leaves, the squirrels started to store nuts and the songbirds prepared to migrate. The hawks had to follow their main source of food, and as it grew more difficult to catch quarry, first the two remaining young Cooper's hawks and then the more expert male drifted away. There was no leave-taking and there were no regrets as Ishmael saw them go. Now that the mating season was over, the bond that had held her and the male together was gone. Yet if the male were still alive, he would almost surely return to the grove next spring. He knew the territory, knew Ishmael and finding a suitable new range and another mate would be difficult. The hawks were not strictly monogamous in the same sense as the Canada geese—the death of one would immediately leave the other free to find a new partner, while if one of a pair of geese dies the other will never mate again—yet once a pair of hawks had mated, even though they separated during the winter, they would seek each other out again in the spring. Too independent to want to be constantly together, there was still a bond between them based largely on mutual convenience yet with possibly a somewhat deeper tie of shared experience and emotions.

Ishmael could not migrate. Her injured wing could not endure the long flight south, for after even an hour or so of steady flying it tended to buckle under her. She was forced to remain behind and get through the winter as best she could.

For a while, she had no particular problem. Larger and stronger than the male, more expert in hunting than the young hawks, she was not dependent for food either on small birds or on awkward fledglings. She could take pheasant, grouse, rabbits or squirrels and none of these migrated. As a last resort, there was always the chicken yard, but after her experience with Whitehackle, she would go there only if desperate from hunger.

Although she could take large quarry, Ishmael much preferred game that was more easily killed. With rare exceptions, hunting to her was a business, not a sport or a challenge. True, when as the result of a special combination of circumstances she went into that murderous frenzy peculiar to the accipiters that Persians have named "yarak," she might attack almost anything, but such spells seldom occurred. Given any kind of a choice, Ishmael only went after quarry that could easily be handled. She was not a coward and in defense of her eggs or young she might even attack a human, but the amount of energy she was forced to expend in killing large game hardly compensated her for the return. When she killed the cock pheasant, she had been so exhausted that she sat on the dead bird for nearly an hour before breaking into him. As she could not store food, she had only gotten one meal from him—exactly what she would have gotten from a pigeon.

Ishmael's favorite technique was "still hunting." She would station herself well up in a convenient tree and sit motionless for an hour or more, her keen golden eyes watching every movement in the forest around her. She hunted by ear as well as by eye and would turn her head instantly at any rustle in the dead leaves, at a bird call or at the angry chittering of quarreling squirrels. The distress call of any bird or mammal would bring her to the spot instantly, for this meant an easy kill. This type of hunting enabled her to obtain food with the least expenditure of energy, and as food grew scarcer she needed to conserve all the energy possible.

When still hunting failed, there was no help for it but to cruise around looking for prey. Unlike the big buteos, she did not soar high above in great circles but kept below treetop level and flew in a direct line. She would give three or four hard flaps, glide for several yards and then flap again, going at a speed of some thirty miles an hour. When she came to a hedgerow she would parallel it for a few feet and then suddenly shoot over it in hopes of finding some unsuspecting quarry that would panic at her unexpected appearance. From time to time she would swing up to the top branches of an isolated tree and sit there motionless, surveying the country before starting out again.

Unlike a mammal, Ishmael had very little reserve store of fat to draw upon, for she had to be lightly built in order to fly, so a fast of even forty-eight hours was a serious matter to her. For a while her luck held, and then came a period of two days when she was unable to make a single kill. Anxious, for she felt her strength waning and she did not dare to become too weak, Ishmael thought of the farm. She was still not prepared to venture into the barnyard itself, but during her reconnoitering flights, she had noticed two broods of yellow ducklings, led by their Muscovy mothers, going to the pond shortly before sunset. It might be possible to pick up one of these ducklings without much risk. So on the evening of the second day of unsuccessful hunting, Ishmael headed for the pasture.

She knew exactly what route to take. She sped through the woods, swung around the covered bridge which provided excellent concealment, and glided along the stream, keeping the willows between her and the farm. At the corner of the pasture was a gigantic cherry, now two-thirds dead, and Ishmael swung up to pitch on one of the bare branches.

Here she froze into immobility, watching the pond. She was a little early and the mother ducks were still in the barnyard with their broods. The only birds she could see were the geese and the old Muscovy drake who was grazing with them. Ishmael settled herself to wait.

Then she saw a motion among the scrub willows that had seeded themselves at the edge of the pond. A mallard duck was leading her brood down to the water. This mallard was a young bird and had had her brood very late in the season, so late it was improbable any would survive. The ducklings were half grown but still could not fly. The mallard was taking them down to the pond for a swim before the Muscovys arrived, as she had discovered from experience the bigger, more aggressive domestic fowl would drive her away.

Ishmael watched the ducklings critically. She was quite sure they could not fly and so their only defense from her would be to reach the water. They were quite close to it and there was no time to lose. Without resorting to her usual circuitous tactics, she shot off the branch headfirst and flew across the pond directly at them.

The mother mallard, intent on watching out for the Muscovys, did not see the hawk, but from a willow came the hard rattle of a kingfisher. Then the duck turned her head and saw the brown-and-white form racing toward her. Shouting her alarm quack, she ran for the water, followed by her terrified brood. There was a high bank there and the duck family tumbled down it—all but one. He was the last and weakest. He saw he could not make it and did the next best thing: he dropped down and lay motionless in a patch of dried grass that perfectly matched his brown feathers.

Ishmael made a grab for the ducklings as they reached the water, but they dived instantly and she shot up with empty talons. She had seen the remaining duckling on the bank and knew he was still there somewhere although she could not see him. Swinging to and fro, she raked the grass with her hind talons, trying to make him move. These strafing tactics were too much for the duckling and he tried to burrow deeper into the patch just as Ishmael swept over him. Ishmael saw the motion out of the corner of her eye as she passed. Instantly the hawk pivoted on one wing, turned and grabbed blindly at the grass where she had seen the motion. One of her talons caught the duckling by the wing and held him.

Now that concealment was no longer possible, the duckling set up a pitiful, shrill quacking not unlike the high trilling note of a baby chick in dire straits. His mother answered him from the pond but she did not dare to return and face the hawk. The Muscovy drake had no such qualms. The distress call of the mallard was identical to the distress call of a Muscovy duckling, and the old warrior waddled swiftly to the attack, his neck vibrating back and forth as he hissed furiously.

Ishmael saw him coming. He was far too big for her to handle and she tried to fly off with the duckling. She did not have a good enough grip and the duckling pulled loose. Before Ishmael could seize him again, the drake was there. With a murderous hiss, he struck at her, his neck shooting out like a rapier, and Ishmael was forced to spring back. She was still reluctant to leave the duckling, but now the drake was standing over the baby and she knew it was useless. When he struck at her again, she was forced to take off.

The drake stood glowering at the vanishing form of the hawk until the predator was out of sight. Then he looked down at the duckling he had rescued. The baby was no longer giving the alarm cry and the drake saw it was brown rather than yellow. He killed the little interloper with one savage peck and returned to his grazing.

There was a numbing frost that night, the first of the season. With her reduced vitality, Ishmael nearly froze to death. When day broke and the heat of the sun partially restored her, she knew she would have to eat that day or die. There was nothing for it now except the chickens in the barnyard.

5.

MAN-FIGHTER

Compared to Ishmael, Whitehackle had a simple mind. True, he was capable of surprising feats of memory; he knew every chicken in the flock—and with the young broods coming along there were now nearly a hundred of them—and could identify most of the other domestic birds on the farm as individuals. However, unless such knowledge was constantly reinforced, he tended to forget and was quite unable to remember events that had happened several weeks before. A few techniques, mainly connected with fighting, were indeed permanently impressed on his mind. He would always remember his beak hold in close combat, the drake's style of attack and how the hawk had been able to hold him off with her long legs. But he did not look into the future and was incapable of planning either an attack or a defense. He lived from day to day.

Ishmael, on the other hand, could remember events that had occurred months before, down to the smallest detail. She could recall the exact spot where she had caught a certain quarry and would revisit the place, perfectly duplicating her previous actions in hopes of achieving the same result. By the same token she would never return to the cornice of the building where she had been shot and for the rest of her life could visualize the place perfectly. She also had the power to combine various methods learned by experience and apply them to a new situation, whereas the cock, once he had learned a certain system, tended blindly to stick with it. Ishmael was able to plan a raid, taking into consideration such items as time of day, where the best cover would be, the habits of her quarry and the manner of her attack. Ishmael was a strategist; Whitehackle only a tactician.

The day after her failure to get the mallard duckling, Ishmael was determined to take a chicken. She knew that she must carry the chicken off to avoid another fight so it could not weigh too much. She had kept the flock under distant observation and had spotted many half-grown birds well within her lifting capacities. She also knew that the chickens were in the habit of gathering in the turnaround at a certain time to eat gravel, and with her built-in "mental clock" Ishmael could tell time in relation to the sun perfectly.

A few minutes before the chickens' gathering time she started for the farm, following her usual route of first flying to the clump of wild cherry trees around the sinkhole and from there going to the high branch of the buttonwood tree. When she started out, she was her usual cold, calculating self, but by the time she had reached the buttonwood, a curious metamorphosis had taken place.

Ishmael was hungrier than usual and hence more determined to obtain food, but her hunger was not the hunger of starvation which weakens and causes listlessness. She had been flying strenuously for the last two days and the activity burned up energy that now had to be replaced by food. If she had eaten absolutely nothing during that time, her stomach, which was now crying so imperiously for fuel, would have passed its peak demand, the digestive juices would have been sluggish and she would not have been so fiercely keen. However, Ishmael had killed a wood mouse that morning and the lean meat kept her stomach juices flowing without really satisfying them. She had recently cast and the mouse's fur had effectively cleaned out her stomach and crop, so the slimy deposit there that tended to make her apathetic was gone. Lastly, there had been a cold snap and the cold acted on Ishmael like a shot of adrenalin. This combination of circumstances—intense exercise, hunger but not starvation, and cold—produced yarak in the bird, that special mental condition somewhat corresponding to the manic state of a manic-depressive. This meant that Ishmael was prepared to take any chances and attack any quarry no matter how formidable. Instead of being the crafty raider, Ishmael was now utterly reckless.

Rather than sitting motionless straight up and down on the limb with her wings closed and feathers laid flat, Ishmael now bent over, her wings partly open and hunched forward, her neck feathers raised and her tail spread. With a terrible intensity of expression she was watching for the slightest movement of any living thing on the farm below her. So tense was she, so keyed up and so on hair-trigger, it was barely possible that she might have attacked the dog himself. Only the accipiters, alone among all raptors, pass into this strange state so closely resembling the berserk frenzy of the Germanic tribes, also creatures of the deep woods.

To Ishmael's astonishment and rage, there were no chickens on the turnaround that afternoon. With the coming of autumn, the farmer had decided to open the sheepfold and had thrown in several bales of old timothy hay as bedding. There were weed seeds in the timothy and the chickens had taken full advantage of this windfall. They were all in the sheepfold, filling their crops and invisible to Ishmael. The hawk continued to wait, growing more furious by the second and unable to understand what had happened to the flock.

An arrogant young cockerel dared to dispute with Whitehackle a stalk of broom sedge and the cock promptly attacked him. After one feeble attempt at a buckle, the rash youngster fled into the barnyard with Whitehackle after him. From her lofty perch, Ishmael saw the chickens through the thinning yellow leaves of the elms and the dark green of the privet. She was off the limb and after them with unbelievable speed.

The cockerel ducked around Whitehackle and returned to the fold, clucking in fear. Whitehackle let him go and was preparing to follow when the pigeons feeding around the salt block exploded upward with a hard beating of wings as they put forth their maximum effort. Whitehackle recognized the sound as meaning danger and turned to look as the hawk shot in over the post-and-rail.

Because the hawk was low and headed straight for him, Whitehackle could not immediately identify the bird, as he was guided by the overhead silhouette. So the hawk was almost on him before he realized his danger. As Ishmael dropped her secondaries and threw out her legs for the bind, Whitehackle went up in a fly. Unprepared for such tactics, Ishmael grabbed blindly and got the cock by the elbows of both wings. This was quite all right with Whitehackle who promptly struck left and right with his spurs. Both birds came crashing to the ground, Ishmael trying to hold the cock off with her long legs while Whitehackle tried to get close enough to use his spurs again.

The weight of the heavier bird threw Ishmael over on her tail but she still was able to hold off the cock. She let go of his wing with one foot and managed to get him by the hackles.

Whitehackle went over her, trying to straddle the bird so he could use his spurs, and Ishmael fell on her back but did not lose her grip. In spite of her long legs, Whitehackle forced her down by sheer strength and began to shuffle. Ishmael well remembered that murderous tattoo and instantly let go, tearing herself loose. Fully aware that on the ground all the advantage lay with the cock, she bounded into the air and darted over him, giving him a raking blow across the back with a hind talon as she went. Instantly the hawk did a wingover, and before the cock could turn, she flashed over him again, ripping feathers from his back this time with both talons and leaving two bloody strips.

Now the dog was there. Disregarding the furious mammal, Ishmael turned and came in again, determined to kill the cock no matter what. Again she raked him, but the dog leaped up to meet her and Ishmael only barely saved herself by a tortuous twist. The punishment she had taken and the dog's presence shocked her out of her unreasoning fury, and she banked away, whirling around the chicken house and gliding down toward the pond. Here she met one of the Muscovy ducks with her brood of anxious, yellow ducklings. Ishmael was going so fast she passed over them but instantly spun around in midair, turning vertically to the ground and, pivoting on one wing, she dropped right in the midst of the brood. The ducklings were barely able to give a few terrified quacks when Ishmael was off again, a duckling firmly gripped in her feet. Ignoring the familiar black walnut, she flew deep into the woods before gorging herself.

For a week or so the chickens remained wary, and even a pigeon diving suddenly into the barnyard from an unusual angle was enough to set the hens cackling and put Whitehackle on the alert. Gradually the flock relaxed as the memory of that terrible day faded away and they resumed their usual routine. This ability to forget danger was not altogether stupidity; if quarry brooded over impending disaster they would become nervous wrecks. Whitehackle was no more afraid to pursue his usual routine than most people who have narrowly escaped an automobile accident become afraid to drive their cars.

Except from as determined and resourceful an enemy as Ishmael, the flock had little to fear from hawks. Their close organization baffled most predators. The flock always stayed together and even the smallest chick, once it found itself alone, immediately set up a shrill peeping that was instantly answered by the mother hen. While some of the flock were feeding, others kept a lookout, so it was almost impossible to take them by surprise. Actually it was generally easier for a hawk to catch a pigeon than a chicken, for in spite of the pigeons' speed, they did not have a highly organized pecking order. They were organized as mated pairs, not as a flock, and no pigeon permanently accepted the superiority of another pigeon. As a result, there were constant quarrels among them, usually among the unmated females, and during these fights the pigeons were oblivious to everything else and especially vulnerable to a winged predator.

With the chickens, once the pecking order had become firmly established, each bird knew its position and usually accepted it, so fighting was kept to a minimum. The only trouble came with those hens low in the pecking order who were inclined to be unnecessarily brutal to those at the very bottom; the hens higher in the hierarchy were far more tolerant of inferiors, knowing their own positions to be unassailable. But here Whitehackle was able to interfere, while there was no head pigeon to rule the roost. Whitehackle's complete authority also prevented protracted fights among the young cocks which would have left both combatants weak and easy prey for a predator. Being closely united, the flock had the advantages of food calls and warning signals, and individuals did not have to travel great distances looking for mates. Lastly, they all enjoyed the protection of the cock who was the strongest and probably the most intelligent bird in the group.

There was just enough competition among the various members of the flock to prevent boredom without having any violent conflicts. This competition centered mainly around food and resembled a game rather than a struggle for existence, as there was ample food for all. Even so, when the farm wife called "Here, chick-chick-chick-chick!" and threw grain from her cupped apron, each chicken rushed to the place and tried to eat as much as possible to prevent the others getting any. A single hen, even though surrounded by plenty, would have grown thin and indifferent to food without this stimulus. There were still arguments over dust-bath cups and roosting places, and whenever a hen got an especially succulent morsel like a grasshopper, she was always chased by all the other hens as frantically as though they were all starving and that was the last grasshopper in the world.

By autumn, every member of the flock had grown to know each other intimately and also to develop a special set of relationships with the other birds that were not simply that of superior or inferior. Each hen showed dominance, tolerance, avoidance, respect, fear or affection in varying degrees toward every other bird. The flock was not a conglomeration of brainless automata but an association of highly distinctive individuals, each with her own special traits. The farmwife understood this perfectly and knew the individual members of the flock almost as well as the birds knew each other. She knew which hens were good mothers, which were inclined to wander, which were flighty creatures constantly getting themselves wedged into small cracks in the corncrib from which they had to be extricated, which were lazy, which picky about their food, which too timid to leave the protection of the barnyard, which so aggressive they would dare to stand up even to Whitehackle, which shy and which tame. She even knew most of their voices, and the warning call that meant a possible distant danger if uttered by the old white Wyandotte brought the woman out at once with the shotgun, but the same cry given by the flighty young Plymouth Rock meant little or nothing.

The way of life in the barnyard was not rigid but changed according to circumstances. As with all animals, the fowl were greatly influenced by the seasons. Now that autumn had come, relationships gradually altered. The young chicks were growing up and beginning to take their places in the group. Unlike the doting male Cooper's, Whitehackle was far from being a devoted father. He was far more interested in the process that led to the conceiving of the chicks than to the chicks themselves. Unfortunately, the chicks did not realize this biological fact. They had discovered that Whitehackle was an excellent scratcher-upper of food and so trailed after him hopefully. Whitehackle was too lordly to bother with the chicks yet they got on his nerves. He enjoyed scratching up food and giving his imperious food call that brought the hens running. At such times, he would proudly strut around, looking the hens over as they were busily picking until he had made his choice and treaded one of them. Now whenever he scratched and called, he was immediately inundated with squalling chicks who devoured the grain before the hens could get there. That wasn't Whitehackle's idea at all. He considered the chicks an unmitigated nuisance, and when he paced majestically about, pursued by the devoted train of youngsters, he would give an irritable "hmmm-humm" mutter that might be translated as meaning "Get away, boys, you bother me." Still he was too kindly or too pompous to drive them away.

Even so, he regarded the chicks as part of his responsibility. The pleasant relationship that had existed between the chickens and the peafowl was badly ruptured when the young chicks had first hatched. The peafowl were carnivorous and regarded the tiny chicks as distinctly eatable. They seldom dared to attack a hen with a brood outright, for they knew from experience that the hen's shrill alarm cry would bring Whitehackle to the rescue and then both he and the hen together would attack the would-be kidnapper, coming in from both sides. Even more to the point, the hen's cry would also bring the dog and the woman to her aid. Even though the dog ordinarily left the peafowl alone, under these circumstances he was quite capable of tearing out a mouthful of feathers while the woman laid about her with a clothes prop. Unlike the chickens who did not seem capable of associating cause with effect, the peafowl understood perfectly that they were being punished for wrongdoing and would leave the chicks alone for a day or two after such an attack.

The peafowl were crafty, in their own way, especially the cocks, and they hit on another scheme. If they spotted a hen and her chicks scratching down by the old limekiln and so well away from the house and barn, they would start to stalk her. First a cock would tiptoe cautiously to the edge of the tobacco drying shed and peer around it to make sure the woman and dog were not in sight before starting after the hen. Even then he would not launch an all-out attack but walk just behind the apprehensive hen with a stiff-legged gait as though on stilts, hurrying her along in hopes that a chick would drop out of convoy. The anxious mother was never quite sure whether the peacock really had evil designs on her brood or whether he simply happened to be going in the same direction and wanted her to get out of his way, so instead of giving an alarm call, she would cluck worriedly and increase her speed. Pretending great innocence, the peacock would continue to follow, turning every way she did, and always hoping for a straggler.

If none dropped out, he would finally lose patience and start pecking at her to increase the pace. Then the hen would begin to run, dropping chicks left and right as she went and giving the "kaaaah!" cry for a ground predator. This cry always brought Whitehackle speeding to her help. Because of his great size, the peacock could have handled Whitehackle easily enough, but the dog usually followed Whitehackle. Then the peacock would go rocketing up, screaming in a succession of quick, hard jerks like the pheasant he was until he was high enough to flatten his wings and glide to a tree or to the carriage-shed roof. As he flew by, the distraught hen's alarm cry would often shift to the prolonged scream that meant an aerial predator.

Not unnaturally, the relationship between the chickens and the peacocks became strained during this period and quite unlike the comradely give-and-take that had existed before the hatching period. But now it was autumn and the chicks were too big to interest the peacocks. Besides, autumn was a time of bountiful harvest and there were far more interesting foods about than chicks. Picking at their droppings, Whitehackle found that the peafowls' mutes contained traces of raspberries, elderberries, pokeberries and other delicacies that greatly inter-ested him. He took to shadowing them, and although he could not walk as fast as they did, he learned their sources of supply.

The peafowl were expert foragers and knew the country well. Like the chickens, they seldom flew, preferring to walk with long, swift strides that covered a surprising amount of ground. As the cocks had molted their long trains during the summer, they were unhampered, and the hens with their broods of turkey-like young followed them. Even so, they usually did not make good time, as they were intensely curious creatures and stopped to stare at every white stone, unexpected piece of farm equipment or puddle of water that reflected the sun's rays, so the less curious chickens could keep up with them. Also, Whitehackle soon learned to recognize the honking call that the peafowl made when separated, so even when he could not see them he knew where they were. Sometimes the cocks would get so far ahead of the hens and their broods that the honk call would not carry far enough, and then the cocks would give their shrill, penetrating scream designed to carry through miles of Indian jungles and over Himalayan peaks. When Whitehackle heard that, he gave up, for it meant the birds were too far away for him to catch up with his hens.

The chickens would follow the peafowl into areas where they would not have dared to venture by themselves, for they knew the bigger birds afforded them protection. When nothing could be seen of the chickens except their red combs bobbing up and down among the weeds as they fed, the peafowl stood well above the cover and could see any approaching danger. Their alarm signals meant nothing to the hens, who did not speak a cluck of peafowl, but long ago Whitehackle had learned the warning cries of all other denizens of the farm and knew as well as the peafowl the meaning of their low, deep "wok-wok-wok" call—it was the equivalent of the chickens' "cut—cut—cut, cattah!" which meant a distant danger. But, if the danger came on, the peafowl did not have any equivalent for the chickens' cry that meant an imminent attack. Instead, they ran fast and low through cover, taking care not to attract attention to themselves. It took some time for Whitehackle to grasp this trait, for when danger threatened, his tendency was to stand his ground until he could see the attacker or at least learn from the cries of the other chickens if it was a ground or air predator, so he knew whether to fly into a tree or dive under cover. This business of sneaking off as soon as an alarm was sounded confused Whitehackle, as he did not know where to go or what the danger might be.

The peafowls' size and the very considerable spurs on the cocks protected them from predators who would have been formidable indeed to the chickens, and as the peacocks attacked any suspicious-looking stranger on sight, the chickens were comparatively safe in their company. No crows, hawks, jays, owls, opossums, weasels, skunks or mink cared to molest the smallest chick when the peafowl were about. Even the peahens could be pugnacious, especially when they had chicks themselves. Once when the combined flocks encountered a stray cat, one of the peahens rushed straight at the animal and, lacking spurs, jumped up and down on top of her until the cat fled, but of course even the peacocks could not fight off a stray dog or old raccoon.

Most exciting of all was to go mousing in the hayfields. After being allowed to dry in the fields, the hay was piled in haycocks and then the Belgians dragged the wagon from stack to stack while the waiting men swung great forkfuls of the perfumed grass over the cart's sides. The little Mennonite boy was in the wagon and his job was to distribute the hay evenly, but he was often nearly smothered by the avalanches that poured in on him from all sides even though he was protected by his broad-brimmed hat. As the steady sweep of the pitch-forks ate away the haycocks, mice would trickle out, darting about like black beetles as they tried to burrow under the stiff spikes of the stubble. The peafowl followed the wagon while the chickens followed the peafowl. When the peafowl saw the men attack a haycock, they would form a circle around it and wait with their heads cocked on one side for the mice to flush. As the haycock melted away, the peafowl would gather closer, heads down, eyes tied to the diminishing stack, bent forward and poised on their marks. Then when the short-tailed meadow mice rushed out, the peafowl were on them like ratting terriers.

Mice were too big game for the hens and even the biggest of the young cockerels were nervous of them, but Whitehackle was almost as good at this sport as the peafowl. Although smaller, he was quicker than they were and was often able to run in and snatch a mouse from under their beaks. True, the peacocks chased him and sometimes took away his prey; but when there were plenty of mice in a stack, the peafowl were so busy making their own kills that they left him alone.

As it neared winter, the farmers had to come in earlier from the fields, since it grew darker sooner and they were creatures of the seasons as much as the animals. Halloween was almost here when the hex doctor might be persuaded to tell stories of trolls and witches and brownies so fascinating no child could resist them and so terrifying no child dared to go home in the dark afterward, which meant that an exasperated father would have to hitch up the buggy and go get him. There was a white crust of frost on the green grass in the mornings and the lawns were drifted yellow with elm leaves. The sumac had been burned bright scarlet by the chill nights but as yet most of the trees had not turned to their full, brilliant autumn colors. Foraging was harder. Only the pokeberries were left now to stain the chickens' droppings, while it was a lucky hen indeed who found as much as an ant. On warm nights came the rasping of the katydids, the last of the insect noises except for the stray cricket who always seemed to find a warm crack in the hearth where he could spend the winter. To supply protein for the flock, the farmwife ladled up thick masses of buttermilk and flung it against the sides of the chicken house where it clung like whitewash so the hens could pick it off. She could not put it in trays, for then they scratched dirt into it, scratching being an important preliminary to either eating or drinking from a chicken's point of view. Even the cockerels went around with white combs from rubbing against the buttermilk, and this caused a series of new fights, as they did not recognize each other. A cock judges another by the size, shape and color of his comb.

One mother hen solved the protein problem by taking her brood of half-grown chicks to the dog's dish every morning at the same time. When the dog had finished eating, there were always plenty of chick-sized morsels and the dog good-naturedly let the chicks pick at his dish. Presently the rattle of their hard beaks on the tin got on his nerves and he would finally walk away. There were also eggshells at the pig troughs, a splendid source of calcium, and the hens would break up the shells for their chicks by tossing the shells up and letting them fall again and again until they splintered into convenient sizes.

The flock was not left entirely to its own resources, for the farmwife brought grain to them twice a day in her cupped apron. The ducks with their broad, heavy feet also came and would have trampled the young chickens in their eagerness to get the food had not the hens and Whitehackle beaten them off. Even so, the chicks were often so hacked that it took several minutes of gentle, reassuring clucking to bring them back. The broodless ducks would also trample the ducklings had not their mothers protected them. Determined as the mother ducks were, they did not dare to molest the drake who marched ponderously in and took his share without fear of repercussions. The geese were fed corn in the barnyard and prevented from entering the turnaround by the closed gate, as they would have walked over everyone. Unable to fly and too large to squeeze through the privet hedge, they were obliged to wait their turn, honking with impatience.

As autumn progressed and the flock became almost entirely

dependent on the farmwife's food, complications increased. The hens were able to fill their crops easily and quickly. This left them with a great deal of free time, and several of them developed the bad habit of feather picking that left them almost bald. Then when the woman fed them in the evening, the hens high in the pecking order filled their crops first and went to roost in the privet hedge while the hens lower in the system were eating. As a result, the top hens got the best places and formed a compact mass that generated so much heat they were quite comfortable even on the coldest nights. The inferior hens were forced to roost outside the charmed circle, and it became obvious that when winter really set in, many of them would freeze. The farmwife tried to overcome this difficulty by moving the flock into the chicken house. This was only a partial success, as the top hens went in first, divided the best perches among them and then, having established territorial rights, were extremely aggressive toward the others. When this situation finally adjusted itself, other chickens who had been roosting in trees, in the carriage house and among the outbuildings began to come into the chicken house to escape the cold. This meant new adjustments and new arguments as each fresh chicken arrived. In the flock of ninety-six hens, there were 4,560 possible pecking combinations, depending on age, weight, aggressiveness, and at what time an individual chicken had decided to come to the house. The cockerels also had their own pecking order. The farm-wife finally solved this last problem by butchering the cockerels.

Whitehackle hated to be locked up, and as he was the farmer's favorite, he was given special privileges. When the cows were milked in the evening, Whitehackle not only was allowed in the barn, but also after the milk had been strained, a little was poured from the strainer into a bowl for his special benefit. Whitehackle loved milk and came back time after time for additional tipples. The barn cats, too, appeared from nowhere at milking time, and when the stall doors opened and the cows came trooping in, each going to her own stall and at once plunging her head into the well-filled manger, the cats would glide forward and sit expectantly until the farmer shot a squirt of milk into their mouths from the full udders. After the cows had been turned out, Whitehackle could be lured into the chicken house with a handful of corn. The dog always came to watch the chickens being put away and, if by any chance the farmer forgot to shut the door, would bark angrily. Only after he was sure that his charges were safe would the dog retire contentedly to his own house.

The farmer took a special delight in the gaudy, arrogant rooster and used to stage mock fights with him. Whitehackle would charge the man fiercely, head down and ruff extended, and the farmer would catch him under his extended wings and toss the bird over his head. Even before he hit the ground, Whitehackle would twist around and come running back for a new throw. The man always tired of the sport before the cock. The bird developed powerful wings and strong legs from the exercise, but it also added to his natural aggressiveness, for Whitehackle would have been hard put to say whether he was playing or fighting with the man.

Whitehackle had always been a "man-fighter," and now this trait began to develop to alarming proportions. He would attack any stranger who entered the barnyard, and when the veterinarian came to examine the cows, he refused to go near the barn unless the farmer was with him. Whitehackle by mistake had even attacked the farmer himself when the man was wearing an overcoat and the bird did not recognize him, so now the Mennonite always called to the cock as he approached the barnyard.

Although the farmer's wife fed him, she did not play with the cock, and since she was considerably smaller than her husband, Whitehackle had no fear of her at all. Also she was not in the barnyard and barn nearly as much as her husband, so Whitehackle decided that she was a *persona non grata* in those parts. As long as she stayed near the house and the turnaround he ignored her, but when the woman entered the barnyard for any purpose, he was likely to attack her. The trash cans were near the barnyard, and once when the farm-wife went toward them to empty a wastepaper basket, Whitehackle attacked her so savagely that she saved herself only by throwing the basket at him and running. After that, she made her husband empty the trash. The farmer considered all this a great joke but his wife was not so amused. The climax finally came when there was trouble with the cucumber pump and she went to the pump by the horse trough to fill a bucket. Whitehackle rushed at her and, going up in a fly, drove one of his spurs through her dress into her kneecap, leaving a black-and-blue bruise that made the woman limp for several days.

It was not only the pain but also the humiliation of being bested by a chicken that hurt the woman's pride. She angrily pointed out to her husband that when the laying season began she could not collect eggs and fight off Whitehackle at the same time. She was also afraid for her eyes, for several times Whitehackle had gone up into her face. But Whitehackle, the hawk-fighting cock, was the farmer's great pride and his one subject for boasting when he met with other men. The woman did not dare to demand the rooster's death, but she secretly determined that by Thanksgiving Whitehackle would go into the stewpot by one means or other.

Indian summer had been brief that year and in the middle of November there was a killing frost. The next morning the man set out extra early to bank his celery, lettuce and beans with mulch to protect them from the cold. He took the dog with him, for he also intended to dig out a woodchuck that had been destroying his turnips.

All unconscious that his days on earth were intended to be so brief, Whitehackle led his more ambitious hens in their morning search for food. The sudden cold snap had killed the last insects and frozen the few remaining berries so hard that the birds could not eat them. Although they had enough scratch feed in their crops not to need any other food, Whitehackle considered the commercial scratch unappetizing and uninteresting. He would penetrate to the far end of the truck patch before being convinced that the good autumn days had really come to an end, and turning back.

The chickens were not the only creatures who had been caught off guard by the unexpected frost. A fox, returning late from an unsuccessful night of hunting, smelled the delicious warm odor of the flock. Making a wide swing, he crept almost on his belly through the mulberry bushes that fringed the stream and saw the chickens coming back across the pasture. They were well scattered and a little white pullet was less than thirty yards away. The fox lay motionless, studying the situation and making sure there were no humans in sight before he charged.

Whitehackle was on the other side of the carriage house, headed back for the barnyard, when he heard the alarm cries go up. First came the loud "alet!" of the chickens, then the "put-put-put" call of the turkeys and lastly the chatter of the guineas, who for once had been caught off guard. Whitehackle spun around and raced back. As he rounded the carriage shed he saw the chickens in trees, pointing with their beaks in the direction of the attack. He dove under the post-and-rail into the pasture and saw the fox struggling with the screaming, flapping pullet.

The sight of a struggle always inflamed Whitehackle and he darted across the field, his legs going like pile drivers, his head down and his ruff extended. The fox did not wait to receive him. He had his mouth full of wildly struggling pullet, and now that the alarm had been sounded, he had no desire to stay in the exposed pasture longer than necessary. He turned and loped off, carrying his head high to keep the pullet clear of the ground.

Whitehackle followed him. Even though the fox was handicapped by the thrashing pullet, he could easily outdistance Whitehackle, but when he came to the woven-wire fence covered with honeysuckle at the far end of the pasture, he was delayed. A woodchuck in the next field had dug a hole under the fence so he could graze on the sweet pasture grass, and the fox had entered the field through this hole. He had trouble getting back through it with the pullet in his mouth, and here Whitehackle caught up with him.

The fox had his head in the hole when Whitehackle arrived, and was helpless. The cock promptly went up in a fly, straddled the thief and drove both spurs into his body. The fox's soft fur offered no resistance to the twin stilettos, and when Whitehackle began to shuffle, he was in serious trouble. Putting forth all his strength, he tried to force himself through the hole, but with Whitehackle's spurs locked in his sides he could not make it. After taking terrible punishment he wriggled back, still with his jaws locked on the dying pullet, and ran along the fence with Whitehackle after him. Had the fox been willing to drop the pullet and use his teeth on the cock, Whitehackle would have been finished, but the fox refused to let go of his still-flapping prey. Instead he ran beside the fence, looking for some way over it, Whitehackle running and flying after him.

From the house came the wild ringing of the alarm bell to call back the farmer and the dog from the truck garden, for the woman had heard the screams of the poultry. The fox found a spot where the weight of the honeysuckle had dragged down the fence and with a run he was over it and in the rough, uncut grass covering a hillside. Now he was safe and he slowed his pace.

He had not counted on Whitehackle. Ordinarily the cock would never have left his territory, but now his blood was up. His enemy was fleeing and he could still hear the gasping "Awk! Awk! Awk!" of the pullet. Beating with his wings and scrambling with his strong legs, he went over the fence and followed the fox.

Far behind them they heard the farmer's shout and the voice of the dog. Help was coming and Whitehackle redoubled his efforts. The fox was tiring now, for the pullet weighed some four pounds and he weighed only ten himself; he was little bigger than a large cat. Although nearly dead, the pullet was still able to flap feebly and delay him, yet he did not dare to stop and kill her. This part of the hill slope was covered with honeysuckle and poison ivy that made going difficult, but Whitehackle with his spreading toes crossed the vine mat easily. As the fox swung to one side, hoping to find better footing, Whitehackle overtook him. Instantly the cock flew up and struck the fox twice on the head with his long spurs. The blows made the fox stagger, but now he heard the dog yelping eagerly on his trail and he kept on, trusting to the safety of the woods.

Whitehackle continued to buffet the fox who could now go no faster than a walk. The cock's spurs were dripping blood, but he was also tiring and his beak was open. The fox wormed his way through a mesh of blackberry vines, while Whitehackle, for once using his wings, flew over them and was waiting for him on the far side.

The fox had had enough. He was suffering from a dozen stab

wounds, several over an inch deep, and one had perforated his eardrum. He felt sick and dizzy. Dropping the dead pullet he turned to snarl at Whitehackle, and when the cock went at him in a hurricane of flapping wings and thrusting spurs, he turned and ran. Whitehackle paid no attention to the dead pullet. Instead, he continued to follow the fox, but now free of the pullet's weight, the fox could run and he was gone in seconds. Still with hackles spread and head belligerently outthrust, Whitehackle watched him go as the man and the dog crashed into the woods. The farmer saw the white form of the pullet and lifted it. Then he looked around for Whitehackle, expecting to find him dead. Instead, he heard the cock's victory crow.

There was no question of killing Whitehackle now. He returned triumphantly on the farmer's arm and even the woman regarded him with almost reverent awe. From then on, he was known throughout the country as The Fox Chaser.

6.

THE HUNTRESS

As the death grip of autumn spread over the farming country, Ishmael lived alone among the dried leaves of the forest that gave her little shelter. Not for her were the cozy comfort of the flock, the protecting chicken house, the regular meals. Friendless and alone, she could expect no help from any living thing, and the slightest miscalculation—a broken feather that left a gap in her wing, a slip when she bound to dangerous quarry, a too-quick decision to try for better hunting territory or a reluctance to leave a depleted range—could well mean the end for her. Ishmael had few natural enemies but life itself was the greatest of enemies.

From her favorite haunt deep in the woods, Ishmael glared out at the hostile world from eyes that were turning a deep orange as she became an adult. Penetrating though her sight was, she did not solely depend on it. At the slightest rustle among the dead leaves, the most distant birdcall, the faintest mouse squeak, she turned her head to look toward the sound while keeping her body rigid. Her pupil movement was not as flexible as that of a human, so although she had eyes on either side of her head, she was constantly twisting her neck about to concentrate her gaze in new directions. She could turn her head entirely around and look straight down her own back, so without moving her body and attracting attention to herself, she could see every point of the compass.

Autumn was not so entirely hopeless a time for Ishmael as it seemed. It was a long cry from the lush days of early summer when the woods were full of clumsy fledglings, but now there were no constantly famished young hawks to feed. There was still quarry even though in greatly reduced numbers, and Ishmael had fewer competitors, as many raptors had migrated. Also the cover was going—a most important consideration. The once impenetrable hedgerows were thinning out and the underbrush on the forest floor shrinking so that game had fewer places to hide. Although it was chilly now, Ishmael actually enjoyed the bracing weather unless the cold became paralyzingly intense. Then, too, cold tended to slow her quarry and weaken it.

Still, life was harder than in the bountiful summer and the shortening days left her fewer hours of sunlight for hunting. The game was now dispersed over a wider area, and with her injured wing Ishmael could not easily cover great distances to look for quarry. In cold weather, two-thirds of the food Ishmael consumed went to maintaining her body heat, so she must eat half her weight every twenty-four hours. In warm weather, her demands were not so critical.

Then suddenly finding food became incredibly easy, far easier than it had ever been before, for this was the hunting season and the gunners crippled enough game to support every hawk in the state all winter long if the raptors had only been able to store it. After the men had left for the day, Ishmael would glide from her hiding place far in the forest and, after a brief check from some good lookout tree near the forest edge, start quartering the fields. She did this very systematically, covering every square yard and diving down to slash with her hind talons at any tussock of grass where a bird might be hiding. She did not have to look long before coming on a pheasant, quail or grouse that had been wounded but not killed by the gunners and so was condemned to a lingering death. These crippled birds had no chance to escape and Ishmael brought them quick relief from pain, for in the wild there is always a clean kill or a clean miss; no wounded escape to die slowly. The hunters seldom got more than half the birds they hit, for the majority came from the city, had no dogs, were poor marksmen and would take any kind of a long shot on the remote chance that the hit bird would drop where it could be recovered. Even a mortally wounded bird can still run and shows an incredible ability to hide in cover that seemingly wouldn't conceal a sparrow, so by the time the men had gotten their limit, they had left many cripples. Like all hawks, Ishmael never killed more than she needed for food, so having made her easy kill she retired to the woods, leaving the rest of the dying game birds to other predators. Even the slow-moving buteos could kill these cripples and for the only time in their lives gorged on pheasant. The buteos were protected but the hunters often shot them and showed the birds' crop contents to each other as proof that all hawks live almost entirely on game birds and certainly the hawks ate little else at this time—the only time that hunters were around to shoot them and examine their crops. If the hunters had shot the turkey vultures, skunks and opossums they would have been full of game bird, too.

Unhappily for Ishmael and the scavengers, this golden age did not last indefinitely. Ishmael, even though regarded as a blood-thirsty killer by the humans, never killed if she could obtain food in any other way, and when there were no longer any dying birds left by the gunners she discovered another source of easy food: a television tower. Night-flying birds on migration hit this tower by the hundreds and the ground around it was littered with their bodies. This tall, invisible pillar of woven steel was a perfect deathtrap and killed far more birds than Ishmael and all her kin. Regrettably the local owls knew all about this spot and being night birds had the first choice of kills, but there were generally plenty of corpses left for Ishmael to fill her crop. But as the weeks went by and the migration ceased, even this formerly reliable source of food failed. Then there was nothing for it but to hunt.

Luckily it had been a good year for rabbits, as every farmer knew to his cost when he examined his vegetable patch in the mornings, and Ishmael had become an expert rabbit hunter. Generally Cooper's hawks do not hunt full-grown rabbits, as the rabbits weigh twice as much as even a female hawk, but Ishmael was an exceptionally large female. Her injury had not affected her size, for like most birds, when she left the nest she was as large as she would ever be, but as her injured wing had made it difficult for her to catch flying quarry, she had been forced to concentrate on rabbits. Rabbits were the easiest of all quarry to overtake but among the most difficult to kill. A kick from the hind legs of a tough old buck could disembowel a hawk, and unless taken exactly right a rabbit can roll on a hawk and break vitally important feathers. A hawk with a hole in her wing is in as bad a situation as a plane with torn fabric, for the air rushes through the hole when the bird tries to stop or turn and throws her off balance. Rabbits, then, were regarded as big game as far as a Cooper's was concerned and dangerous game at that.

During the grand days of hunting season, Ishmael had never bothered to hunt rabbits but she had observed them and memorized their haunts and habits. Now she set out to put her knowledge to use. The rabbits stayed near brush piles, the foundations of deserted buildings and bundles of abandoned wire which made ideal brier patches for them. Evenings and early mornings were the best times to look for them, as they were afraid of the buteos during the day and the great horned owls at night.

This ability to observe prey habits, plan a campaign against them and employ fairly ingenious hunting tricks to capture the quarry made Ishmael more "intelligent," from a human's point of view, than Whitehackle because she seemed to think more like a human and, to humans, thinking like a human constitutes intelligence. Yet whether Ishmael's brain was more developed than the cock's would be difficult to say. In order to survive, Ishmael had to catch living prey and a wide variety of prey, for she could not become too specialized, as the different types of quarry obtainable were constantly varying. This meant that the hawk had to know the habits of many game animals and how to capture them. Whitehackle with his comparatively limited diet did not need to make this effort. Under different conditions, the accipiters might have become like the fast falcons who live almost exclusively on highflying birds but are virtually unable to take quarry on the ground and so use limited hunting skills, or even like the Everglade kite who will eat nothing but one species of snail and seems quite stupid. As Whitehackle was practically nonflying and did not need to outwit his quarry, he did not develop skills. Given greater mobility and the need to use his wits, Whitehackle might have proved capable of surprising feats. Even so his ability to direct the functions of the flock—a power utterly beyond Ishmael—was impressive.

Ishmael had several types of flight. To amuse herself, she would sometimes soar with widespread wings and tail like a vulture, letting the air currents take her where they would, only occasionally giving a few quick flaps when she began to drift out of the current. When traveling from one place to another with a definite goal in mind, she flew straight with her typical flap-flap-flap—long glide—flap-flap-flap style that had a wavy nature as her momentum from the flaps diminished and she dipped down. When on a reconnaissance flight to obtain information for future use, she flew in much the same way but far more slowly, higher to get a better view of the country, circled frequently and lit often to study the lay of the land. When actually hunting, she kept low, went very fast and often swung out to the side or shot up momentarily to look for prey. The small birds knew all these flight patterns well and paid little attention to the first three, sometimes even attacking the hawk, as they knew that she was not keen, but when they recognized the hunting flight, they were panic-stricken.

Ishmael made a brief check of her range one evening, using the reconnaissance flight. Had she found a rabbit well away from cover, especially a small rabbit or one that seemed weak, she would have tried for him, but no such rabbit appeared. However, she noticed several rabbits in the apple orchard and decided to try there at dawn next morning.

Ishmael arrived at the orchard just at sunrise, coming in fast and low and deliberately swinging around so the sun would be at her back, allowing her to see while blinding the quarry. She had meant to pitch in a tall locust she had spotted the night before and watch there for rabbits, but as she swung up toward the tree, she saw the white flash of a rabbit's tail racing for cover. Ishmael had cut down her speed preparatory to lighting on the branch. Now she twisted her wings slightly, stopping herself in midair, and then keeping her wings extended slid sideways toward the rabbit as though down an inclined plane. Steering with her long tail, she angled her glide to cut him off from the root fence.

Even while running away, the rabbit had never taken his eyes from the hawk, for he could see nearly straight backward. As the hawk slid to intercept him, he turned and streaked down a wagon track, going all out. On the smooth track he could make better time than in the tall orchard grass, and he knew it. Pursued by a fox who would have been more handicapped by the tall grass than the bounding rabbit, he would have avoided the track, but with a hawk it was different.

The rabbit went like a brown flicker, but now Ishmael turned, brought her wings in close to her body and turned loose her rush. Compared with the hawk, the rabbit seemed to be standing still. But this was an experienced old buck who had been chased by hawks before. As Ishmael lanced in for the bind, the rabbit stopped dead and the hawk whistled over his head. Instantly she banked around, extending her wings at right angles and spreading her tail to its fullest extent to brake her forward motion, at the same time turning her head to watch the rabbit. He had doubled back and was heading for the root fence again. Once among the roots, he was safe.

Using the momentum of her upward swing to give her additional speed, Ishmael veered around and turned loose another savage rush. This time as she came in she rose slightly, so if the rabbit stopped again she would have enough altitude to drop on him. Instead of stopping, the rabbit waited until the hawk was almost on him and then dodged. Ishmael struck the ground where he had been, but the rabbit had been turned from the fence and was still in the open. Taking a few running steps the better to launch herself, Ishmael leaped into the air and slanted after him.

The grass was high in this part of the orchard and the rabbit disappeared into it. Ishmael flew a few feet above it, turning her head to and fro, trying to find the quarry, but the rabbit had vanished. Afraid that he might have doubled to the right or left and be escaping, Ishmael dropped her tail, threw back her wings and shot up to the branch of an apple tree where she sat bending forward and watching the expanse of grass below her.

Abruptly she stiffened. The tops of the grass were waving near the evergreen windbreak. Ishmael plunged through the branches, never taking her eyes from the moving line of grass blades. She crashed into the grass, missed, rose on fast-beating wings, hung in the air for a moment, dove again and once more came up. The rabbit was dodging back and forth through the cover and knew the runways there better than she did. The hawk soared for a moment to get her bearings and then swept upward. She had discovered that she could not go in at an angle; the grass held her back. Making a complete loop in the air, she dove straight down. She hit the rabbit, knocked the breath out of him and was able to get her killing grip on his head without trouble.

Ishmael took some half a dozen rabbits that fall, four of them young bunnies who had not learned the way of the wild yet and two old-timers who had begun to slow down and were not agile enough to avoid her rush. By then, the rest of the rabbit population had learned to be on the lookout for her and were too strong and smart to be caught without more effort than they were worth. However, later in the winter she caught several more. By then they had so overgrazed their range that they were forced to travel considerable distances from the safety of cover to feed, and so became more vulnerable. The rabbits would have had trouble believing it, but Ishmael was really doing the rabbit population a favor in keeping them thinned down, as otherwise they would have destroyed their own range so completely that most of them would have starved to death before spring and not left a sufficient breeding population.

Every morning now the close-clipped pasture grass was sugared with frost and paper-thin ice formed over the water trapped in the horses' hoofprints. Then as winter progressed, the rising sun no longer melted the frost in the mornings. The cold sank deeper and deeper into the damp earth, turning it to iron. Before starting on her rounds, Ishmael had to wait until the sun was well up and had warmed the surface of the earth sufficiently to make updrafts to buoy her in the thin, clear air. Having reduced the rabbit population to a point where hunting them was no longer profitable, she turned toward other prey.

This had been a good year for crops, which meant it had also been a good year for mice. The mice lived on the grain and there had been so much lush cover that they had been virtually immune from predators, so they had multiplied by the million. Now the grain had been harvested, winter had destroyed the cover and the mice were desperate. They had taken to girdling the trees and bushes and the devastation they wrought was astonishing. Whole districts took on a blighted look as the mice gnawed away the protecting bark from the shrubs.

Ishmael seldom troubled with mice. They were too small and too hard to catch. Also, they were largely nocturnal, so she left them to the owls who were most grateful. Then one morning she awoke feeling light-headed and curiously alert. It was almost like being in yarak but with a subtle difference. The insane desire to attack was not in her, yet she craved action. The atmosphere seemed lighter somehow, the air pressure was not so great and she could fly more easily. The barometer was dropping sharply.

Suddenly Ishmael had a passionate desire to eat. She knew something was going to happen, exactly what she did not know, but she wanted to have a full gorge when it did.

Slipping off the tree, she headed for the orchard. There might still be one unwary rabbit there. If not, she would check the hedges for sparrows and then the walnut and hickory trees for squirrels.

As she approached the orchard, she saw a sight so incredible that she cast up and swung away, not trusting her eyes. The whole surface of the ground seemed to be moving. Circling around, Ishmael gradually realized that thousands of field mice were leaving their burrows and starting for higher ground. Oblivious to danger, they were exposing themselves in full daylight in their panic-stricken efforts to escape some danger that they sensed.

Ishmael waited no longer. She rocketed over the mass, dropped her long legs and, with a mouse in each foot, headed for an apple tree. She bolted them in a series of quick gulps and went back for more. Now there were other raptors. In winter the hawks no longer had small, fixed ranges; they went wherever the action was. A soaring redtail saw Ishmael drop into the field and, rightly guessing that she must have found a rich source of food, swung around and followed her. A redshouldered hawk saw the redtail and followed. Sparrow hawks were attracted by the big buteos' actions and hurried after, so in an astonishingly brief period of time, twenty hawks were diving on the fugitives.

There was no quarreling among the raptors, for there was plenty for all. The mice made no attempt to avoid the hawks. Driven by what seemed to be a blind mania, they rushed on and on, crossing the open road in a black flood and hurrying on toward the distant hills. Foxes materialized from nowhere and joined in the hunt, running through the mice and tossing them up with a quick snap as they went, each mouse falling with a broken back, several in the air at one time. Still the mice made no attempt to take to their holes. They hurried on for the hills as though nothing else mattered.

Ishmael gorged herself. Then she perched in a tree until she could pass the food from her swollen crop down to her stomach, afterward flying down to fill her crop again. More and more hawks were sweeping in from miles away. Able to see for great distances and being highly mobile, they were the most efficient of all predators for a situation like the present, and the mouse population began to melt away under their constant attacks. Replete, Ishmael sat in an apple tree and watched the mouse horde vanish toward the purple hills, its progress marked by the wheeling, circling, diving raptors.

The next day the curious lightness in the air was even more pronounced, and though Ishmael still had a partial crop she went hunting again. As though driven by the same force that caused the mice to make their blind rush toward the high ground, Ishmael felt an unreasoning craving to gorge herself over and over again. There were no more live mice to be found, but she came across several scavengers battening on the dead mice left by the foxes. One was a weasel. She caught him with a mouse in his teeth and ate them both.

The following day she was still possessed by the urge to eat all she could as though to lay up supplies against a famine. There were neither rabbits nor mice available, so she went bird hunting instead. At noon she saw the white end feathers of a mockingbird's wings flash among the pokeweeds and, making a quick bank, shot after him. There was no shelter among the weeds but the mockingbird managed to make it to a clump of dogwood. Ishmael followed him in and, although much bigger than the mocker, steadily gained on him, threading her way through the interlocking branches without ever taking her glowing orange eyes from her quarry. Ishmael could focus simultaneously on a branch six inches away and on the mocker thirty feet ahead. Her broad, oarlike wings enabled her to rush through the thicket at fearful speed while her long rudder-like tail was constantly turning and twisting to guide her among the twigs and branches.

Seeing that he was doomed if he stayed in the thicket, the mocker burst out and made for the open pasture. Ishmael was positive she had him now, for the pasture was as bare as a billiard table, but the mocker made for a flock of grazing sheep. Dropping to the ground, he ran under a ewe and crouched there trembling. If Ishmael had been in yarak she would have followed the mocker anywhere, but the sheep daunted her and she checked off and pitched in a tree. The mocker stayed where he was, and although Ishmael made several strafing flights, coming as close as she dared to make him fly, the mocker refused to budge. Ishmael did succeed in frightening the ewe and making her break into a clumsy trot, but the mocker ran under her and refused to be flushed. Ishmael had returned to her tree and was trying to think what to do when a rabble of starlings flew around the corner of the barn and, lighting in the field, began noisily to eat and fight. Ishmael leaped into the air, turned and diving between two branches came almost straight down on the flock. The flock fragmented, screaming, but Ishmael picked off one and killed him on the ground. She started to eat him there, too, but the sheep gathered around her in a fascinated circle and made her nervous. She continued to feed, the hot flesh steaming in the cold air as she broke into it, while the curious sheep came closer and closer. Finally Ishmael could no longer stand the strain of their wide-eyed scrutiny and took off, carrying her prize with her.

The barometer dropped sharply during the night. When dawn came, there was a strong breeze that delighted Ishmael, and she rode the wind with a mad joy like a surfboarder, glorying in the sensation of speed without having to make any effort on her own part. With outstretched wings and tail she let the freshening wind whirl her around, confident that whenever she wished she could pull out of the gale and take refuge in the woods. The gray-black scud clouds raced low above her, and through their tattered wisps the turquoise blue sky still gleamed, studded with the dead white of cumulonimbus clouds that remained so motionless that they seemed to be painted on it. Ishmael was still enjoying herself when the storm burst around her. Almost beaten to the ground by the force of the rain, Ishmael fought her way to the woods, tail closed and wings held close to her body to give the storm a minimum amount of sail to work on. In the woods, she pitched in a linden and waited for the storm to pass.

Instead, it increased in intensity. The tops of the trees bent like buggy whips and occasionally came the tearing crack of branches ripped loose or the groan of a tree torn up by the roots. Frightened and unable to keep her perch against the wind, Ishmael dove down through the rain and, keeping as close to the ground as possible to avoid the force of the storm, flew to a grove of pines planted as a watershed to hold the soil. Under the mat of branches, she was protected from the hurricane and even managed to sleep a little.

The storm raged all that night and the next day. Ishmael was grateful for the full gorges she had acquired, for now her fat stood her in good stead, as she could not hunt. On the following day, there was still a strong wind and the rain was falling steadily but without its former fury. Late that afternoon the rain petered off, and the evening sky, instead of being a dirty gray, flushed scarlet. Tomorrow would be a good day. As the sun touched the horizon, Ishmael from her pine fortress could see small birds flying, probably going to roost. Taking advantage of the flat lighting that was perfect for hunting visibility, Ishmael wriggled her way through the pines and launched out into the damp air.

She found herself in a flooded world. There were pools every-where. Ishmael headed for the orchard but that was all one great lake. If the mice had stayed there, not one would have escaped. She flew slowly over the fields, looking for familiar landmarks, but the entire character of the land had changed.

A spinning group of dots caught her eye. A flock of teal were circling one of the rainwater pools, preparatory to landing. There was no cover for Ishmael to make her usual stealthy approach, but as it was almost dark, she used another device. Imitating the rapid, hard wingbeats of the teal, she came in as though she were a duck joining the flock. So perfect was her imitation that the teal paid no attention to her until she was among them. Then Ishmael dropped her charade and flung herself at one of the teal. The teal, even though obviously taken entirely by surprise, folded one wing under his body and did a barrel roll just as the hawk struck. Ishmael flashed over him, getting in one rake that did nothing but send a feather leaping up. She heard the teal hit the water and, knowing he was safe, swung away and went for another bird. This teal tried to mount with Ishmael rising fast under him. As Ishmael had widely separated primaries and a light wing load, she could fly almost straight upward for a considerable distance before losing airspeed and stalling out. The teal was also trying to fly straight upward, but with his comparatively heavy body and tight wings, he felt himself losing airspeed. He turned to level off, confident that in the straight-away he could easily outfly his pursuer, but as he changed his angle of flight to the horizontal, Ishmael came up under him. With every feather fully extended and wings and tail so stretched out that she seemed almost circular, she came to virtually a dead stop in midair and, shooting out her long legs, she bound to the teal. They came somersaulting and flapping down into the pool. Had they fallen into deep water, Ishmael might well have been drowned, for one set of talons was locked in the teal's body and she could not have released them in time. They came down on the bank and the teal made a desperate effort to reach the water, dragging Ishmael along with him. Ishmael managed to grab a tussock of grass with her other foot and, thus anchored, held the struggling bird until he dropped exhausted. Then she cautiously let go of the tussock and, with one quick grab, seized the teal by the head. The teal was too heavy to carry, and by the time Ishmael had finished feeding, night had come on so that she had to wait for the moon to rise before she could see to fly back to the woods.

The teal turned out to be the last waterfowl flight of the year. With the rabbits reduced and the mice gone, Ishmael was soon starving again. But it is the Cooper's hawk's extreme versatility and ability to outwit different types of prey, whether ptarmigan in northern Canada or lizards in the Mohave Desert, that has enabled her to maintain such a wide range. Ishmael now had to find some sort of prey suitable for her style of hunting. She found it in three coveys of bobwhite quail who lived on a 150-acre tract. Quail were the perfect quarry for Ishmael; they were just the right size. It was not by chance that one of the Cooper's many names is "quail hawk."

During the summer and early autumn, Ishmael had not bothered the quail. There were not too many of them that year, for the quail had suffered due to the increase of mice, as they were in competition for the ragweed seeds. In addition, one of the coveys lived in a thickly overgrown field of broom-sage which was so dense that the quail were as safe from the hawk as though protected by barbed wire. The broom sage was surrounded by soybean plantings where the quail fed in the early morning and evenings. Food and cover were so good that the covey seldom ranged more than a quarter of a mile, and although a man with a dog could put them up, they were quite safe from Ishmael.

The second covey lived in an aster-goldenrod bog which was also impenetrable and there was plenty of Lespedeza growing around it. Ishmael had a little better chance with this covey, as it took so long for the quail to fill their crops with the tiny seeds that they were forced to remain in the open. The third covey was in an elder swamp that formed such an interlacing cat's cradle of resilient stalks that the quail were safe in its cover, but these fed in wheat stubble where they were highly exposed.

During the summer, the quail had broken up into pairs and scattered over a wide area to raise their young. So well did the parents and tiny brown chicks conceal themselves that the Cooper's hawks never knew that they were about. But when autumn came, the quail changed their social organization. They began to form coveys of twenty birds or so, composed of adults and the now-grown young quail. With winter coming on, they had to huddle together for warmth. At night, each covey would find shelter in some protected spot and form a circle with heads pointing out. In this formation, it was impossible for a predator to take them by surprise, so the quail were able to make up for the lack of summer cover.

Although the quail had nothing like the iron discipline which Whitehackle imposed on his flock, they did have a pecking order and leaders. The head quail knew the range and how many birds it could support during the long winter months, and when the covey reached what they considered to be the maximum manageable size, they drove away all surplus birds. These unhappy exiles wandered around helplessly, trying to find their own range, but all the best territories had already been preempted by one or the other of the three coveys. To survive, the quail had to have cover, a constant supply of food not too far away and running water that would not freeze. Such combinations were rare, especially as the tidy Pennsylvania Dutch farmers were strong believers in "clean farming" and conscientiously burned all brush heaps and patches of weeds while keeping the hedgerows trimmed down to a minimum. To make matters worse, the highway department had sprayed the roadside thickets with a weed killer, so even this refuge was gone.

As a result, the ostracized quail were doomed. Some would starve, others be frozen in the snow or so coated with ice that they could not fly, for they had to keep together for mutual warmth, yet there were no remaining territories that could support a full covey. As their resistance weakened, diseases broke out among them and these diseases would have been transmitted to the healthy coveys and caused epidemics had it not been for the predators.

Of all the quail predators, Ishmael was the most terrible. She paid little attention to the regular coveys, for experience had taught her that only by chance could she break through their alarm system or find any far from cover. The wanderers were a different matter. They had no cover, were forced to expose themselves constantly in the open to find food and were not organized. As winter set in, quail formed over half of her diet, whereas before they had formed only a small fraction of it. Her style was to rush suddenly on a group of the scattered fugitives and force them to fly. Her expert knowledge of prey flight instantly enabled her to tell the weakest bird, and that was the bird she pursued. This bird was usually suffering from some disease, so Ishmael unconsciously yet systematically weeded out the culls, much as the farmer's wife butchered the surplus chickens that did not come up to par in order to maintain the standard of the flock.

As the supply of surplus quail grew less, Ishmael's interest in them diminished by the same ratio, for they became increasingly difficult to catch. Some of the covey quail also died for one reason or another, and the head quail then allowed the strongest and best of the refugees to join the coveys to keep them up to strength. By midwinter, this process was complete; there were no quail outside the coveys, and as the quail in the coveys were practically uncatchable, Ishmael would ordinarily have been forced to turn to other quarry.

This year several things went wrong. The covey quail in the elder swamp found themselves in serious straits. The vast horde of hungry mice, unable to find sufficient food, had chewed the elder stalks so the elders died and destroyed the cover. The heavy rains had flooded the swamp, driving out the quail. Generally the authority of the head quail provided valuable leadership, as these old birds knew the range, the best feeding grounds and how to avoid danger, but these senior citizens were also highly conservative and faced by unaccustomed circumstances were not able to adjust themselves to the new conditions. Instead of altering their way of life, they insisted on keeping the covey on the edges of the now-useless swamp. Then came the final blow. Hunters with experienced bird dogs had found this covey and ruthlessly harried it. Unlike Ishmael, who took only the surplus exiles and only the weakest of them, the hunters preferred to find coveys, as a covey offered more shots. When the covey first flushed, they would drop two birds and then with their dogs search out the scattered members. By the time they had gotten their limit, the elder swamp covey was dispersed and driven hopelessly far from its familiar haunts.

But the gunning season was of limited duration, and once it was over, the quail had no more to fear from man. Now Ishmael took over. This once well-organized, safe covey was now composed of dispossessed fugitives and at her mercy. When she was hungry—and in winter Ishmael was constantly hungry—she had no mercy. She had to eat, and the displaced quail were the readiest quarry available.

The quail lived in terror of her. When one of the big, slow-moving buteos passed over, they would freeze for a moment or two or at worst trot into the sumac until the hawk had passed, but at the sight of Ishmael they would plunge into the deepest tangle they could find and stay there for half an hour or more, trembling. Even the sight of a mourning dove would paralyze them for several minutes. Ishmael learned to know the "wheat-wheat-wheat" rallying call of the covey quail when they had become separated and were trying to find each other, and the sound would bring her gliding in on silent wings from half a mile away. Even if the covey was well out in the open, she would circle around to get between the quail and the cover before launching her attack. She learned to watch for the white throat marks of the cocks as they strained themselves up on tiptoe to look around. She also found that, even though the quail were expert dodgers, they had no staying power and would drop within thirty yards. On the ground, they could not avoid her.

But the quail were no fools and soon learned to know her tactics. They could seldom see her approach—Ishmael was too experienced a hunter for that—but often some other bird would give the alarm. Once when she heard the familiar "wheat-wheat" call and was circling around behind a grove of thorn trees she meant to use for cover, two jays started screaming at her. Ishmael heard the quail stop in midnote. Then came silence. Ishmael pitched in one of the thorn trees and waited. She could see nothing, but there came the patter of tiny feet among dead leaves as the quail hurried toward the windbreak of evergreens planted on the north side of the orchard. Ishmael instantly took off and circled the evergreens with no success. Apparently discouraged, she turned and flew away, pursued by the taunting jays. She shook off the jays by shooting at full speed through some maples, dropping almost to the ground and then making a U turn and doubling back while the white bellies of the jays flashed above her as they kept on in a straight line, still screaming. Barely touching the frozen weeds, Ishmael kept on toward the evergreen line, but a few yards from it she dropped to the ground and walked in. She stood motionless and listening intently until she heard the quail call again. She made a quick jump onto a low branch and froze there until an unsuspecting quail walked right under her, calling "wheat—wheat—wheat" anxiously as he went.

Even during winter the farmers were about enough to see Ishmael's harrying of the quail. There was not a man among them who did not have fond memories of going quail shooting as a boy, usually under the tutorage of their grandfathers, for their parents had been too busy bringing in the autumn harvest. Their wives loved the cheerful, chunky little birds as much as the men and regarded the quail rather in the light of songbirds whose musical "Bobwhite! Bobwhite!" had made pleasant many a long summer evening. That Ishmael was rapidly depleting the covey there was no question, and the men went out to hunt down the killer with rifles and shotguns.

In spite of her wariness, Ishmael would have been doomed if the search for her had started a few days earlier, but by the time the men set out, the few surviving members of the covey had found shelter in some cornstacks that a thoughtful farmer had left standing. The Pennsylvania Dutch still stacked their corn in the old-fashioned way, row on row of tepee-like cones, and not even the most scientifically trained conservation expert could have devised a better device for maintaining game birds over the winter. The stacks provided both food and cover for the birds, and as a final touch, the farmer had been wise enough to leave the stacks beside a running stream that never froze. If the head quail had led the covey from the worthless elder swamp early in the season, the birds would have found the stacks and been safe, but the old birds had waited too long. Now that the remnant of the covey quail was safely housed, Ishmael ignored them and turned to other quarry. The men knew well where the quail were and waited by the stacks for several days. When Ishmael did not appear, they then watched the other two coveys in the goldenrod bog and broom-sage field, but Ishmael had never paid any attention to these, as she well knew they were safe from attack. Finally, the men gave up, deciding that the hawk was too smart for them.

If they had come back a week later, they might have gotten her, for Ishmael began to haunt the vicinity of the cornstacks. She was not after the quail but after pheasants. The pheasants also liked the stacks and, being bigger than the quail, drove out the smaller birds. The remains of the covey were still able to survive by grabbing up grains of corn when the bullying pheasants were elsewhere, but then came a heavy snow. The pheasants took full possession of the few stacks and the quail were finished.

Ishmael had gone hunting early that morning and was cruising around, hoping to find some half-frozen creature in the drifts that could be readily caught. The wind had left cups in the snow around the bases of the trees, and as she flew Ishmael veered to and fro, checking each of the cups on the chance that a rabbit might have sought shelter there. Actually she passed several rabbits, for the snow showed blue under the shadows of the trees and this combined with the brown pelts of the bunnies made an unusual color combination that confused her. Then, too, sleighs with jangling bells were scudding along the roads with what seemed breathtaking speed to the excited children in them, and the strange sights and sounds made Ishmael nervous. She checked off and flew across the field where the cornstacks stood, intending to try some oak trees that still had acorns for squirrels. On her way across the field, she caught the gleam of scarlet against the snow where a cock pheasant was breaking through the crust after a buried cob.

Ishmael promptly altered her flight to the labored beat of a crow in case the pheasant looked up and saw her before she had the stack between them. Then she did a wingover, dropped and came in low. Quail could dart in under the protection of the dried stalks in the flicker of a feather, but the pheasant was far too big for that. Swinging around so she had both the wind and the slope of the ground in her favor, Ishmael turned loose her rush.

She came in too fast and the cock saw her at the last instant. He dropped flat in the snow and Ishmael whistled over his head. Immediately the cock hurled himself into the air with a roar of wings, giving his stuttering alarm scream at the same time. The sudden noise momentarily startled Ishmael and that gave the pheasant just enough time to get under way.

Ishmael whirled around and was after him, but the cock was going all out, and with her bad wing Ishmael could not overtake him. She did not try. Knowing that pheasants have little endurance, she followed at a comparatively easy speed, waiting for the cock to drop.

The cock knew precisely what the hawk had in mind and had shaken off other hawks who tried this same trick. He headed for a grove of sugar maples on a hill while Ishmael trailed him, expecting to see the bird drop into the cover and try to hide there. Instead the pheasant suddenly rose and went over the grove. This maneuver was so entirely unexpected that Ishmael was caught off guard. The pheasant had taken advantage of his momentum to make a quick upward swing to clear the treetops, but Ishmael had not time to do the same. Instead she made a rapid dip and then, with a twist of her tail, shot up with hard-beating wings. She had dropped below the level of the trees, so the pheasant, looking back, did not see her and thought the hawk had given up the chase. Confident, he went into a long glide beyond the grove, heading for a wheat field.

Ishmael had not given up even though she had lost ground and altitude. She kept on across the grove and saw the cock ahead and below her. Giving a few quick, hard wingbeats to build up speed, she slanted across the field with closed tail and wings held close to her body. The pheasant saw her coming but his energy was exhausted and he had to land. To come down in the open field with a hawk after him would have been suicide, and he was barely able to make it to a net of blackberry vines along the roadside. Making himself as small as possible, he wriggled in among the vines, but Ishmael was only a few wing-beats behind. The tangle was so thick the pheasant could not go far in and he was enmeshed and helpless. He gave Ishmael no trouble when she arrived.

Ishmael got another pheasant from the cornstacks the next day. Then the others left that area. It was barely in time to save the quail, for they could not have stood another night without food or shelter. They hurriedly moved back into the stacks and what was left of the covey managed to pull through the rest of the winter.

With no main source of food available, Ishmael had a hard time. The local birds that did not migrate—the cardinals, blue jays, nuthatches and titmice—knew her and her habits too well to be caught. She was able to pick up an occasional squirrel or starling and sometimes a pigeon if she caught the birds on the ground and was able to come in from a height before they could get away. Even so, she would not have made it but for the winter visitors—the crossbills, waxwings, juncos, purple finches and snow buntings. These birds were strangers to the district, did not know about her and did not know where the cover was. These, together with the odd pheasant, rabbit or grouse, pulled her through.

It was March again and spring was coming. The city dwellers knew nothing of it, for the weather was as fierce as ever, and even the farming people could scarcely see any difference in the days. But the animals knew, especially the birds. The days were stretching out second by second, minute by minute. The sun hung for a little longer each day before dropping behind the trees. For the first time in eleven months, Ishmael began to feel restless and long for companionship. She visited the grove of hardwoods where the white oak stood with the ruins of the beloved nest still wedged in the crotch, but except for an occasional flock of crows, there was no sign of life there.

Then—then it happened. As she awoke one frigid morning, she heard, so faint and far away that she could not be sure it was not the cry of some other bird, the "kik" cry of the male Cooper's. Instantly Ishmael was in the air, flying as hard as she could toward the grove. She pitched in the oak, looked around and then called "ca-ca-ca." There was no answer, so she called again. No, he did not answer and he did not come. Lonely and discouraged, Ishmael prepared to leave.

A flash of blue and white like a giant jay flickered through the skeleton branches. He was coming, flying low and burdened with a still-warm brown creeper. He would not come to her without a gift after these long months of separation.

Now the days of loneliness, hunger and anxiety were over. The quick little male fed them both and Ishmael happily reverted to her former spoiled state. They drifted through the woods on their courtship flight as the sun grew stronger and the daylight longer, until one day the male laid the first twig in the crotch of an eighty-foot beech and Ishmael showed she was ready for another nesting season.

7.

THE BARNYARD

The long winter months when Ishmael struggled to kill or die were a time of peace in the gentle barnyard. Highly sensitive to radiant heat, the barnyard fowl were sluggish in winter and the cold months were almost a time of semihibernation. The chickens did little except survive until spring. As food and water were provided for them, their main interest was keeping warm, and even this was no great problem. Due to their high body temperature, at night they generated enough heat to keep the chicken house quite cozy, especially for the high-ranking members of the pecking order. Whitehackle always saw to it that he roosted at night between two fat, comfortable hens who acted as his personal hot-water bottles. In case of a particularly bitter spell or when the snow piled into soft drifts that made walking impossible, he and his flock would sometimes retire to the spacious barn. The cattle kept the lower part of the barn as warm as a newly baked pie and the chickens could roost on the rafters. Occasionally he would venture up to the hayloft, that vast ghostly expanse where the pigeons sat in rows along the overheads, watching him with their alert, inquisitive eyes, and there was often a feather of snow forced by the high north wind through the cracks in the sidings. But the loft was cold, and unless he found a stray mouse or an overlooked ear of wheat in the straw, he soon returned to the warmth and *gemütlich* atmosphere of the lower part.

During the cruelest cold spells, even the hardy guinea fowl consented to come into the sheepfold where the geese had already formed themselves into a solid phalanx in one corner, hissing and snapping at any sheep who crowded them. Only the peafowl refused to take shelter under any conditions and insisted on roosting on the barn roof even in the worst storms, although by morning they were often covered with two inches of snow and in sleet storms were so coated with ice that they could not fly until the sun melted their frozen mail. However, in subzero weather they would roost on the chimney of the Gegusse eise Kessel to keep their scaly toes from freezing.

Beyond calling his harem to roost every night with an imperative crow, Whitehackle had no duties during the winter. He and his flock were starved for protein, as the cows would not come in fresh until spring so there was no milk to spare. When the sheep began to lamb in midwinter and the afterbirths were dropped, Whitehackle went nearly mad with excitement, searching out the pinkish-white membranes like an alcoholic searching for whiskey. In spite of the farmer's care, sometimes a ewe would lamb in the field and Whitehackle with the more venturesome chickens would gather around her, so raging with impatience to get at the afterbirth they would rush in and pick at the writhing, newborn lamb while the mother was cleaning it. They could tell by the ewe's action when she was about to give birth and would stay with her even after dark. Once as a result Whitehackle got locked out of the chicken house, and when morning came, his mutilated comb had frozen. The farmer's wife rubbed it with glycine and turpentine so Whitehackle suffered no ill effects. However, after that he was more careful not to miss closing time. By now he had made friends with the woman who had put herself out to get in his good graces, impressed not so much by his victory over the fox as by the fine, big breasts of his cockerel offspring, which made them sell for premium prices at the market.

As the days grew longer and warmer, the first spring green came. The poison ivy extended its soft, liverish-colored tendrils and the skunk cabbage unfolded its jade cups. The woman collected forsythia wands and put them in bottles by the windows to force them along. She also collected green tansy and put that in the chickens nests. The tansy, unlike the forsythia, was not just for nice; it kept down the lice and mites.

The wild geese began to arrive. The old geese who had nested on the farm before stamped off on their flat feet to their former ranges, paying no attention to anyone, but the transients were more polite and went over to meet the domestic geese, curtsying with their necks apologetically. In the uplands, the quail broke up into pairs for the nesting season and virtually all the hens were laying. In the farm markets, the price of eggs dropped sharply.

Once again Whitehackle led his dutiful harem out into the greening pastures. Now that the frost was out of the ground, he could sometimes scratch up a worm, and whenever he found such a wriggling, appetizing delicacy, he always gave the rolling food call for the benefit of the eager hens, who came running. True, by the time they had arrived Whitehackle had usually eaten the worm himself; still it was a nice gesture. But if greedy, Whitehackle was always unfailingly chivalrous to his hens, even though his chivalry sometimes took curious turns. The farm boy was fond of the crust of newly baked bread, especially when spread with thick churned butter, but did not care so much for the soft inside. He amused himself by making the bread into little balls which he tossed to the chickens, while eating the crust himself. Whitehackle always made sure he got most of the pellets and his gluttony annoyed the boy, who decided to teach the rooster a lesson. He got some soft soap, made that into pellets and threw one to Whitehackle. Whitehackle promptly bolted it and then stood rigid. He retired to be sick while the boy threw bread to the grateful hens. Chastened but still hungry, Whitehackle returned. After that, whenever he picked up a pellet, he held it in his beak long enough to be able to taste it. If the pellet turned out to be soap, he called over the hens and gave it to them.

Then the annual spring fights started among the males. With the defeat of the drake, Whitehackle had only one serious challenger to his position as overlord of the barnyard, yet until that issue was again settled there would continue to be tension that disturbed the orderly organization of the poultry. This challenger was the turkey gobbler, an impressive fellow who seemed to be a curious mixture of several birds and even some mammal. He was of a bronze color and had a fine tail, which if not up to the peacocks' fantastic trains still made an impressive show when he spread it. He had purple feet, his head was naked like that of a vulture but covered with folds of skin and carbuncles which grotesque as they were looked quite appropriate on him. But what seemed utterly incongruous was his snood, a single pencil-like finger of skin that hung from the crown of his head. Ordinarily this snood was only a couple of inches long and a dull white in color, but when the gobbler was excited, especially sexually, the snood quadrupled in size and turned a bright red. Then there was his beard, a long, wiry tail that protruded from the center of his chest. This beard hung down somewhat like a moose's bell and was definitely made of coarse hair, not feathers. It was incredibly inappropriate on a bird.

When the gobbler's head turned blue and he started to gobble for the hens, the farmwife knew that trouble was starting. The gobbler's first fight was with the peacocks. The gobbler could breed the peahens and the peacocks could breed the turkey hens and although both drew the color line, the possibility was still there. As the gobbler was heavier than the peacocks and inclined to be something of a bully, he usually started the trouble. The peacocks were much faster than he was and preferred to run, leaving the pompous old gentleman to strut around before his hens with spread tail and chest thrown out. This year, two of the peacocks attacked him together, pinning him into a corner of the barnyard where he could not escape and, flying back and forth over him, lashing with their spurs. Had not the dog interfered, they would have killed him. The poor old bluffer was humiliated in front of his hens and forced to limp off to hide in the barn where the peacocks, unable to use their wings in the confined space, dared not follow. The gobbler spent a week in the barn, sneaking out after the peacocks had gone to roost to snatch a few oats and a mouthful of water before darkness. By then he had recovered enough to come out by day. He carefully avoided the peacocks but badly needed to show his superiority over something. He picked Whitehackle.

They met in the narrow runway between the carriage shed and the milk house. It was all the gobbler's fault; he deliberately attacked the rooster. Head held high, his feathers sleeked back and uttering his trilling war cry, he charged straight at the smaller bird. His snood seemed to leap from his head, so rapidly did it protrude and flush scarlet.

In the open, Whitehackle could easily have avoided the charge, but in the confined space he was trapped. He tried to go up in a fly, but he could not go high enough and the gobbler knocked him down. Before the cock could get his legs under him, the gobbler jumped in, feet thrown forward and toes spread to claw him. Whitehackle managed to squirm out of the way and then ran, with the turkey after him.

Once clear of the runway, the cock turned to fight. Unlike two cocks who stand facing each other with lowered heads, the birds circled, leaning slightly away so as to be able to jump clear of a blow. Although the gobbler had spurs, he preferred to use his beak, mainly because he was too heavy to go up in a fly. He grabbed for Whitehackle several times, the cock always twisting clear. Then Whitehackle decided to try his spurs. He went up in the air but he could not quite reach the gobbler's head, and the turkey's heavy plumage, which almost amounted to plate armor, was too much for him. As he came down, the gobbler pecked him savagely on the head and made him stagger. Instantly the heavier bird rushed the cock and nearly bowled him over. Once he got the rooster down, he could rake him to shreds with his long claws.

Whitehackle felt the gobbler's pile-driver blows stabbing down on his comb and knew he must shield his head at all costs. Closing with the much bigger bird, he thrust his head under the turkey's wing to protect it. This would have been a suicidal act if Whitehackle had been fighting another cock, for it left him blinded and helpless, but the gobbler kept striking at him with his beak, lacerating his back but doing no other damage. His head protected, Whitehackle was now able to get his beak hold and, leaning back, swung up his spurs and hooked them in. The feathers under the gobbler's wings were soft down and offered no protection to the horny spikes. The gobbler yelped like a dog as the double blow went home. Whitehackle struck again, at the same time twisting his head to and fro to pull out feathers. This was too much for the gobbler, still sore from his encounter with the peacocks. He turned and stumbled off, dragging the smaller cock with him until Whitehackle let go. Then dead to all shame and the contemptuous looks of his hens, he ran to the barn and hid himself in the darkest corner while Whitehackle crowed proudly.

The farmwife had witnessed the fight and turned away with a sigh. During the winter she had hated the gobbler for bullying the ducks and chickens. Twice in her anger she had kicked him so hard that she had been afraid he had been seriously hurt. Now that he was defeated and broken, she was sorry for him and resented Whitehackle's victory. Later, she got the old gobbler a dish of corn and some water and watched pityingly while the shamed tyrant ate and drank humbly before slinking off to hide behind a stall.

With the defeat of the gobbler, a period of peace and prosperity descended on the barnyard. The spring advanced with a rush that year. One day the carriage ruts were caked with gouts of dirty, crusty snow, dead brown grass matted the pasture and the underbrush was lifeless fagots. A few days later the warm sun rose on a green world, the chimney swifts were zigzagging over the eaves, the martins were seeing what damage the winter had done to their houses, and the first daffodils gave color to the high banks. Flocks of migrant redwinged blackbirds covered the marshy areas like mosquitoes, and robins made their quick little runs across the muddy lawns. The peacocks now had trains like cascades of flowers and displayed to everything, even inanimate objects like large white stones. Throwing their arched trains forward over their heads to envelop the object of their devotion under a canopy, they would shiver with ecstasy, making the hard quills of their soft brown back feathers rattle like drumsticks. The peahens, who had vanished for the last few weeks, now reappeared trailed by brown balls of fluff that looked almost exactly like pheasant chicks. When the mothers went to roost at night in trees, they would take one or two chicks on their backs and then fly up, calling to the others. Heaven help any chick, no matter how small, who could not scramble up the trunk and then jump from limb to limb until he reached his mother.

Then came a fearful and completely unpredictable disaster. The sun set one evening on meadows glowing with the soft green flush of early growth, the hard outlines of the naked trees were softened by the nipples of new buds and the men came back from the fields in their shirt sleeves. As the dropping, bloody sun glared from behind the bars of the tree trunks, a cold wind hissed through the eaves of the barn, carrying with it a handful of tiny snowflakes. The flakes increased in number until it was impossible to see the barn from the kitchen windows. The anxious farmwife threw her husband's coat over her head and went out to lure the chickens into the barn with corn and even tried to tempt the peafowl down from their perches on the roof, but they refused to stir.

For three days the storm tossed against the closed wooden shutters of the farmhouse windows, and when the sun rose, a frozen sea of white, motionless billows covered the world. Paths had to be dug to reach the barn, and when the woman went out with kettles of boiling water to melt the frozen water dishes, she walked along alleyways cut through the drifts that were higher than her waist. The farm was entirely isolated, for not even on horseback could the men break through the windblown soft, white masses that filled the lanes. It was a freak spring storm, but surely almost at once the temperature would rise, the snow would turn to water and pour off into the streams. The farm people waited.

The temperature did not rise. During the day it remained in

the twenties and at night dropped to the low teens. The pumps froze and the men had to break the ice covering the pond to get water. The electric wires were down and the women got out the old kerosine lamps and candles reserved for such emergencies, while the men dragged in cords of wood from the woodpile to keep the fireplaces going night and day. At first it was fun to be so completely cut off from the rest of the world, like being on a desert island, and the novelty of it kept the family gay. But as day after day passed, the situation grew more serious and the children became more restless, for the snow was so deep that sledding and the usual winter sports were impossible. Still the cold held and a weird silence settled over everything. There were none of the usual farm noises, for the stock could not leave the buildings, the wild birds were huddled deep in the woods and the drifted roads were empty of carts.

The chickens spent their time happily enough in the warm barn, eating and sleeping, under the protection of the charm written over the tack-room door "Ito, alto Massa Dandi Bando, III, Amen J.R.N.R.J." The barn was built in the sheltered lee of the hill and the thick snow served as a blanket to keep out the wind and cold. Behind the century-old stone walls, proof against famished fox or stray cat, nothing could harm the chickens and they waited peacefully in their little world-within-a-world for the thaw to come.

In an old dump hidden under a jungle of frozen honeysuckle lived a wisp of murder. No one suspected his presence, not even the boy who knew every muskrat hole in the sides of the pond and nearly every meadow mouse's tunnel in the pasture. This brown flicker of energy whose body was scarcely six inches long was the Angel of Death to small animals. There was no hole he could not enter, no tree he could not climb, no rabbit so enduring he could not run him down. It never occurred to the farming family to wonder why this dump was not a breeding place for rats; the tiny assassin kept them down. He was a weasel, and had been created for one purpose and one purpose only—to kill, kill and kill. He killed when he was hungry, he killed when he was gorged, he killed from necessity, he killed for fun. To the hordes of small rodents, he was the Ultimate Check on their astonishing fecundity. Compared with him, Ishmael was a conservationist.

For weeks now, perhaps months, the weasel had lived in the catacombs of the dump, never venturing a yard from its shelter. Now, he suddenly decided to move. Perhaps the storm had destroyed his food supply, perhaps he was cold, perhaps he was bored. For whatever reason, shortly after sundown he flashed from the dump and undulated across the snow, going in a series of bounds by humping himself up in the middle like an inchworm yet moving with fearful speed. He had not turned white, for he was not far enough north for there to be snow on the ground all winter, and was still in his brown summer coat. There was snow on the ground now, however, and he showed up against it with vivid clarity. The weasel knew it and he crossed the open stretch as quickly as possible, which with a weasel is very quick indeed, and vanished into the woodpile beside the barn.

For a while there was no movement in the pile while the weasel darted about among the logs, checking for prey with his exquisitely delicate nose. Finding none, he lost interest in the pile and decided to go elsewhere. The pile had lain dead and motionless in the fading light, a shapeless mass faintly lighted by the snow. Now the weasel's snakelike head popped out for an instant. It abruptly vanished and seemingly instantly appeared at another point four feet away. Again it dematerialized and flashed out at another place almost at the same time. It seemed as though there were half a dozen weasels in the pile. Satisfied there were no enemies about, the weasel risked a dash to the barn. Even his string-thin body could find no crack in the stone foundations and he ran back and forth in a fury of exasperation. Then he found a slightly warped side board. Standing up as straight as a tent peg so his white belly showed, he managed to reach it. Then elongating his rubber-band body, he poured himself through the hole. He was in the barn.

Here he was in a weasel's paradise. There were many places where stones had fallen out of the walls and here the pigeons nested, as well as along the beams and under the eaves of the overhang. Many of the crude stick nests held fat helpless squabs and the weasel could climb almost like a squirrel. There were also the chickens, ducks and some poults.

The weasel touched none of them. Ceaselessly he hunted for rats. The old structure was veined with rat tunnels and the weasel threaded his way through them, his tail trembling and fluffing out with anticipation as he drank in the rich, intoxicating scent. When the rats sensed his presence, they went stark mad with terror. The floorboards of the loft trembled as they fled through their passages to escape the slim death. In one passageway under the feed bins, six desperate old male rats turned on their pursuer. There was an open space here the size of a basketball and they waited in ambush. Intent on the ecstasy of the hot scent, the weasel rushed into the midst of them. The old males fought desperately, gouging with their chisel teeth, but the weasel fought like a lambent flame. He was everywhere and nowhere and his long fangs went through tissue and bone like a rapier through cardboard. Two of the rats died and the rest ran.

There were several nests of writhing, newborn rats in the barn. Their mothers were willing to die defending them and die they did. Some of the rats fled the barn across the snow to be killed by owls, foxes and hawks, but many, trusting to their speed and knowledge of the raddle of passageways, stayed on. They grew gaunt from lack of food and never dared to sleep more than a few minutes at a time, for the brown vampire was constantly searching for them. In his quest, he glided under sleeping chickens, slid over eggs and squabs and leaped from back to back of the poults without ever offering to molest them. The farmer noticed that there was no fresh earth at the ratholes and the greasy black marks where the rats rubbed themselves against the floorboards had dried. He wondered what was happening and filled in the holes.

One night the weasel was hunting as usual for rats. He was neither more nor less hungry than usual and followed his customary route. Undulating along a beam, he slipped under a sleeping hen as he had dozens of times before. As always happened, the hen gave an irritated cluck and half spread her wings. One wing slightly slapped the weasel. Instantly he had her by the throat.

The hen's scream of terror ended in a gargle as she strangled on her own blood. The next hen awakened and began a puzzled clucking. At once she was attacked. For the next hour the tiny terror raged through the barn, killing blindly, drunk with blood and death. He killed until the screams of the chickens awakened the dog and his barking awakened the farmer. The light from the lantern showed a holocaust of dead or dying chickens and a little brown shape crouched on the body of a hen, staring up with bloody jaws. The farmer was too stunned to move and the dog did not see the weasel. The little fiend slipped through the open door and escaped across the snow.

The farmer was half mad with grief and despair, for there were fifty-eight dead chickens. Most were eatable, but many of his best laying hens were gone. Worse yet, the weasel was sure to return. The man and his son spent the whole of that day nailing boards over every crack they could find in the chicken house, and that night all the chickens and as many of the ducks and turkey poults as possible were put inside. Even so, nothing but concrete cinder blocks could keep out a weasel if he were really determined. Half a dozen times that night the farmer and his wife awoke, thinking they heard the squawking of terrified chickens or the dog's barking. They need not have worried. On his way back to the barn in the early-morning light, the weasel had attracted the attention of Ishmael as she swept low over the honeysuckle tangles. The weasel never knew what hit him.

Whitehackle had survived the attacks because he roosted high in the barn and the weasel had not gotten to him. The death of half his flock troubled him only slightly and then only for a few hours. The next day he had spent some time looking for some of his favorite hens and was mildly puzzled and annoyed when he could not find them. Afterward he adjusted easily to the new conditions. Polygamous, one hen was much like another to him; his only relationship to his harem was to guard and breed them. The monogamous pigeons, on the other hand, would have felt deeply the loss of a partner, while in all probability a goose who had lost a mate would mourn alone forever.

If there were to be eggs to sell that spring, the lost hens had to be replaced. The farmer drove his wife to the Green Dragon Auction near Ephrata where the woman was able to pick up a number of potentially good laying hens for fairly reason-able prices, although this was the wrong time of year to expect bargains. She bought whatever looked good to her without regard to breed—Plymouth Rocks, Leghorns, Wyandottes and a Cochin China. Prices being what they were, the couple could not hope to replace all the hens killed by the weasel, but they did secure two dozen hens and pullets after several trips.

The arrival of these strangers turned the formerly peaceful chicken community into a state of anarchy. Each new arrival had to establish her position by combat and this kept the chicken house in a constant uproar. Worse yet, after the newcomer had learned her way around the barnyard, rested and had a chance to study those above her, she was often able to stage a second round and reverse previous decisions. As the pecking order depended on brains and bluff quite as much as on strength, the issue was not simply that of brute force. It depended on whether a chicken knew how to use both feet and beak in a fight, could puff up her neck feathers at the same time she extended her wings to give the impression of size, or obtain additional height by holding her head erect and jumping to come down on her opponent. Whitehackle could not be everywhere to break up these fights, and to make matters worse, new hens were constantly arriving whenever the farmwife was able to pick up a few good-looking chickens. Fighting was continuous, the birds ate less and were constantly recuperating from wounds. The formerly stable, contented society was destroyed.

The cold finally broke and was followed by a period of steady rains. The chickens, confined to the buildings first by the snow and now by the rain, became restless and irritable. At first they showed their boredom by feather picking, which left some of them with bald patches. Then when the rain still continued, they turned to more vicious forms of sublimation. The more powerful hens began to attack the pullets, not as part of the pecking system but to pull out their feathers and pick the raw ends. Once they had acquired a taste for this perversion, they gradually became addicted to it, occasionally killing a small pullet and picking at the body as fiercely as Whitehackle picked at a mouse. Even the setting hens became affected by the madness. Some of them had laid soft-shelled eggs, as the farmwife had not been putting out ground oyster shell regularly,—she could not reach the stores where it was sold, because of the snow—and their systems were deficient in calcium. These eggs were easily broken when the hens settled down to brood, and the hens started to eat the broken eggs, for both the protein and the calcium they supplied. Then they broke good eggs and ate them. As the flock was highly imitative, perfectly normal chickens were caught up in the cannibalistic mania. The woman did all she could to prevent these depraved habits, making sure that there was always plenty of ground shell, putting out trays of laying mash covered with wire so the chickens could not scratch the mash out, and putting porcelain eggs or even empty spools in the nests and keeping the eggs in the cool springhouse to be reset when the hysteria had passed. Curiously, although the hens could detect fine shades of motion and identify each other by almost microscopic differences in appearance, they could not tell a spool from an egg, for in such matters they responded to the general element of a figure, not to the specific conformation.

The position of the hens low in the pecking order was pitiful indeed, although they were equally ruthless to each other. After being attacked by one of the dominant birds, a weaker hen would usually resort to tidbitting, attacking a still inferior hen with a pointless rage or, if so near the bottom she could find none lower, taking out her fury on sticks by stabbing them with her beak while giving vent to the deep, guttural sound that can only be expressed as a growl. At other times these unhappy underlings in an alien world where everyone seemed to be their superior indulged in aimless preening, directionless running up and down, scratching steadily or collecting brightly colored pebbles.

Only the presence of Whitehackle prevented the total disintegration of the flock, and gave the oppressed low-caste hens any hope. It was quite possible that the all-powerful cock might show a special interest in one of these humble ones and make her favorite of the harem. As the cock's whim was law, not even the most aristocratic dowager dared to question little Cinderella's sudden rise to power, and didn't little Cinderella make the most of her newfound position! Admittedly she seldom remained favorite for long, but anyhow she had had her moment of glory. This was quite a common occurrence, as Whitehackle was far more drawn to respectful females who instantly crouched down at his approach, duly bending their heads and twisting their tails to one side to receive him, than to the haughty hens high in the order who had such a good opinion of themselves that they stalked around head in the air as though they were cocks and crouched only reluctantly. Such aristocrats were so used to forcing others to crouch in their presence that they found it difficult to abase themselves even to a cock. Whitehackle liked his females weak and willing, so he tended to ignore these matrons. As a result, they often became increasingly more masculine, tried to crow with cracked voices, attempted to tread the young pullets and, naturally, would not lay fertile eggs. Ordinarily there would not have been such a great disparity between the top-ranking hens and those in the lower echelons, but the old-time hens who had survived the weasel's attack had highly vested territorial and seniority rights in the barnyard and so regarded themselves as vastly superior to the newcomers who arrived frightened and unsure of themselves. As the result of constant attacks, the newcomers became completely hacked and never had an opportunity to acquire confidence. Given time, Whitehackle would be able to correct the situation, but as long as the flock was crowded together in small quarters, fighting was almost unavoidable. Once the weather broke, the situation would improve, but meanwhile deadly enmities were developing and the inferior hens came to hate their new home and longed to escape.

At long last the rains stopped and the chickens ventured out on the muddy, steaming ground. The farmwife had converted the tobacco shed into a laying house as she did every year, keeping an old iron stove going in the middle to provide warmth and installing laying boxes. To her surprise and disgust the new hens refused to use the facilities thus provided. They spread out through the farm, even going as far as the woods to nest—anything to escape from the dominance of the older hens. In such a situation, they were at the mercy of predators.

Some of the worst predators were the peacocks. These beautiful but sadistic birds loved to torment a sitting hen. They would pick at her until they forced her to leave her clutch and run clucking with apprehension to the protection of the barnyard and Whitehackle. The peacocks never bothered the eggs and there seemed to be no point to their molestation except pure devilment. If the farmwife found the nest in time, she covered it with a coop, so although the peacock would spend long hours roosting on the coop with his head cocked on one side, hoping the hen would emerge, he would finally be forced to give up. However, some of the nests were so well hidden that the woman did not find them, the peacocks would drive off the hens and the clutch would grow cold. As the nests were so scattered, Whitehackle could not protect his wives.

Slowly, however, Whitehackle was able to bring order to the disrupted society. With plenty of tender young pullets available, Whitehackle ignored the opinionated old dowagers who either learned to yield to him or were forced into sterile, sullen isolationism which ended in the stewpot. By the time the first little peeps emerged from the shell, the flock was well on the way toward a peaceful reorientation when the hawks appeared.

This time it was not Ishmael alone who was the raider; the male hunted with her. This was not a question of an occasional raid and a single chick lost. Rather the two hawks came daily and each made a kill. Each day there were fewer and fewer of the little chicks to answer their mother's anxious calls, and not infrequently the mothers themselves vanished and only a ring of feathers told the tragic tale. Unable to keep constant watch over the flock, the farmwife resigned herself to a second disaster, and this time there would be no more egg money left to buy new stock. She could only wonder what evil force had driven the hawks to forsake their natural prey so entirely and concentrate on her chickens.

But if the woman had given way to despair, not so Whitehackle. The fierce determination that in the cockpit drove him to fight on to the last stroke of the steel gaffs, and the last peck now sent him ranging to and fro over the farm, always ready to dash to the rescue whenever he heard the alarm scream. He now no longer had any fear of the hawk, for he had twice beaten her in beak-to-beak combat. The hawks, on the other hand, avoided him, preferring to launch their cutting-out raids when he was in some other part of the farm. For a while they were successful, but as the remaining young chicks grew bigger, they became too much for the little male to carry off and finally put an increasingly heavy strain on Ishmael. She could kill them easily enough but she had to eat them on the ground and there Whitehackle might find her.

Whitehackle also sensed the changing situation. Several times he had almost caught one or the other of the hawks plucking their fresh-killed prey. Each time so far, the hawk had been able to take to the air before Whitehackle could reach the murderer, but their luck could not hold forever. The male seldom killed now, it was nearly always Ishmael; and even when she killed in the open, she had the habit of dragging her quarry under a bush for concealment. In that position she could not fly straight up and might well be trapped. Whitehackle forgot about eating, forgot about his morning crow and even neglected to breed the hens. Someday he would catch that hawk on the ground where he could get his spurs into her. He was not trying to avenge his hens but to attack a trespasser on his range who continued to defy him. Whitehackle spent all his time patrolling the farm, waiting for his moment of vengeance that was sure to come.

8.

THE LAST FIGHT

It had been a hard season for Ishmael and her mate. The freak blizzard had decimated the small bird population and then the long period of rain had made hunting difficult, for the hawks could not fly with wet plumage. Even when the rain stopped and the pair began their long-delayed nest building, there was little game. Although the Pennsylvania Dutch refused to use insecticides, other farmers were not so scrupulous, and for the last few years planes had been spreading tons of the smoky poisons over the countryside. The small birds ate the dead and dying insects and became sterile. As the poison was not in sufficient concentration to kill, there was no sudden decline in the number of adult birds, but each year there were fewer and fewer fledglings to take the place of the birds who failed to return from the long migratory flights. Still, the steady falling off had not been drastic enough to be noticed by humans or to affect the hawks.

The combined effects of the late blizzard and the heavy rains would have been a serious blow to the birds under any conditions, but in their reduced numbers it was a major disaster. Naturally the seed eaters were less affected by the insecticides than the insect-eating species, but as all birds ate some insects, they were in greatly reduced numbers and the bad weather was the final blow. Ishmael laid only two eggs that year as though sensing that raising the young hawks would be more difficult, but even so the male found himself unable to feed his family. Ishmael grew increasingly impatient with him and her angry "Hurry up!" call—a series of shrill "waaas"—got on the male's nerves so that he turned sulky. Devoted though he was, the male Cooper's could not stand constant nagging. Ishmael sensed the difference in his attitude and wisely decided to change her tactics. Leaving him in charge of the nest, she went hunting herself. Sure of the powers that had carried her through two barren winters, she started out confidently, but she quickly discovered why her mate had failed. The few birds around were smart old-timers who all seemed to be hawk-wise. Empty taloned she returned to the nest and her waiting family. The starving cries of the fledglings sent her into spasms of desperation but by then it was too dark to hunt.

As soon as it was light, she started out again. The crying of the young hawks was growing feebler, and unless they ate that day, the young male who was the weaker of the two would probably die. Drifting through the woods, hunting at random, which was quite unlike her, Ishmael heard a whir of wings and saw a cock grouse barreling through the trees, flushed by some passing predator. She banked after him, but the grouse saw her and went all out. The two birds were flying in a stand of hardwoods, and the grouse crashed through the brittle twigs in a series of explosions that sounded almost like rifle fire. Ishmael zigzagged after him, right on his tail, but each time she struck, the grouse managed to make a snap roll and avoid her. Finally when he was over thick cover, he fish tailed into a sideslip and dropped straight down. The moment he hit the ground he started to run. The raging hawk beat to and fro over the tangle and even landed, scuttling back and forth, trying to find a way in, but the grouse had outwitted her. After she had flown away, he came strutting out and marched up and down, giving a proud "peep-peep-peep" in triumph over his smartness.

When Ishmael swept back to the nest, the young were too weak to do more than raise their heads and call faintly. The male hurried over when he saw her come in, expecting her to have prey, but when he saw that she was empty clawed, he lit quietly on the opposite side of the nest. For a long while the two hawks sat motionless regarding their dying young. Then as though a signal had passed between them, both birds took off together, flying silently together through the woods.

Leaving the youngsters alone and undefended was unthinkable by the hawks' standards, yet only by working together could they hope to make a kill. Unlike the buteos, who often hunt together as a team, Cooper's hawks prefer to hunt singly, each hawk using his or her special tactics developed by long practice. The male usually hunted small birds, depending on his agility and speed, while Ishmael concentrated on larger quarry, as she was comparatively slow on turns but had great strength. Being solitary birds by nature, they did not like cooperative hunting, yet now they had no choice and would have to combine their talents.

As they flew, they heard the distress call of a hysterical robin. The male was ahead and he instantly altered his course toward the sound, with Ishmael following a few yards behind. They saw a red squirrel whisking around a nest while the robins dove at him, screaming with rage and anxiety. Ordinarily, it was hard for either of the hawks to catch a squirrel; squirrels were too quick at dodging around a tree trunk and actually seemed to enjoy the game, taunting the frustrated hawk with jerking tail and a contemptuous chittering. But with two hawks working together, this would be different.

The robins fled at the first sight of the hawks but the squirrel could not fly. The male Cooper's made no effort to chase the red wraith, he merely circled the tree, making sure the squirrel did not get away. Ishmael came sweeping in, threading her way through the branches without ever taking her eyes from the quarry. The squirrel was engaged in teasing the male but when he saw Ishmael he made a frantic effort to escape. He dodged around the trunk, but with a hawk working both sides, he was sure to be caught eventually. He did not dare to jump to another tree, for one of the hawks would seize him in the air. He took the one remaining course—he let go and dropped straight down, keeping as close to the trunk as possible so the hawks could not dive at him without hitting the bark. Headfirst, Ishmael plunged after him while the slighter male swung away to give her a clear field. Not having the big, bushy tail of his gray cousin which acts as a parachute, the squirrel hit the ground hard and it took him a second or two to recover. That second was all that Ishmael needed. She took care to grab the squirrel by the head, as once when she was a young bird she had been badly bitten. One clench of her mailed foot armed with curved talons was enough.

The famished young devoured the squirrel and still clamored for more, so the hawks set out again. They not only had to feed the young but also themselves, for if they grew too weak to hunt, the young were doomed. To conserve energy, they pitched on the black walnut at the edge of the grove that served as a watchtower overlooking the open fields, and waited.

Luck was with them and they did not have long to wait. A grackle came slanting down to feed among the sprouting oats with wings spread and tail cocked at a forty-five-degree angle.

Both hawks regarded him gravely but made no motion, as both knew he was too close to the multiflora hedge that bordered the field to make a successful flight. Then Ishmael could stand the strain no longer and leaped into the air with a thrust of her powerful legs. She was scarcely clear of the tree when the watchful grackle saw her and darted into the wickerwork weave of the hedge while the frustrated hawk cast up and landed on a telephone pole.

Now the male had an idea and took off, flying straight at the hedge. He was so small that he could go nearly anywhere the grackle could, but ordinarily this would have done him little good, for the black bird would have waited until he was enmeshed among the thorns and then slipped out. The male Cooper's began to rake the hedge with his hind talons, forcing the grackle lower and lower until he was almost on the ground. Then the male dropped and ran in after him. Forced from his refuge, the grackle had no choice but to take his chances in the open. Ishmael had been leaning over the edge of the pole, watching intently, and as the grackle started across the oats, she dropped on him. The grackle threw himself on the ground, beak open, wings spread and Ishmael overshot him, but by now the male had extricated himself from the brambles and he finished the business.

The grackle plus the squirrel satisfied the two young birds, and now, despite her hunger, Ishmael was afraid to leave them alone, so the male went out hunting on his own. He returned to the plucking log with a starling, and Ishmael was so ravenous that she actually attacked him to get the precious food. The male dropped the starling hastily and disappeared again. He did not return that evening but at least Ishmael had a gorge.

Several times again that spring the parent hawks were forced by necessity to leave the nest and young unprotected and go hunting together. On these expeditions they were invariably successful and Ishmael would immediately seize whatever quarry they obtained and speed back to the nest. After feeding the young hawks, she would remain with them while the male did his best alone. Only if he were entirely unsuccessful would Ishmael reluctantly leave the nest and join him, although she suffered agonies of mind every minute she was away from her precious fledglings, with bloody assaults from murderous owls, crows and raccoons always a possibility.

The young hawks were growing stronger now, although their developing feathers were stripped at the base with the ugly mark of hunger streaks where the blood had been pulled out of the growing feathers to nourish the depleted bodies. As the babies grew stronger, they also grew more combative and frequently fought, picking at each other especially in the soft ear openings. Small sores developed and now a new danger threatened. In spite of the spraying, it was a bad year for screwworm flies and these flies were sure to lay their eggs in the nest and perhaps in the sores. When the eggs hatched, the larvae would feed on the birds' blood and slowly kill them. Ishmael, for all her cunning and courage, could not prevent this disaster, but the male hawk could. He noted the presence of the flies and substituted sprays of wild cherry for the pine sprigs he usually used to ornament the nest. These sprays were not just for nice. As the sprays rotted, they gave off a mild mist of cyanide gas powerful enough to drive off the flies but not strong enough to bother the fledglings. The male watched the sprigs carefully, substituting fresh sprays when the old were worn out, and so the babies survived, the flies finally completing their larval period and crawling out of the fledglings' ears and pupating at the bottom of the nest.

By watching the male, Ishmael learned much about small bird hunting. A song sparrow generally headed at once for cover, a vesper sparrow (easily identified by his white wing edges) would try to ring up and get above a hawk, so with a song sparrow it was important to cut him off from the nearest hedge but with a vesper it was better to rise at once to meet him. Mockingbirds were tricky fliers but often they would leap around on the ground, beating with their wings to send up insects. In this position they were easily caught. When a redstart alighted he always made a 180-degree turn to look for danger. A perching hawk should remain absolutely still during this time, for the redstart could not identify a motionless predator. When the redstart began to feed, then the hawk could attack but always alter the flight pattern, as even at a distance the redstart could recognize the typical Cooper's form of approach.

Ishmael was now in her full mature plumage. Her brown plumage had disappeared with the last molt, her back had turned slate blue, her creamy white breast was heavily cross-barred with tawny lines and her legs and ceres at the base of the beak were butter yellow. Her eyes had turned to a deep orange, almost a red, and the black bars on her tail stood out vividly. The neutral-colored brown feathers of her youth which had blended with the dark bark of trees and had served as camouflage to hide her from both enemies and prey were now no longer necessary. Swift and experienced, Ishmael needed to fear no predator and could take her quarry by superior flying ability and skill. Now it was more important that she look well in the eyes of a mate to perpetuate the species, and the dun-colored immature hawk had been transformed into one of the handsomest of birds.

The hawks worked out a schedule so rigid that an observer who knew their habits could have told almost to the minute where the pair would be at any time of day. At daylight, they flew to a stand of maple and beech trees that, to reach the light, grew as straight and tall as telephone poles. A road covered with talcum-powder-like dust ran past the grove and beyond that was a pasture covering a low hill. Below the stand was a swamp. This was ideal hunting ground for the hawks. From the top of the tallest beech they could command a large sweep of territory and have altitude on anything that got up. The trees hid them and if starlings came down in the pasture to feed, the hawks could drop down below the level of the hill and shoot over it suddenly, taking the feeding birds by surprise. The pair would sit motionless here for an hour or two before trying another territory, but they were seldom disappointed.

This morning the two sat quietly yet intent on the world around them. From the swamp came the "didadiddit" chuckling call of a cock pheasant, the whimper of dove wings as a flock arrowed past, the raucous cries of crows in the distance, the bawl of a cow and the buzz of a yellow jacket circling the remains of a starling dropped by Ishmael the day before. Then high above come the cries of a V of Canada geese as each bird signaled his position in the formation and was immediately answered by the next in line. From a distant hill came the baying of dogs after a rabbit. The sound was strikingly similar to the cry of the geese, as the dogs were also signaling their relative positions to each other as they ran. The hawks were watching for the pheasant who had called, turning their heads just enough to take in the whole spread of the swamp. A fox was also after the pheasant, but he was using his nose to trail the bird through the goldenrod. A man passed below them, interested in the cock and following the bird's prints in the soft dust of the road. He did not see that the cock had gone to the swamp and kept on along the road. The hawks sat frozen as long as he was in sight. After he had gone, they stretched and shifted from one foot to the other.

Ishmael saw a flicker of red pelt among the cattails, and opening her wings slid down to a mulberry growing near the edge of the swamp. Flying from tree to tree, she followed the fox as he wormed his way through the tangle, as she knew from experience he was almost sure to flush something. At last a meadowlark leaped up. Before the bird had ceased towering, Ishmael slanted past, reached out almost casually with one leg and took him.

Ishmael was hungry and refused to share her kill, but later both birds moved to a sassafras clump by the dump. They were on the edge of a wheat field here and, sitting silently, the hawks could hear a rustling among the serried rows. They waited for a sight of the potential quarry, and then the male, who was still hungry and highly tense, got a quick glimpse of a brown shape. The male was in screaming yarak, crest up, wings partly open, waiting for any motion. Brief as the brown flash had been, it was like pulling the trigger of a gun. He was off his limb and hit the wheat almost at the same instant. There was an explosion among the stalks as the male rolled over and over, clinging to a large rat. The rat writhed around in the hawk's grip, his two yellow incisors showing clearly in his cleft upper lip as he gouged at his attacker's leg. So fast that the eye could hardly follow the motion, the hawk let go with one foot and grabbed the rat by the face, effectively muzzling him. With spread wings and tail he was able to hold the rodent down, although the rat lashed from side to side, trying to throw him off balance. Ishmael came down to help but the male screamed "ca-ca-ca!" at her and hung on until the rat was dead. He gorged on it but allowed Ishmael to have what was left.

If it had not been for the demands of the young, the two hawks could still have managed reasonably well, but finding enough wild game to provide food for the ravenous young birds was impossible. The hawks were forced to scout the farming areas, looking for domestic fowl. Yet their first raids were not on poultry but on pigeons. Every barn had its quota of pigeons, but these wary and fast-flying birds had been almost impossible for the hawks to catch working alone. The pigeons usually sat on the sunny south side of a barn's peaked roof, but always left two or three sentinels on the other side in case of a surprise raid. Ishmael had occasionally been able to catch a pigeon by coming in very low on the north side and shooting suddenly up before the sentinels could see her. As she came over the eaves, the sentinels would take flight, but before they were high enough for the others to see them, Ishmael would be up and over the barn peak and down on the rest luxuriating in the warm sun. She had to be quick, for once in the air the pigeons could easily outfly her. The little male had never attempted this trick, although he could occasionally take a pigeon if the flock were feeding on the ground and he could come down on them from a tall tree.

Under any conditions, the odds were so much in favor of the pigeons that the hawks seldom bothered with them, but now the two birds were hungry and willing to try anything. One afternoon while flying from the beech grove to the dump, the pair passed the open double doors of a barn loft, and the male saw some pigeons feeding among the chaff on the floor. It looked like too good a chance to miss and he checked off to make a dash at them. The birds scattered and the male concentrated on a tough old cock pigeon who flew straight ahead into the barn. The hawk followed him, only a few wingbeats behind.

Ishmael saw the pigeon flash out an open window in the far end of the loft and then bank sharply around the barn with the male Cooper's still after him but thrown off balance by the unexpected maneuver. With her astonishing memory for anything connected with hunting, Ishmael remembered that she had flown this same pigeon some weeks before and how he had fooled her. After flying through the window and circling around the barn, he had ducked back through the double doors and then, shooting up, had hidden himself among the beams of the loft. She was sure that he would try the same trick again, so as soon as she saw him go out the window, she quietly flew over and lit on one of the open double doors. Sure enough, the pigeon came barreling around the barn, having gained a comfortable lead on the pursuing male, and dodged into the loft without noticing Ishmael. She waited until she saw him go up on a beam and then dove into the barn, swinging up at a sharp angle and turning over on her back at the last instant. Before the pigeon could find a hiding place, she had him.

An hour later when the Amish farmer who owned the barn came to close the doors, he saw on the loft floor the typical ring of feathers left by a feeding hawk. The farmer was delighted, for he hated pigeons. Their droppings destroyed hundreds of dollars worth of hay, yet there was no way to keep them out of the loft. Even with the doors closed there were spaces under the eaves where the pigeons could slip in, and they roosted in the barn at night. He did not dare to shoot them for fear of blowing holes in the roof, so he was forced to take his losses. He had no poultry, unlike the Mennonite farmer who owned Whitehackle, and regarded hawks as God's own instruments for vermin control. He devoutly prayed that the Cooper's would return.

His prayer was answered. The hawks worked out a system to outwit the alert pigeons. Flying low, they would come in toward the barn from the north, using a windbreak of cedars for cover. At the last minute, they would divide, Ishmael swinging north past the double doors and the male going southeast, swinging up toward the pigeons on the roof. The flock would take off, flying west, and, as the male was above them, drop to put the barn between them and the hawk. They would meet Ishmael coming around the corner and going at her top speed. The flock was trapped between the two hawks and either Ishmael or the male was almost sure to make a kill.

The hawks drastically depleted the flock to the huge joy of the farmer who computed that the predators were saving him two hundred dollars in spoiled hay. The pigeons, however, were by no means fools and after a few weeks of harassment virtually deserted the barn. This was splendid for the farmer but not for the hawks. They especially liked pigeons; there was plenty of meat on them, yet the pigeons could not fight like game birds. They went looking for a fresh supply.

They found it near a new house built by a factory laborer who worked for a firm in New London. The man's hobby was raising homing pigeons and he had a loft near his home. The house was in the woods, and the homers, returning from a race, would come dropping down through the trees with open wings to land on the loft's platform. These purebred homers could reach speeds of seventy miles per hour, and ordinarily the hawks could not have caught them any more than they could have caught bullets, but among the trees it was different. From their high black walnut lookout tower, they could see the tired pigeons coming in from a long race. Promptly the hawks would fly to the woods and take up positions in trees overlooking the loft. As the pigeons drifted in through the branches, the hawks would attack. It was usually Ishmael who catapulted down, grabbed the pigeon as he was in the act of landing and carried him off through the trees. The furious fancier tried standing guard with a gun, but the action of the hawk was so fast and the man was so afraid of killing his pigeons that he never got in a shot.

The hawks had learned that they were quite safe at the Amish man's farm and often perched on the edge of the barn, waiting for one of the few remaining pigeons to come out from under the eaves. Here they allowed humans to get quite close to them.

One day while driving past, the factory worker saw the hawks on the barn roof. Gunning his car, he raced home, got his rifle and hurried back. The hawks were still on the barn and he crept up behind the cedars, confident that at last he would get rid of the raiders.

He was raising the gun to take aim when he heard a loud yell and a charge of shot splattered around him. Frightened and cursing, the man turned to face an equally furious Amish farmer pointing a shotgun at him. The man could not speak Pennsylvania Dutch and the Amish farmer knew no English, so neither could understand the other. Frustrated, the factory worker returned to his car and drove off. Raging, he reflected that even a dumb Dutchman should have enough sense to know that hawks killed pigeons and so ought to be exterminated.

The irate Amishman watched him go, shotgun over arm. He could not understand this outlander. Even a dummkopf city man should have sense enough to know that hawks killed pigeons and so were a valuable asset to the countryside.

The shot had alarmed the hawks and both birds had had sufficient experience of firearms to be in mortal terror of them. They never came back to the barn.

Although the young were now branchers and hopping from limb to limb of the nesting tree, they still had to be fed and they were even more ravenous than as nestlings. There simply was not enough game to sustain them. The pigeon fancier was not the only new resident in the district. Factory after factory was fleeing the city to avoid constantly higher taxes, lack of warehouse space and shortage of attractive housing for their employees. To accommodate these factories, huge areas of woodland were leveled, new highways cut across farms, and streams turned into sewers, and the water level was constantly dropping. It had become increasingly difficult for the area to support birdlife, even in greatly reduced numbers. Only the artificially maintained poultry could continue to exist, and so the Cooper's hawks were forced to turn to this one remaining source of food.

Whitehackle's farm became their prime target. Because of the influx of new chickens following the weasel's raid, the social organization had become demoralized and the hens with their broods were spread over a wide area. Under these conditions they were extremely vulnerable to predators, and the hawks knew it. So they concentrated on this farm.

As long as the chicks were so small that the raiders could swoop down, snatch one up and fly off with it, the hawks' job was easy, but as the chicks grew larger and heavier, carrying them became more difficult. The little male abandoned the attempt entirely and was forced to resume hunting the few remaining small birds. Ishmael, however, continued to haunt the farm. Even if she could not carry a chicken, she could kill it, gorge and then carry part of it back to the nesting tree.

Still, as Whitehackle got the flock more and more under control, it became increasingly hard for Ishmael to find a lone chicken so far from the others that the creature's alarm cry would not bring the cock down upon her. She had no wish at all to face those terrible spurs and that murderous beak, so as long as Whitehackle patrolled the barnyard, she was constantly frustrated. If she were able to come down from behind him, Ishmael was confident that she could kill the rooster as she had killed many a cock pheasant, by grabbing him by the head and the base of one wing, but the cries of the hens would bring the dog and the humans down on her. So Ishmael bided her time, sure that eventually she would find him alone.

Her opportunity came in July when the dewberries were ripe. Whitehackle loved dewberries, and as they grew on the ground attached to long, spider-like creepers, they were easy to reach. When ripe, these berries were even sweeter than the tiny wild strawberries, for they had no tart taste. Unfortunately, none grew close to the farm, and Whitehackle had to go looking for them on the distant hillside below the grove where the hawks nested. Always wary on these expeditions, Whitehackle lost no time filling his crop and then hurrying back to the safety of the barnyard.

One afternoon he stayed out a little later than usual and the sun was dropping before he started home. Ishmael was returning from an unsuccessful day of hunting and saw the slanting light strike the cock's plumage full, making him blaze like a heraldic device. Whitehackle did not see the hawk alight in the tall black walnut tree, but he was dimly conscious that the birds had abruptly stopped singing. The sudden silence made him nervous and he paused to look around, standing by a clump of bushes heavily overgrown with a dense mat of wild grapevines.

This was the moment for which Ishmael had long waited. The cock was alone and far from the barnyard. She dove from the branch and came rushing down on set wings.

Whitehackle heard nothing, but a shadow leaped up before him: the terrible silhouette of the broad wings and headless body. At the same instant he received a tearing, raking blow that made him reel. At the last instant, Ishmael had flunked the hind and decided to strafe instead. Knocked over on one side, Whitehackle saw the hawk shoot up in front of him and do a wingover to come in again. When she attacked for the second time, he was ready for her.

He went up in a fly, meeting the hawk in midair and knocking her down. They hit the ground a few feet apart and Whitehackle instantly charged, head down. Ishmael was braced on her tail, her legs thrown out before her, but as the cock came in, he too flunked the impact and went up in another fly, intending to straddle her. As the cock rose, Ishmael went farther and farther back, raising her talons as she did so to hold off the rooster, until as Whitehackle reached the top of his fly, the hawk was flat on her back with her legs extended straight up in the air. When Whitehackle saw what he was coming down on, he tried to veer off but it was impossible. All he could do was to drop his own legs to meet the threat. The two birds locked talons and rolled on the ground, buffeting with their wings and striking with their beaks.

They tore apart and stood facing each other, Whitehackle with lowered head and extended hackles, the hawk with open beak and bent legs. Ishmael spread her wings and raised her crest to appear more imposing and edged in sideways, hoping to make the cock run so she could seize him by the back. Whitehackle refused to be bluffed and attacked, going up just enough so he was clear of the ground and could use his spurs. He was two and a half times as heavy as the hawk and she went down. Mad with triumph, Whitehackle went up in fly after fly over the hawk's body, lashing wildly with his spurs instead of straddling and shuffling, so Ishmael was able to get to her feet and bound into the air. Instead of escaping, she twisted around and came back, delivering such a savage blow with both rear talons that Whitehackle was knocked down. Spinning around, Ishmael came in with outstretched legs, intending to get her head and wing-base grip, but Whitehackle rolled over on his back and extended his legs to meet her. The birds had now reversed their positions; the hawk was in the air coming down on top of the cock and he was on his back trying to hold her off. As Ishmael fell on him, Whitehackle with a down-pulling movement grabbed her on either side with a spur.

Ishmael gave an involuntary cry as the breath was driven out of her lungs by the blow. They writhed on the ground side by side with one of the cock's spurs caught in the hawk's body. Then Ishmael wrenched free and sprang back. The leap took her among the bushes and under the overhanging mesh of grapevines. She was trapped.

Head down, hackles spread, Whitehackle moved in. Frantically, Ishmael tried to fly but she was knocked back by the vines. She went up again, but again the resilient vines flung her down and this time Whitehackle grabbed her head feathers with his beak and held her down. Moving a little to one side, he delivered three pile-driving blows with his beak and partly stunned her. Ishmael lay helpless, waiting for the end. There was no question what the end would be, for when she got a quarry down, she always killed. That, obviously, was the whole purpose of overcoming one's adversary.

Whitehackle stood over her, beak ready, wings partly open, legs bent and his cone-shaped ruff fully extended. He stood there as though frozen. Ishmael lay and watched him, panting with open beak but making no other move. She was finished and knew it.

After a long, long time, Whitehackle straightened up, stepped back and, curving his body into a fishhook, gave his victory crow. Then he proudly strode away, high-stepping as he went.

Ishmael continued to lie on the ground, staring after him. She could not believe that he would not return and finish the job, but Whitehackle headed back for the farm. He did not fight to kill, only to establish territory. Killing for the sake of killing, even to protect his flock or in self-defense, was an action contrary to his instinct. As long as the other bird acknowledged his mastery by bending the head or lying limp, he was entirely satisfied.

After a while, Ishmael managed to roll over onto her feet,

walk out from under the vines and fly away. She was dazed and bewildered but she was alive. She never went near the farm again. Whitehackle had triumphed.

It was to make little difference which bird won the long struggle, for shortly afterward the Mennonite family migrated West. Even though their family had lived in the pleasant, rolling Pennsylvania valley for over two hundred years, conditions had now become intolerable. The new highways cut up the country, the factories and housing developments loaded the quiet lanes with traffic that made travel by buggy virtually impossible, and taxes rose. A motel equipped with swimming pools, a deluxe restaurant and a golf course opened, with its main attractions special tours through the Pennsylvania Dutch country. Tractors pulling five and six sightseeing vans, each as big as a Pullman, toured the country, while a guide using a loudspeaker system pointed out the Plain People as though they were animals being exhibited in a zoo. Their children were forced to attend the new schools, and when the parents protested, state police were sent to chase the youngsters through the cornfields and arrest them. The covered bridge, long a great source of pride, was smashed when a diesel trailer truck loaded with sheets of metal tried to cross it and the old wooden trestle could not stand the weight. Sadly the Mennonites, Amish and Dunkers sold their farms as factory sites or to real-estate promoters, loaded their possessions in wagons and departed for Iowa or Kansas where there was still unspoiled country.

From her black walnut lookout, Ishmael watched the Mennonite family leave the old farm where as a brown youngster she had taken her first game. In the back of the wagon driven by the boy were stored crates of chickens. From the top of one crate protruded Whitehackle's head. Perhaps he saw her, for as the wagon disappeared down the lane he crowed defiantly.

Shortly afterward, the two young hawks left the grove. It was doubtful indeed if they could survive with so little game and their wings heavily streaked with the fatal hunger streaks that weakened the feathers. They were the last hawks to be hatched in this ruined area.

A few weeks later, the parent birds heard a shrill, angry whine coming from the grove, a hideous, mechanical sound they could not identify. It was the scream of power saws cutting down the great trees, some of which had stood since colonial days. The grove had been sold and the hilltop was to be "improved."

Without a home, without food, the hawks could not remain. The male was the first to leave, and in spite of her bad wing, Ishmael followed him. Going by easy stages, she could still travel. They, too, headed West. Perhaps in Canada or somewhere else in the wilder parts of the country, they could still find a home where they could live undisturbed for the remainder of their lives.

AUTHOR'S NOTE

Having worked with hawks for thirty-five years and with fowl for twenty, I thought that I had an adequate background when I began writing this book. I soon found out how wrong I was. I would like to thank some of the people who helped me:

Earl C. Schriver, Jr., of Baden, Pennsylvania, who not only told me a great deal about the nesting habits of the Cooper's hawk but also very kindly gave me a female Cooper's so that I was able to renew my acquaintance with these remarkable hawks.

The Biological Sciences Curriculum Study of The University of Colorado, who generously sent me their film, *Social Behavior in Chickens.*

I would also like to thank the gentleman who gave me Whitehackle. He has asked to remain anonymous, as he still fights cocks.

Most especially I would like to thank Dr. Heinz Meng, Professor of Biology at State University College, New Paltz, New York, whose treatise on the Cooper's hawk seems to me to he the definitive work on the bird. Dr. Meng was kind enough to read my manuscript and correct several errors. I would also like to thank Professor A. M. Guhl of Kansas State University, Manhattan, Kansas, who is, I think, the foremost authority on chicken ecology. Professor Guhl most generously also read my manuscript and made several helpful suggestions. At the same time I would like to stress that neither of these gentlemen is responsible in any way, shape or form for my interpretations of the mental processes of birds.

On only one matter do I claim to be an unquestioned authority. I know more of what happens when a Cooper's hawk decides to tangle with a Whitehackle gamecock than anyone else in the world.

My description of the hawks' singing "duets" during the mating season is taken from Dr. Meng's treatise. I have never heard it myself nor can I find any reference to this curious custom in any of the literature on the birds. However, Dr. Meng describes this ritual in considerable detail.

It seems incredible that a cock would attack a fox, but there have been a number of such cases; indeed, on one occasion a gamecock actually killed a fox. In *The Sporting Magazine*, June, 1821, p. 141, occurs the following (here condensed): "A cock bred by J. H. Hunt of Compton Pauncefoot, Somerset, was put out to walk at one Adam's in that country. A fox seized a hen in the barton and her cries drew the attention of the cock who discovering the fox in the act of carrying off his prey, flew at reynard and at one blow killed him on the spot and saved the life of the hen." Capt. L. Fitz-Barnard in *Fighting Sports* (London: Odhams Press, n.d.) says "Another great cock belonging to an old friend of mine was known as the Fox-Hunter, and he earned the name, for he was seen chasing a fox that was carrying off one of his hens." In *Cock-Fights and Game Fowls from the Notebook of Herbert Atkinson* (Bath: George Baynteen, 1938), the author says (p. 31): "Instances have occurred of my own birds attacking foxes carrying off their hens. I gave Mr. J. Walker a white cock to mate with some Pyle hens he had. One morning early he found a fox had visited him and the cock and one hen was missing. Occasional white feathers enabled him to trace them to a large wood behind the house. Here he saw a woodman and made inquiries. The man related that as he went to work at early dawn he saw a fox hurrying along with a white hen in his mouth, and running and flying after him a white cock. Mr. Walker, proceeding in the direction indicated, came on the dead hen which the fox had dropped, and had just decided that the cock must have been killed also when he was agreeably surprised to hear him crow at a distance, and further search found him quite unharmed, but there was blood on his spurs. Evidently he had made it so hot for Mr. Reynard that he dropped the hen and bolted. I could state other incidents of game cocks chasing and flying at foxes in defense of their hens, and also attacking dogs."

Earl Schriver first suggested to me the possibility that male raptors put wild cherry sprigs in the nest because when the sprays rot, they generate cyanide gas that drives off screwworm flies. I frankly found this too hard to believe, but since then I have heard it from several other sources. Whether the hawks put the sprays there with the deliberate purpose is hard to say. In *Eagles, Hawks and Falcons of the World* by Dean Amadon and Leslie Brown (New York: McGraw-Hill, 1968) a number of other theories to account for the hawks' action are discussed.

Conservationists may feel that I have unduly emphasized the role of the Cooper's hawk as hunter, especially as the hawk is rapidly becoming exterminated over much of its former range. I feel that the time has passed when we can dismiss the feeding habits of predators by saying, in an effort to deceive sportsmen and game commissions, that they eat only harmful rats and mice. The role of the predator in nature is far too complicated and important for that well-meant deception. I find it hard to believe that anyone, after reading this book, would want to speed the destruction of this interesting and typically American bird.

D. P. M.
April, 1968

ABOUT THE AUTHOR

Daniel P. Mannix was an award-winning American author and journalist, as well as a magician and filmmaker. Mannix's magazine articles about his experiences in the carnival, where he performed under the stage name "The Great Zadma," became popular in the mid-1940s and were compiled with the assistance of his wife in the book *Step Right Up!* His dozens of books and extensive essays range in subject from children's animal stories, environmental issues, and hunting accounts to historical examinations of the Hellfire Club, the Atlantic slave trade, and the Roman gladiatorial games. Mannix was particularly interested in the Wizard of Oz canon and composed a biography of L. Frank Baum for *American Heritage* magazine in the 1960s.

DANIEL P. MANNIX

FROM OPEN ROAD MEDIA

Find a full list of our authors and
titles at www.openroadmedia.com

FOLLOW US
@OpenRoadMedia

EARLY BIRD BOOKS
FRESH DEALS, DELIVERED DAILY

Love to read?
Love great sales?

Get fantastic deals on
bestselling ebooks delivered
to your inbox every day!

Sign up today at
earlybirdbooks.com/book